14 Horror S[

An Anthology of Zombies and Death

By Rachel Swenson

If you like my book, please leave a review. I would appreciate it. Thank you!

Table of Contents

Zombies Attack

" This is it. We can't hold them back much longer," Sarah said. "Just keep shooting them!" Craig yelled in despair. "There HAS to be a way out."

Craig and Sarah were driven into a corner. The hordes of zombies were running at them, drooling and bleeding along the way, making gruesome noises and frightening motions. Craig had a gatling gun, an easy but efficient AK-47, and Sarah had a big shotgun. Both of them were firing away at the approaching creatures, reloading and shouting for nerve. Craig was wearing his hat backwards, and Sarah had a small backpack on her back.

" Well, where is it then? I don't see an escape! Do you?" Sarah screamed. Craig took a look around for a minute. "There!" he said. "The vent!" With that being said, Craig and Sarah turned around and jumped into the vent, crawling through the spooky space that could give any person a claustrophobic heart attack.

" Go! Go! Go!" Craig shouted as he watched Sarah go first. Although he didn't want to be an annoyance, he wanted she would crawl a little faster.

They were stuck in a high school. After the illness basically took control of Fang City, they left to the supermarket, looted whatever they could, and established camp in the high school classrooms, thinking that they were safe. And they were ... for a while ... until they were found.

" This teaches us to be more careful when we head out next time," Craig said.

" Hey, simply because there happened to be a zombie in the women's restroom, doesn't mean this is all my fault, fine!" Sarah said in disappointment.

" I am not saying that. I am just expressing my worry about the next hiding place we find. We need to become more secluded, and wait out the end of this episode of horror. The zombies are all over, and we can't afford to take risks," Craig added.

" Well, what do you suggest?" Sarah asked.

" A bank. Find supplies and hide in the safe-deposit box. For now, till we find something better."

" Sounds good, but let's get out of here first. I think I already killed about 20 in a few minutes, but they keep coming," said Sarah.

" Let's take the emergency exit and after that just follow me. I know the quickest way to get there," Craig explained.

" Yep!"

Sarah left the building as quick as she could, followed by Craig. They blocked the exit and ran through the alleys.

" Did we lose them?" Sarah asked, panting and attempting to catch her breath.

" I think so. Let's keep running until we are really there," Craig replied.

" Easy for you to say. You were a basketball player. I was part of the chess club," Sarah said.

" Ha-ha! I thought chess was a sport! That's what you told me!"

" Yes, but ... Ughh ... I am worn out. Can we stop briefly for several seconds?"

" Okay," Craig replied. "But no more. We need to get to a safe location."

After a fast pause, Craig and Sarah ran into the closest bank. They silently opened up the door and held their guns in front of them, ensuring the environment was safe. They slowly moved towards the vault.

Locked.

" Right, genius. How do we open it?" Sarah asked.

" The code has to be around here somewhere. I mean, everyone is gone. Aha! This must be it. Let's try it."

Craig tried to open the vault, but it would not budge. There was no chance of opening it. He yanked and pulled with all his may and started kicking it in frustration.

" Hey, take it easy," Sarah said. "That's not going to help. Let's go to plan B."

" What is that plan B?" Craig asked. "We can find an air-raid shelter. Some of these homes have one. They were built during the Cold War, so they MUST have SOMETHING."

Craig concurred and they left the bank. They saw some money lying on the floor, but cash was no good here. There went that idea ...

" Look out!" Sarah screamed.

Craig turned around and shot a zombie in the chest. Takadakadak! His gatling gun fired a few rounds, all precise hits.

" Thanks. Now let's get moving."

Craig and Sarah came to the old part of town. They knew there may be a higher risk of encounters with zombies, but Sarah's idea about the air-raid shelter actually wasn't bad. After searching through some houses, they found one with a basement. It was great, since it had a food storage, comfortable sofas, a bed, and enough space to move around.

" Aaahh ..." Sarah said in fulfillment as she fell on the bed. "This is what I am talking about."

Finally, they were safe, or so they thought ...

Chapter 2: Let's Get Out

Craig and Sarah stayed in the air-raid shelter for 5 days. They opened cans of food, ate the leftovers, and read some of the books that were on the shelves. The only thing that almost became an issue, was that there was only one bed. Clearly this shelter was produced for couples, but Craig and Sarah were not even in a relationship.

Craig was 21. He had been a sports fanatic, always trying to be the best at everything. His entire life, he had spent many hours practicing basketball shots, trying to slam-dunk the ball, and playing non-stop with his friends.

Sarah was 19. She secretly had a crush on Craig, but he was too oblivious to see. Sarah always looked up to him, although there was no need to. Sarah was extremely intelligent. She had won chess tournaments, built her own websites, and learned how to generate income online. She normally had high grades in school and studied world history and geography. If there was any area in the world you would bring up, she could tell you something about it.

But now they were stuck together, something that Sarah didn't mind. Craig, though, was concentrated on survival and didn't even want to get close. Yes, Sarah was appealing, but his mind was on other things. Besides, she was his best friend. It would be so strange to take it any further, right? That's what he thought at least.

" I am happy the toilet works," Sarah said. "Could you imagine being here without a restroom?"

" Yes," Craig said. "But we are lacking food. I have to go get some at the convenience store right across the street. I know there is some over there. I saw it when we came here."

" Please beware," Sarah said. "We don't want to alarm anyone. Nobody can know we are here."

" No worries," Craig replied nonchalantly. "I'll be back before you can blink your eyes."

As Craig took off, Sarah feared the worst. They had felt safe before, only to get up by several zombie hordes and needing to run for their lives.

Craig took his AK-47 and pointed it in front of him. With every silent move he made, he squinted his eyes and concentrated as hard as he could to see if there was any motion. He left the house they were hiding in and walked across the street, as silently as he could ... until ...

" What was that?" Craig thought nervously.

Nothing.

Or ...

Wait ..." Whaaaarghh!" he heard an ugly zombie cry out. It was coming right at him. Craig didn't think twice and shot it instantly. Bull's eye! But the sound set a disaster in motion.

Unexpectedly lots of zombies came running towards him from around the corners of the surrounding streets.

" Oh no, what did I do?" Craig said as he backed out and kept firing at them. He was outnumbered. There was nothing he could do but go back downstairs and hide.

" Open up! Faster!" Craig yelled.

Sarah opened the hatch. "Did you get the food?"

" No time at all for questions. Let me in and shut the hatch! Quickly!"

Craig climbed up down the ladder when he felt a yank on his shirt. "Waaaah! Let go!" Sarah climbed up and punched the zombie in the face. "Take that ugly head!" The zombie let go and Craig safely got down. The hatch was closed, but now what?

They were stuck. The zombies had found their hideout. There was nowhere at all to go. They had no food or drink. They had shelter, but they wouldn't make it through for long. And the only way out seemed blocked by zombies. They had to go out somehow and contribute to their limited supplies. If only there was a way to slip past them ...

Sarah buried her head in her hands and sobbed, "How long is this going to go on? Just how long can we endure this? Is there any hope?"

" Now, now," Craig said calmly and courageously. "We will find a way. We always do." He put his arm around her. That sufficed. She felt safe. Not that she tried to make him do that on purpose, but it was convenient for now.

The apocalypse? All of it began when they were in school. The bell rang.
TRIIIIIIIIIIIINNNNGGGGGGG!!!!!!!!!!!!!
" Finally, I am so finished with school," Craig said to one of his friends.
" Hi, Professor Fisher. Anything new today? Created a time device? Cured cancer?"
one of Craig's good friends said mockingly.
" Go home, boy," Professor Fisher reacted as he walked along.
Craig's good friends started chuckling.
That Professor Fisher ... such a nut job ... always in his own little world, trying out this or
that. One time, they remembered, he created soap that would glow in the dark. He was
so excited about it and presented it to the class. When somebody turned the lights off,
the soap ended up being black and was less noticeable than anything or anyone else in
the room. Another time, he claimed he had an instant cure for fever, making it so that
the body's temperature level would rise instantly when taking one pill. When a man at
school tried the pill, he had the influenza for 5 days and had to stay at home.
Craig felt a little bad that Professor Fisher had become such a bullied instructor, but in a
way, he was such a weirdo that it was to be expected in the first place.
As Craig walked home, he ran into Sarah.
" Hi," Sarah said shyly.
" How are you?" Craig asked.
" Good. And you?" Sarah said with a smile.
" Fine," Craig said as he was about to leave.
" Listen, Craig ... I was wondering if ..."
But before she could finish her sentence, they heard a loud BOOOOOOOOM! Coming
from the school building. The entire floor was shaking for a second just because of the
blast.
People began running everywhere.
" Wha- ... What's going on over there?" Sarah asked.
" I do not know. Wan na go see? Let's go!" Craig said enthusiastically.
Sarah followed Craig to the school. When they came closer, they saw a lot of people
gathered in the corridor and the chemistry classroom. They were in a pretty happy state
of mind after such a remarkable sound. Everybody was chuckling. When they weaved
their way through the people watching, Craig and Sarah watched Professor Fisher
attempting to tidy up glass, scorched fluids, and compounds on the floor of the room.
Certainly, he had experimented with something and failed significantly.
" Poor Professor Fisher," Sarah said.
" You are right, but it actually is kinda' amusing," Craig said as he could not hold in his
laughter entirely.
Craig and Sarah each went their different ways. Sarah never completed her sentence.
She didn't get around to asking Craig what she wanted.
The next day was supposed to be a routine school day. Both of them went to the
chemistry class. That was their first class. They were early. It was a gorgeous day. It
would be another fifteen minutes before the rest of the class would appear.
" Hey, decided to be early?" Craig asked Sarah as he saw her walking into the
classroom.

" I guess we had the exact same idea," Sarah answered.

But when they went into the class, they saw Professor Fisher lying on the floor. There were glass urns and bottles everywhere; there was a certain odor to the room they could not put their finger on; and there were documents all over the desk with solutions and doodling in a weird handwriting.

" Professor, are you all right?" Sarah asked when she came closer.

" Professor ..."

All of a sudden, the Professor looked at them. Those eyes! Sarah got surprised and stepped back. The Professor's eyes were green inside, and the bags under his eyes were bleak and scary. His whole face had somewhat degenerated and was wrinkled 10 times more than before. He was drooling a bit and his hair was messed up.

" Professor, what's going on? What is wrong with you?" Sarah asked again, but she wasn't sure if she should stick around.

" Let's go. We'll tell the other instructors," Craig said as he backed out towards the exit.

Craig and Sarah went through the hallways. They told the teachers something was wrong with Professor Fisher. The teachers said they should stay in the teachers' room. They waited ... And waited ... and waited ... Then they heard noises ... lots of scary sounds ... yelling and growling and panting ...

" Let's lock the door!" Craig said. "I do not trust this one bit!"

They locked the door and watched through the window. All of a sudden they saw lots of people coming through the doors in the lunch area. They were in panic. They were injured ... or so it appeared. No! They were sick and aggressive! What was going on?!!!!

Craig had always played zombie computer games. He came to a quick conclusion.

" They are zombies! They need to be! It's real! There are real zombies!" he screamed. "Let's get out of here as soon as we can!"

Then they heard gun shots.

Bang!

Bang!

Takadakadak!

They watched as 2 police officers with heavy armory entered the lunch room, killing zombies as they moved forward. This went on for about twenty seconds, until every zombie was dead on the floor.

" Hey!" the officers yelled as they waived to Craig and Sarah. "Are you kids okay?" Craig gave him a thumbs up. "We'll get you out of there!" one of them said.

The officers came to the door. Craig and Sarah opened the door. "Let's go. It's trouble out there," one of the officers said. But then something awful happened. Both officers got assaulted from behind. 2 zombies were concurrently biting each officer, making them drop their weapons. Craig and Sarah stepped back. They watched in horror for two seconds because they didn't know what to do. Then Craig decided. He saw it was going nowhere at all. These officers were as good as dead. He stepped forward, picked up the two guns, and closed the door.

" What! Why did you do that?!!!!" Sarah screamed in panic.

" Th-They were dead anyway," Craig said with an unstable voice. "There was nothing we could do. We need to protect ourselves now."

" Are you insane?! I never used a weapon before!" Sarah screamed back.

" It's simple," Craig said. "I've seen it in movies so many times that I am pretty sure that I know what I am doing."

And that's how they got stuck at the high school.

Back to the bomb shelter. Sarah dropped off to sleep in Craig's arms. They were both exhausted from all the running, shooting, panicking, and the lack of food and water. Craig woke up with a shock. After a deep, quick nap, he suddenly realized the situation they were in. He got up and started planning their escape route. Sarah was still asleep. She could sleep through anything, he observed.

The last chocolate bar from her bag was gone. He saw her eat it before they fell asleep, and it was now empty.

" Okay," he thought out loud, "If we reach the supermarket, we could maybe find some food there. We'll use our school backpacks and fill them up with stuff. Then we get out of there. But where?" He thought for a moment. "Perhaps we just need to find a car and drive out of the city. That would probably be best. If we can get out of town, we could find a place with more people who have not turned into zombies yet."

As he was contemplating his strategy, Sarah awakened.

" What? Where? How?" she asked in panic.

" It's fine. We are safe for now," Craig said, soothing her down. "Let's leave when you're all set. We need to get some supplies and after that find a car to leave town."

After twenty minutes of getting ready, Craig and Sarah opened the hatch, hoping that the zombies were gone, and they were.

" We need to be as quiet as possible. The more sound we make, the higher the threat of having a whole horde storm at us," Craig whispered.

They snuck through the city streets and came to the supermarket, avoiding the occasional zombie on their course. When they came, Craig and Sarah simply went to the food area and found an entire lot of canned food left.

" Let's stuff these in our bags," Craig said. "That's the only way we'll have the ability to survive for a longer amount of time." He thought for a second. "And make certain you get a can opener!" he added. Yeah, that would be the day, having a huge food supply and nothing to open up the cans with.

Craig and Sarah put as many cans of food into their backpacks as they could. One of the cans of food rolled on the floor after Sarah mistakenly dropped it. "Whoops," she said. That should have been it, but the can rolled outside the grocery store doors and set off the alarm.

" Weeeeeeeeeeeh!"

" O-oh" Sarah said with a sheepish face.

Within seconds, numerous zombies came running into the store. Craig and Sarah ran as quickly as their legs could carry them.

" There!" Craig pointed at a little surveillance room.

They went into the room and locked the door. That should keep them out for at least a long time. Pfew! That was a close call.

" I'm sorry," Sarah said.

" It's fine. Everybody makes mistakes," Craig said. "Hey, what's that?"

Chapter 5: One Specific Zombie

In the corner of the room stood a zombie that didn't look half as ugly as the other ones. He just looked at them, didn't move a muscle. It was as if he didn't even have the desire to assault them. Craig was going to shoot him, but then he hesitated.
" Notice how that zombie isn't even coming near us?" he whispered to Sarah. "He doesn't have red eyes like the rest either. Hey you!" he said to the zombie. "Why aren't you assaulting us?"
" I am not like the rest," the zombie said.
The zombie talked? Yes, it talked. Sarah and Craig were pretty surprised.

" Describe what's going on here, or I will blow your head off," Craig said, as he and Sarah pointed their weapons at the zombie. "Why aren't you like the rest, and how do we find a cure for this illness?"
" My name is Calvin," the zombie said. "I am immune and invisible to the zombies, but I need you to help me find the cure. I know it must be in the high school someplace. The one who created it, probably knew something about a remedy."
" We'll get you there," Craig said courageously. "Just let me kill these frustrating creatures first."
Craig was loading his weapon and Sarah was loading hers.
" Ready? 3, two, one ..."
" Wait!" Calvin said. "Look!" He pointed at the cams. They were still working! How convenient!
" Aha!" Craig said. "We can wait for them to move to different areas of the supermarket and after that we'll slip out. We can observe everything in this control room. Thanks for the idea, Calvin. You are pretty wise."
" I know a lot more," Calvin said. "I have been studying physics and chemistry for years. That's why I am positive we can find the solution to this disease in the school labs. We just need to get there, but I am too scared to get going by myself."
" That makes no sense," Sarah said. "If you are undetectable to them and they won't eat you, then what makes you think you are at risk?"
" I do not know that for sure, and there are still people out there hunting down the zombies, so they could shoot me too."
" I think you're right. We'll help you out," Sarah answered empathically.
They waited on 2 hours. They saw the zombies walk around on the video cameras. In the meantime, Calvin explained to them how he didn't get affected in the exact same way. He had been in the school lab and had been exposed to the compound. All the other zombies were bitten. He had never been bitten, just got some of the toxic stuff on his skin and developed into a half-zombie. But when all the zombies began appearing, he hid himself and ran away from the school.
Craig and Sarah listened attentively. After some time, they saw the location should be safe.
" Ready? Let's go," Craig commanded.

Chapter 6: A Unique Group

They opened the squeaking door as silently as they could and snuck their way through the grocery store.

Once they were outside, they had to determine whether to go through the park or through the city. "Through the city is faster," Craig said. "Yes, but for some reason, I think we might find more zombies there too. I say, let's try the park," Sarah said.

" Neither," Calvin said. "Listen, guys, I know how we can hole up and hit the drains. I can tell you exactly where they wind up by the way they are constructed."

Great. A zombie who imitates a smarty pants.

" Your nose must be obstructed," Craig said. "The sewers? Seriously?"

" It's the most safe way to get to the school," Calvin claimed.

" He is right, Craig. I would rather reek than be dead," Sarah concurred.

" Okay, fine. But you better know where you're going. I don't feel like being stuck in such a horrible place."

" Don't you worry about that," Calvin said.

Once they were on the right street, they opened a hatch that took them to the sewage systems. It was pitch black, but Craig had a flashlight from his backpack. He found it in the grocery store, and luckily, it was working. They went on and on, turning left and right till they came to what Calvin called, "The drain closest to the school." They went up, looked around them ... yes ... he was right. How did he do that?

" I assisted with the building and construction of some of these sewers. Here in Fang City, there are all types of little small jobs. I helped out in the drains. Did you do anything like that?" Calvin asked.

" I babysat 3 kids every weekend," Sarah said. "There were two boys and a girl. The boys were a ton of fun, and the girl was still little. I really wonder what happened to them. I still do not know why we haven't examined our own families yet."

" Just because we have been in danger all that time," Craig said. "Survival is the first concern. We will figure it out later. I hope they are all right."

They climbed up and went to the high school. "Let's be even more careful," Craig whispered, "because this is where it all began. There must be lots of zombies around here."

They snuck into the high school, where they navigated their way through the hallways. One of the zombies looked so ugly and vicious that Sarah nearly made a sound, but thankfully, Craig saw what was about to happen and covered her mouth with his hand. " Do not make a noise," he whispered. "We are nearly there. They don't know that we are here till we make a noise, just like in the supermarket."
The trio entered into the laboratory. There they saw the mess that came because of Professor Fisher's failed experiment. They looked all over. It was like a needle in a haystack. Papers were all over the floor ... tons of them. Fluids were leaking all over, and the appliances, glass, and furnishings were all over the floor. There were even several lifeless bodies bleeding and making it messier than it already was.
" This may be something," Calvin said.
" Yeah? What is it?"
" Professor Fisher's journal. It shows the procedure he went through. Let's see ..."
Fisher read out loud from the journal.

I have been testing things to make a potion that could make people invincible. I know which compounds and solutions to use, but I am afraid it will not only turn people into invincible creatures, but that it will also strip them of their humanity, therefore having the wanted impact but having a useless side-effect that might deteriorate mankind.
I hesitate to try it out on myself, not so much just because of what could happen to me, but just because of the repercussions for others.
Oh well ... whatever ... they dislike me. They mock me. They do not care what happens to me. And I don't care if anything happens to me. I am going to try it.
Just as a precaution: If anything significant or apocalyptic were to happen, simply know that the impacts of these transformations can more than likely be undone by using the device on my desk. It sends out an active, high frequency signal that cannot be heard by people but has a lasting impact on the brains of those transformed by this formula. It should work, if my estimations are accurate. Here I go ... for humanity ... Wow ... Craig, Sarah, and Calvin stared at one another for several seconds. Was it truly going to be that basic?

All of a sudden, the door made a noise. One of the zombies had seen them and tried to get in.

" Well, if we are going to try it," Craig said, "we better do it quick. Now!"

" I'm on it," Calvin said as he jumped over the desk and grabbed the device the Professor had written about.

" Beware!" Sarah shouted, pointing to a zombie that leapt through the classroom window. Craig fired his AK-47. "Got him!" But as he did that, the door behind him opened and a female zombie got him, opening up her mouth to bite him.

BAM!!!!!!

What was that?

Sarah shot the female zombie in the face.

" He is my man, ugly wench," Sarah said as if she was copying a one-liner from an action movie.

" Nice job!" Craig said with a smile. "Thank you for saving my life!"

" You 'd do the exact same for me," Sarah said. "Like my style? I know how to kill the competitors. Haha!"

The hordes were still coming. There were at least twenty zombie in the corridor now.

" Rush already!" Craig shouted at Calvin. "We are going to die if you do not do something!"

" Just trying to figure this thing out," Calvin responded.

The zombies were coming closer every second. It was as if everything occurred in slow-motion. Craig and Sarah were firing their guns like never before, but the hordes subdued them. Both of them were knocked to the ground, in addition to their weapons, having several zombies get on them who tried to punch them down much more and bite them.

" Aha! I got it!" Calvin shouted.

Craig was about to lose his face by a zombie with a drooling mouth when ... The zombies stopped. The insane appearance in their eyes had vanished. They started looking around and stare at the environment they were in. Craig didn't wait a second and punched the one on top of him in the face.

" Ouch! Why did you do that?"

Craig and Sarah looked at each other and began to smile. It seemed like the device had worked. The frequency transfigured the zombies' brains. The zombies in the classroom weren't zombies anymore. They were simply people in rags and with unclean faces, wondering what had happened and why they were there.

" Sorry," Craig said to the former zombie. "Just had to blow off some steam. Don't worry about it. We'll explain it later. Thanks, Calvin! You are the MAN!"

Sarah got up and hugged Craig.

" Craig ... I. I." she stammered.

" What is it, Sarah?" Craig asked.

" Do you remember that day of the blast in the classroom, the day before all of it started?" Sarah asked.

" Obviously," Craig said. "Who would not?"

" Well," Sarah continue, "I was about to ask you something, but then we both got sidetracked."

" What is it?" Craig asked.

" I was just wondering if I could give you a kiss," Sarah said.

" Uhmm ..." Craig said as he ended up being a little red.

He had developed some good feelings for Sarah in the process of the whole zombie armageddon, although he had always couldn't admit it. Now he was confronted with what he had been denying for so long.

" Uh ... all right," Craig said in an unstable voice.

Sarah bent forward and kissed him for several seconds.

" This is the first of many," she said as her whole face became red but happy.

THE END

Knowing More

He grew up in a friendly environment, with people from all different backgrounds, races, childhoods, faiths, skin color, or financial situations. The Phila City was a decent place, with a relatively small population. It was peaceful there, and nothing shocking or problematic ever occurred, except for on incredibly rare celebrations.
But things have changed.
A lot.
The residents have changed.
Every little thing is different now.
Every little thing is worse than it used to be.
In fact, a lot of things are going extremely wrong.
Skyscrapers decorate the skies like enormous interrupters of peace, hundreds of lights in the evening and a chaotic crowd throughout the day. Sirens are heard frequently, and the state of the city is overlooked by the regional cops, who are in desperate need of a valiant vigilante to come to the rescue when they cannot.
Demondre is black. His parents were immigrants, as were many others in the previous generation. He is 22 years of age and in the prime of his life. He enjoys being young and energetic, with the flexibility to go any place you want whenever you want. His newfound power has been incredibly advantageous to himself and those around him. Recently, he concluded what he sensed the whole time: He can predict the future. Not like a fortune teller or some kind of soothsayer. Astrology has never interested him in the least.
No, Demondre has the ability to feel what is happening before it does. It normally doesn't consist of everything, and the future always changes, but a certain user-friendly hunch has always helped him comprehend the connection between what happens in the present and what the effects in the near future are, more than others who have similar insights. In this way, he can somehow anticipate some of the most imminent events and the actions of others as a result of their intents and previous experiences.
Demondre discovered he was different when he won games and sports, and when people began asking him things like, "How did you know that?" and "Did you just read my mind or something?"
Things that occurred were seen before they took place, and the strong hunch he got every time some danger came his way, was more than simple coincidence, or so he figured. Now he is armed with a strong self-confidence and a knowledge of his special abilities.
After pondering what he would do with these remarkable emotions, he decided that he would use it to help out others.
" Anyone with more possibilities should exceed the routine and use those alternatives for the good of other people," he reasoned.
Examples abound. He is determined to save some individual occasionally, just to make the city a more secure place. In order to safeguard his identity, he is wearing a mask and a superhero outfit. He does not want his rescue efforts and his heroic endeavors stand in the way of his everyday life as a normal resident.
Last week, for instance, a block caught fire. The cause of it, they learnt later, was a homemaker who mistakenly let her dinner burn while spending hours on the phone and

forgetting on the frying pan on the stove. The fire spread to some other houses beside her. Fire engine arrived within a small time duration, and panicking people ran from the homes.

" Is anyone else in there, madam?" one of the firemen asked another civilian.

" I don't know. I came out because of the smoke," the woman said anxiously. "I thought I was going to die. I'm so glad I am safe, but how horrible."

The fireman approached another woman.

" Is anyone in those buildings?" he asked.

" Oh, thank goodness. You're here! Please rescue my daughter," she wept. "I was attempting to get her, but a burning beam fell between us. I told her I would get help as quickly as I could. Please hurry!"

" Understood. We'll do what we can, madam," the fireman said. "Hey you, you, and you! Follow me into that building. Bring the fire distinguishers. Quickly. There's a girl in there. We need to take her out immediately."

" Yes, sir."

The four firemen got their equipment and ran towards the building. Inside it was a mess. Smoke was everywhere, and items were burning all around them. There was only a small chance this girl would be alive anyhow, but at least they had to do their best they thought.

Getting here in the spaces, they could barely see anything, regardless of their masks.

" There's no chance to make it all the way through," one of them said.

" I do not even know where to go. We have to watch out or one of us will die here as well," another said.

" Ugh ... ughh ... can you see anybody?"

" There! It's a. wait a minute ... that can't be a little girl. Are you seeing this?"

" Hey mister, what are you doing in here? Get out before you can! This place is going to collapse!"

But the shady figure didn't move. He stood there, waiting as if he expected something to happen within seconds. Then it occurred. The ceiling dropped and surrounded the boy with its pieces of burning particles. He still stood there. He didn't move a muscle.

" No, it can't be," one of the firefighter said, expanding the pupils in his eyes while gazing at the scene in front of him.

" Incredible," another said.

" Did you just see that? It was as if he knew exactly where the damaged ceiling was going to fall. He didn't even get scraped!"

" Something's wrong," the head fireman said.

Before they could say another word, the boy used the exact same damaged ceiling parts to pull himself up to the second floor and disappear from the sight of the firefighters. What he was doing they could only guess, but the smoke was becoming too thick and the flames would melt their unique suits. They couldn't stand the heat any longer.

" We have to go," one of the firefighters said.

" We can't. What about the girl?"

" We did our best. There's nothing left to do here. I recognize how tragic it is to leave her alone, but perhaps we can find another method. We have to leave the building. Follow me."

The firemen stepped out of the burning building and walked around it to find a different way to enter it. All to no avail. It looked like the building was done for, and with that everybody inside too.

The mom was sobbing. There was no consoling her. She refused to be comforted. She felt guiltier than ever. Why did she ever leave her daughter when she was her only hope?

" What kind of a mother am I?" she said in sorrow.

" The kind that tries to save her own life, madam ..." the fireman replied. But before he went on, he realized that every word would just contribute to her depressive state. He didn't blame her at all. If only there were a way this could have been stopped, he thought. It was too late now. They tried and they failed miserably. This is the part of the job he disliked so much.

But then there was a noise.

Everybody looked into the direction of the building, raising their look with a restored, small particle of hope. The vapors were thick, but the image soon became clearer. The young man emerged from the flames and the smoking air, holding the living daughter of the mourning mother in his arms. Mouths fell open, hearts started beating much faster, and the mom of the girl came running towards this strange rescuer, thanking him and feeling grateful she could carry her breathing offspring in her arms.

" Thank you," she said. "Whoever you are, I will always be grateful."

" You're welcome," the black guy with the mask said. "Now if you'll excuse me, I have other things to do."

With that, he ran off.

" Wait," the mother said, reaching out her one hand.

But the hero had disappeared. Nevertheless he pulled that off, the firemen would never comprehend it. The chances were so much against him that they considered it a miracle, and so did the relieved mother.

This was just the first of many essential acts to come.

Another case was less daring but equally dramatic. The media was all over it. The moment was tense, and the crowd was anxious. Video cameras were being held by a dozen people, attempting to get a good angle or a decent shot at the unfolding scene. Oohs and aahs were said by many as the masses gazed up at a single man on the edge of a building terrace, some one hundred feet in the air.

" Don't do it!" they were shouting.

" It's not worth it! Think about it!"

The screaming voices were nothing but muffled echoes in the distance. The man didn't care. He had had it. It was over. What else did he need to live for? His partner left him and his dire monetary situation was impossible to enhance. His self-esteem was shattered, as were his purpose and his perspective on joy itself. He was going to jump off. It would be better that way, he told himself. Nobody would lament the loss of his useless life. He was certain of that.

Colleagues stood helplessly by in the windows, not daring to come near the dangerous edge of the edifice. They wanted to prevent this worthless act of anguish more than anything they held dear at that moment, but their incompetence had no limits. They just didn't have the guts to come to the rescue.

Nevertheless, the exact same masked hero appeared again in this apparently helpless scenario. Determined to save this man's life, he leaped up the stairs, running as if his own life depended on it. After reaching the distressed man, he got on the edge of the terrace and stood there, next to him and beckoning him to get his hand.

" What for?" the man said. "My life is meaningless anyway. I have no reason to live."

" You know that's not real," Demondre said. "I dare you to name three people who at least care about you enough to live."

" Are you kidding?" the man asked. "Nobody cares about me."

" What about all those people down there?" Demondre asked.

" They do not care. They just want the news to be amazing enough to get more audiences to watch their channel."

" Well, what about your colleagues?" Demondre asked, pointing at his colleagues in the window.

" I do not think they would be devastated if I died," the man said with tears in his eyes.

" What about your children? Do you have any children?" Demondre asked.

The man paused. He couldn't manage his feelings. He felt abandoned and lonesome, but the caring kids who visited him every weekend were crazy about him in spite of his defects. He knew that for sure. He broke down and wept.

" You know what? You're right. Life is tough, but I do have something to live for," he said.

" Then get my hand," Demondre firmly insisted. "And we'll get you the mental help you need."

The man reached out and tried to grab Demondre's hand.

But he slipped.

He was going to fall anyhow, but not on purpose.

It was a frightening moment for everyone who was watching. But not for Demondre. His brain computed every inch that would move in the near future. He knew where the man was going to hold on and where he was going to let go. In an immediate, Demondre bent over and grabbed the wrist of the slipping man, balancing himself and the taken advantage of individual perfectly before pulling him over the edge and helping him back inside.

People clapped. They were happy this possibly awful scene had ended well, at least in the sense that there was still hope for this desperate soul. People came at the man and accepted him, thanked Demondre, and organized a way for the man to rest and get help. Demondre wasn't going to walk down and give a speech. He knew the price of fame, so he disappeared out the back door.

There is one more story worth mentioning before we start expanding on the main crisis this hero found himself in, and that's a bank robbery.

It took place on a Saturday afternoon. He was sitting on a terrace, taking little sips while enjoying a cool glass of juice. The day was bright and warm. Nothing appeared to suggest the threatening situations the people in his close environment would soon be in. Demondre saw it all happening before it did, though. He anticipated the three gentlemen in suits, hiding their faces behind sneaky masks as they would barge into the bank on the opposite side of the street within minutes.

He wouldn't let them.

This was his moment of bravery.

Out of the blue he stood and walked towards the bank.

"Can I help you, sir?" someone behind the counter asked.

"Ssshhh ..." Demondre said, holding his finger in front of his mouth.

He hid behind a pillar of the costly, elegant interior of the company, awaiting the anticipated bad guys to get in the lobby. His forecasts were right. Pulling guns out of their bags, the trio announced their reason for interrupting.

Shooting in the air, they said, "Ladies and gentlemen, we are here to take the money which is rightfully ours. Move and you die. Stay still, shut up, and you'll live. If we can just all work together, nobody will get harmed.

The normal thing that always happens was something Demondre saw before it occurred too.

"Hey, don't try to be a hero," one of the burglars would say, looking over and seeing a staff member grab his cell phone.

Tagadagadack!

He would shoot the man in the chest with his gatling gun.

It didn't truly happen, but it was going to happen. It wasn't too late yet. Demondre knew it. Within a flash of a second, he turned around the tough column he was leaning his back against and elbowed the burglar in his throat. The surprised bandit instantly dropped his weapon and had fallen over. The other two turned around, but it was too late. Demondre had already disappeared behind another wall.

"Where did he go?" one of them asked in a frightened voice.

"Are you playing games? Show yourself!" the other shouted.

Demondre didn't need a mirror. He didn't need a showing surface area or somebody signaling him when it was safe to attack. He knew exactly when the 2 burglars would turn the other way, and he waited on the precise moment to strike. After about 10 seconds, this is what happened and with the back of their heads facing his direction, the way was free to grab their heads and bash them against each other.

Knockout.

All 3 of them.

The guns were lying next to them on the floor, but none of them had the strength to reach for them, since their level of awareness was that of a sloth.

Before his applause, the hero leapt out of the door and disappeared out of sight.

Anybody who knows about Demondre's superpower to predict the future must be in shock when they hear that he walks away from the honor he could have gotten by an amazed crowd. But experience has taught this young hero the harshness of reality and the impulsive judgments of people.

He has decided to keep himself from the honor of the masses, since he recognizes how fleeting and unstable it is.

Demondre gets back and regrets the impulsive propensity of these simple creatures to condemn and rebuke. He reflects on a previous occurrence that ruined him financially. Whether or not his rightful money is in his pockets, he does not care. He just wished it would have been otherwise. Why do people always trying to get things for free?

This is what took place:

Somebody found eventually that Demondre could forecast the future, at least in a restricted way. He discovered by the little things, like when Demondre played cards, caught a bottle falling on the ground, or avoided a hazardous motorist when he was crossing the roadway. This harmful person did not think it was bad making somebody suffer. He simply wanted money ... as much as possible.

His name was Mike. He devised a little plan and tricked Demondre into losing a lawsuit. The dirty liar ... sad that people get away with those unethical types of strategies.

There they were, sitting in a court room, exchanging spiteful glares at each other. The room was primarily brown, decorated with basic patterns on the ceiling. Crowds of people were curious to see the result of this supernatural phenomenon Demondre was implicated of being able to set off. There were at least 50 people in the court room, in addition to a few in the hallways who were waiting for the end results. The judge possessed a substantial hammer and pounded the pulpit as he pleased, happy to be in charge and having the ability to exercise his occupation.

Demondre's legal representative was as inexperienced as a child, but Demondre didn't have a lot, so searching for a better one was certainly the question.

" What do you have to say in your defense?" the judge asked Demondre.

" Your honor, I never planned to break the system or to get money in a dishonest way," Demondre said.

" But you know how and that's not fair!" Mike's attorney blurted out as he got up.

" Mr. Demondre," the judge continued, "Do you deny the power of predicting the near future?"

" I do not," Demondre boldly announced.

" Then don't you think," the judge continued, "that it's possibly hazardous for you to get in the lotto, no matter how low the price of the tickets? If anybody else had this power, they could exert the same to easily win all the money for themselves."

" But I didn't," Demondre defended.

" He's lying, your honor," Mike said.

" Order!" the judge screamed. "When I want your witness, I will enable you to come to the stand."

" I ask forgiveness, your honor," Mike said.

" Mr. Mike's legal representative, your customer has made a horrible allegation. Are you able to back this claim up?"

" Yes, your honor. Exhibit A here shows that Demondre has bought a lottery ticket, completely aware of which numbers would make him win."

Putting the lotto ticket on the table, he smirked and relaxed in his chair.

" You know I bought that ticket for you!" Demondre shouts. "How dare you use this against me, you backstabbing weasel?!"

" Order, order," the judge demands.

The entire thing exploded. There was turmoil in the courtroom. People were angry, guards were contacted to relax the circumstances. And to make a long story short, the end outcome was that while Mike got a truckload of cash for winning the case, Demondre had to pay a big cost and was forbidden to ever participate in the lottery, and mixed emotions existed amongst the population.

Demondre hasn't done much after that to use his anticipating power. He has kept a low profile. He does not rely on the typical person as much as he used to. Just like any celeb or somebody in the spotlight, there is always risk prowling beneath the surface caused by those who abuse the system and the evil opportunities laid out for them by life.

Demondre wakes up. He finds himself panting because of a terrible nightmare he does not remember. All he knows, is that it has left him anxious and sweaty, even minutes after his awakening. It must have been terrible dreaming about this.

He sits up for a minute or 2, then gets up and gets a cup of chocolate milk. Back to reality. He gazes at the pigeons outside. One of them is silly enough to fly into the glass window.

BANG!

The fat bird slides down after slightly cracking the glass. Ridiculous pigeon. Why would you fly against the window like that? Didn't he see it? Oh well ...

Demondre lives in an apartment or condo, not too far away from his mom and dad, who live about six blocks away from him. Demondre's apartment or condo is small and simple, but he enjoys it.

He loves his own space, with the flexibility to do whatever he wants. Every other day, though, he visits his parents to see if they are doing all right.

This day is no different than any other day, or so it seems initially. Demondre's superpower is limited to the near future, but hardly ever extends into the foreknowledge of things to come hours or days ahead of him. He doesn't mind. All he wants is to be happy and if anything comes his way, he will stand all set to assist.

Ultimately, this day is different than the other days. He feels it. He just does not know what is wrong, or what is going to be wrong. Either way, he makes himself rush to his mom and dad place this time, because his feeling is stronger than ever before.

" Knock knock!" he says as he opens the door.

Empty.

The house is empty.

" Mother! Dad!" he yells, expecting a response.

" Are you here? Remember I was going to come over today?"

No answer.

He walks through the living-room. Every little thing is in its place. Nothing has been moved. The cool little room is tidy as ever. He opens up the door to the bedroom.

What an important difference! What a mess!

Things are turned upside down in the bedroom. The sheets are off the beds, the cabinet has fallen on the floor, and even the mirror has broken into a thousand pieces. This is not like them. Something took place here.

Demondre fears for his father's and mother's lives. The strenuous job ahead of him has now become some kind of investigator project to solve the puzzle and figure out what happened to them.

Before calling the cops, Demondre looks for tracks, anything the kidnappers left. Through the stacks of clothes, the damaged furnishings, and the ripped matrass, he searches and searches till ...

" Hey, what's that?" he asks out loud to nobody in particular.

It's sculpted sandstone.

Demondre bends over and rubs the stuff between his fingers.

" I know where this is coming from," he says. "There is only one place outside the city where you can find chiseled sandstone: the Dead Man's Rocks. Maybe these small grains of sand were in the bad guy's pocket when he took my mom and dad."

He lurks into some other things but could not find anything particular.

" To the Dead Man's Rocks it is," he says.

Demondre heads back to his apartment. He goes through the busy city streets, crosses the crosswalk without waiting on it to become green, and maneuvers his way through the crowds. When he enters his place, he puts on his mask and his superhero outfit.

He takes a look at his old second-hand bicycle. It's a superannuated piece of junk that he just uses to save himself some gas. But this situation needs more severe measures. Forget the bicycle. There is something better in the garage.

" How's it going pal?" he says to another vehicle standing in the corner. Raising the sheet, which is covering it, he thinks about the last time he used this fantastic speed devil.

" Time for a ride," he says in a low voice as he gets on his valuable, glimmering motorcycle. "This is going to be incredible."

The bike is crimson red. Its glossy surface area depicts flames and tiny patterns invisible to the naked eye, unless a person comes closer and shows some appreciative respect to it. Its engine is effective and makes its rider go superfast. Demondre loves this thing. It feels like a dream riding it. It's just more expensive and delicate, which is why he only uses it to get out of the city.

" Prepared to go, bikey?" he says as if talking to an actual person.

He sits down, kicks the engine on, and prepares to speed out the garage door. VROOOOOOOM!

He races through the city and feels alive. Only a couple hours till he gets to the Dead Man's Rocks. This is going to be ...

Demondre was going to say "fun," but he gets held up by traffic. Great another red light. And another, and another. It just happens to be rush hour and Demondre is stuck in a traffic congestion with his motorbike, feeling that the potential of this quick beast of a motorcycle gets untapped.

" What a waste," he says. "It's just like I could arrive faster on foot. If only I had learnt about this earlier, I could have avoided the rush hour. Now everyone is just going to work at the exact same time. Ughh ..."

The long, hard battle to get out of the city is taking a lot longer now. After about 5 hours of sighing and complaining, the rush is finally over.

" Woohoo!" Demondre cheers as he takes off and hits a consistent typical speed of circa 80 miles per hour on the highway leading out of his hometown, heading for the rocky range of mountains. What he will find there, will surprise him, to say the least.

This is it, the Dead Man's Rocks. His parents must be over here someplace. It appears so basic, and yet it is not. Why? Since there are miles and miles of mountains here, all containing the sculpted sandstone he found in his father's and mother's bed room.

His persistence has limits, but his sense of futuristic events helps him find a distinct location on instinct. Demondre searches and searches, and after that senses something happening in one of the mountain caves near him. After about an hour of taking a look around, he finds the deserted cave.

Demondre pulls over, puts his motorbike against a rock, and slips into the cavern. He has to be prepared for anything, he thinks.

" No, I need a different one! Hand me the spruce leaves and the allium!" he hears a voice yell.

" Okay, boss," a seemingly less intelligent voice answers.

As Demondre approaches the light originating from the hollow opening in the cavern, he observes 5 guys, each of them armed to the teeth. He can only think how much the arms and handguns cost that they are holding and keeping in their pockets and holsters.

One of the guys appears like he supervises, giving him the impression of a lab rat, with a white coat and a pair of glasses.

" I need uncommon fern, magenta wool, poppies, and some of that chiseled sandstone from the rocks. That will be the right mix, believe me," the man in the white coat says.

" Hey Kevin, where do you want this stuff?"

" In the corner," the professorsays.

These combos sound unsafe, and they are, seeing that this mean man is putting them into a tube beside an enormous rocket.

Demondre looks around. He analyzes the situation. The rocket (what is that for?), the Professoror whatever he calls himself, and the four armed men. Then there is the ... hey... those are his parents!

On the right side of the cavern, his mother and father are bound and gagged. They can't see Demondre, but Demondre can see them. No one has seen him up until now actually, a practical advantage he is more than ready to use.

" Ha-ha-hah!" the man with the glasses exclaims. "This is it. Let's check it on our guinea pigs."

He walks over to Demondre's parents and dumps the stuff into their mouths.

" Nooooo!" Demondre yells, but it is far too late. Why he didn't see this coming, he doesn't know. His powers left him alone. He couldn't anticipate it. And now this bad guy poured some who-knows-what into his mother's and father's mouths.

" Who goes there?" one of the criminals asks after hearing Demondre's cry.

" Do not bother," ProfessorKevin says. "These two will be ready within seconds."

Demondre keeps hiding. But as he looks above the rim of the rock he is hiding behind, he sees his two parents become something ... well, something different. Their eyes turn red, their mouths start lathering, and their sense of reality appears to disappear as they transform into some monstrous kind of zombies. Needless to say, this new toxin they have taken in has a trigger impact on their aggressiveness.

" Stand back. Let's see what they will do," the professorsays. "Hey, little hero! If you're still there, just come out anywhere you are! We won't shoot you!"

For some reason, Demondre trusts his words and leaves his hiding place.

" What did you do to them?" he asks in anger.

" You'll discover quickly enough, as everyone will," Kevin says laughingly.

Demondre's parents break their bonds and holler loudly.

" Aaaarrgghh!"

After this expression, they storm at Demondre and leap at him, pulling him to the ground and standing prepared to put their teeth into him.

" M-mom. Father. It's me!" Demondre says. "Snap out of it. Please!"

But it is to no avail. They have been changed. They don't have any memory, compassion, or emotions whatsoever; just a blood thirst and a craving for human flesh.

Demondre dodges their attacks and punches one of the thugs in his face before getting his firearm.

" St-stand back," he stammers. "I don't want to kill you."

His father and mother aren't listening. They are only driven by their desire to kill. Neglecting Demondre's remarks totally, they begin another attack and run at their child.

BAM! BAM!

What just occurred ...?

It is as if time stands still for a moment. Adrenaline is flowing through Demondre's blood. His heart pumps faster than an ADD boy on the drums. He holds his breath. Fumes rise from his hot rifle.

He just killed his mother and father.

A sense of loss and unhappiness rushes through his very soul. He still can't believe what happened.

" Hahahah!" the evil Professor laughs. "It works. Prepared to load, boys!"

With no regard for Demondre and his dead father and mother, the man in the white coat puts a mix in the rocket, ready to launch the thing. The Professor pushes the button and launches the rocket.

" There it goes! Hahahahahah!"

" What did you do?!" Demondre cries out. "You've turned my mom and dad into beasts! I had no choice but to shoot them!"

" Not just your father and mother, young man," the wicked Professor says, "But the entire city! Hahah!"

" What do you mean?" Demondre asks.

" I developed a compound that will turn everyone into zombielike creatures like your mom and dad. I hacked the products out of these rocks, and they showed to be quite helpful. People in the city will dislike one another, they will kill one another, and no one will know how all of it began."

" B-but why? Why on earth would you do that?"

" Oh, I have my reasons," the evil Professor explains. "I started out like you. I thought I would help the world by being yourself, but all my experiments got rejected. I had chemistry classes, but they weren't open to my recommendations. Eventually I lost my family, my money. And it's all thanks to those idiots. They took my life away, and now, I am taking theirs. Well, not truly, I'm just the one who shows them a little push. And then when panic strikes, when they're ready to ask for a solution, I will sell them the remedy ... for billions! And they'll purchase it no matter what, as I will have an effective monopoly. It's genius!"

" You beast!" Demondre yells.

" Call me what you want, young man, but you're already far too late. There's nothing you can do to stop it now. The rocket has been launched. I would not advise going into town. It may be a little disorderly there."

" Oh yeah? We'll just see about that!" Demondre says as he runs out of the cavern.

He hops on his motorcycle and starts the engine. Determined to catch up and follow the rocket into town, he hits the gas and figuratively flies through the air, going beyond the speed limitation on the highway to get to his location in time.

He doesn't care about the criminals. He has to let go of his father and mother for a little while till he has the time to think about their deaths. All he has to concentrate on now, is returning to the city to prevent the disaster from dispersing.

The professor was right, though. He is far too late. Hordes of zombies are already roaming the streets. They attack humans, each other, and anything they can get their claws and teeth on. Demondre dodges a few bodies on the street by leaping on his motorcycle over ledges and crisscrossing the bike towards the downtown area. What he sees there, is among his biggest worst nightmares.

The downtown zone is crazy! As Demondre approaches the burning buildings and fuming stacks of particles and dead bodies, he is confronted by hordes of zombies ... numerous zombies. He didn't know the gasses from the rocket would have such an immediate influence. Is there anybody left to save, or has the entire city been doomed to being destroyed?

Painful sounds of terror rip through the routine hustle and bustle city sounds, like a howling ghost screaming and flying through the air. The worst chaos in the city's history unfolds before Demondre's eyes. Viewing the scenes and the bloody results of every resident losing his/her sense of reality makes Demondre shiver.

Random riots and blasts of aggressiveness are thrusting everybody's heart with fear and stress and anxiety. Someone has to do something. This is really getting out of hand. It already became a lot worse!

Packed with a set of combating skills and anticipating powers, Demondre storms at the hordes and begins his fight. He punches one zombie here, kicks another there, and each time, he is able to predict their counterattacks and deviate from the patterns of their strikes.

Is there ever an end to this? What is he even trying to accomplish? Preventing more casualties?

While avoiding countless zombies and knocking down lots of other ones, he is trying to determine how to remove the root of the issue. He isn't sure. It looks like there is no stopping the transformation of all these people, some of which are heaped on the floors and the damaged streets while others are taking out their rage on susceptible victims. The city has never been in such an awful state before. It spreads out like a disease. Innocent martyrs paint the city red with their blood, turmoil breaks the really foundations its largest skyscrapers are built on, and an unclean smell of the dead decorates the senses of all who come near. But it isn't over yet. It has barely begun.

Chapter 8: Catastrophe

Demondre battles his way through some zombies till a certain suspicion catches his attention. He sees it happening before it does: A subway train is about to derail and cause hundreds of people to die or get caught up in the dreadful movements of the city's former civilians.

" I have got to stop this thing," Demondre tells himself. "I know it is coming from ..." he closes his eyes ... "that angle."

He opens his eyes and looks at his finger, as if he didn't know where he is pointing at. He leaps off a stack of building fragments and starts running into the direction of the subway tracks.

Where is the switch?

He has to act quickly, or the collision will turn into one of the biggest tragedies in the city. He looks and looks, but cannot find the silly switch.

Then he sees something behind the wall.

" Aha!" he says, running towards the object.

It's a lever, a substantial one, one that needs somebody to pull with all his strength to get it to move. Demondre pulls as hard as he can.

" Umpffff! Too heavy. Let's try again."

This time it budges.

" Yes!" he cheers.

But his little moment of happiness is based upon a wrong conclusion. The lever is pulled back, but the subway tracks have not even moved an inch.

" What the ...? Why didn't it work?" Demondre grumbles.

In the meantime, the subway train is coming closer. It is racing with a tremendous speed, not able to stop because of the technological error that has happened by coincidence. Demondre is getting nervous. He is uncertain about what to do next. He takes a look around for another switch or lever. There is nothing there!

The subway train approaches.

It's getting closer ...

And closer ...

BANG!

The train derails and glissades over the ground, ending up above the surface area because of the deviating items in its way. Floors collapse, people die, fumes of smoke contribute to the random explosions in numerous places, zombies get run over ... blood and horror portray the awful scene as the so-called hero watches by helplessly, regretting the loss of the lives he could have saved.

" Noooooo!" he shouts.

Chapter 9: Recognition

Demondre gets up. He finds himself panting just because of a terrible nightmare he does not remember. All he knows, is that it has left him anxious and sweaty, even minutes after his awakening. It must have been terrible dreaming about this.

He sits up for a minute or two, then gets up and gets a cup of chocolate milk. Back to reality. He stares at the pigeons outside. One of them is stupid enough to fly into the glass window.

BANG!

Reality strikes.

It hits him like a baseball bat.

What the ...?

He's seen this scene before. He remembers his dreadful dream. This is REAL!!! Is all that stuff with the zombies and the poor victims truly going to happen? Are his mother and father going to be kidnapped?

There is only one way to find out. And THIS time, he's not going to let some traffic congestion or search in the mountains put a time limit on him.

He knows the location. He believes in his dream. It has to be real. Why else would the same fat pigeon from his dream fly into the exact same window?

Determined to prevent the horrible events in his nightmare, he runs downstairs, opens the garage door, pulls the sheet off his motorcycle, and hits the gas.

VROOOOM!

No traffic.

No hold up.

Good.

First, he visits his mother and father. Within a minute, he gets to their places.

Bam!

He swings the door open, letting it crush against the sidewall.

" Mom! Dad!"

" What's the matter, child?" his father asks.

" You need to get out of here. Come on, I have no time at all to clarify. I will tell you later. We are lacking time."

" Uhm ... all right ... if you say so," his father says obediently.

" As long as you'll explain it to us later," his mother adds.

" Naturally, obviously. Now, let's go! We're really in a hurry here."

Both mother and father get on the back of Demondre's motorcycle.

" Oh, this is really dangerous," his mom says.

" It will be all right, mom, for now. I will drop you off at the library. It's on the way where I am going anyhow. Just assure me you'll stay in there until I'm back."

" Okay, I pro ... whoa!" his mother exclaims, since Demondre isn't even waiting for her to finish her sentence. He already hit the gas and has taken off into the direction of the library. After dropping his parents off, he races through the streets to his location in the countryside.

" And now I'll handle you ... Kevin!" Demondre says in a firm, undaunted voice.

He takes off again, avoiding the traffic jams because of the earliness of his trip. He rides his flaming bike out of the city and finds the range of mountains he is looking for within a significant amount of time. He sees the cavern from his dream, but this time, his mom and dad aren't in there, nor has the evil professor completed or evaluated the development of his hazardous compounds yet.

Demondre does not wait any longer. He knows what's going to happen. He walks right up to the goons standing guard.

" Hey, who are you?" the professor asks shocked.

" I'm the one who is going to bring you down," Demondre says with confidence as he keeps stepping forward.

" Shoot him already!" Professor Kevin screams.

Bang! Bang! Tagadagadag!

They really missed. They all missed! Demondre's senses were at a peak. He could feel precisely when and where the bullets would go. Dodging them perfectly, he raises one side of his mouth into a slight smirk as he watches the bullets fly through the air without striking their destined target. With his fists, he gets each of the four guards around the professor, knocking them out one by one and leaving them on the cold floor of the cave.

" N-no! I was just trying to help humanity. |Don't you see? I mean no harm," the professor claims.

Demondre grabs him by the throat and holds him against the stony wall.

" You're a huge, fat phony," he says. "I know what you're intending on doing, but this is where it stops."

He drops the professor on the ground.

" Wh-what are you intending to do?" Kevin stutters.

" Watch," Demondre says in a form of calm anger.

He collects his strength and begins to smash every tube, every piece of glass, every fluid, and every aspect on the chemistry table. The rocket doesn't get spared but bent in half by the effective hands of this superhero.

" No!" Professor Kevin sobs. "Not my experiment! You have not the slightest idea of how hard I was working on that! Do you know what you're doing to me?"

Demondre turns around.

" Yes, I do. And now the authorities are going to think about what they are going to do to you. I'm taking you with me."

Demondre grabs the wicked professorand takes him out of the cave. Dragging him over the rocky ground, he finally takes a look at him, punches him in the face, and throws the knocked out Professor on his bike.

The city has been saved. The illnesses and disasters have been prevented. The sun is rising, birds are chirping, and the cold breeze feels good in his face. The odor of fresh flowers fondles his nose. An enjoyable motorbike ride lies ahead of him.

" I think this will be a good day after all," Demondre says with a pleased face while hitting the gas.

" And I think I will even be in the city so quickly to avoid the traffic congestion."

THE END

Beasts

This isn't it," Calvin the Professor says, scratching his head. "It needs something else. I think I am doing it all wrong. The formula appears correct, but something is still really missing here."

Professor Calvin is a regular lab rat, or simply put, someone who has spent his entire life figuring out compounds and combining chemical fluids and materials. He is astonished by the effects of one fluid blended with another. It fascinates him. It has always fascinated him. That's why he went to university 10 years ago: To study chemistry and biology, primarily chemistry. His final theses and documents were full of complex computations the teachers didn't even comprehend. He always outmaneuvered them, but now it appears like he hasn't followed the right formula. It annoys him.

He has run into issues before, and has even had explosions in his lab, but this time, he has been doing mathematics for days, looked up numerous theories and clinical facts, and he still hasn't figured it out.

His perseverance has its limitations too.

" I give up," he says, throwing his hands up in the air. "I'll continue later."

It's just one of those things that takes forever. It doesn't matter how much effort he puts into it; he just wants to get it done.

" Why does it have to be so hard?" he questions. "I have succeeded with countless experiments and have taken science to a higher level. This formula is just too intricate. There must be something I am lacking, but what?"

He leaves out of the door and returns home, after a long day of 10 hours of work. His marriage partner greets him with a kiss at his homecoming, rebuking him for working overtime again.

" But honey," the Professor says. "This is extremely crucial. Can't you see the turnaround this society will have if we get this mixture working? It will be a transformation."

" I know, but you have to relax sometimes. There's more to life than work," she says. At that moment, his 3 children come running in to the room.

" Dad!" the tiniest boy yells.

" Father, you're home! Finally," his daughter says. "I wanted to show you my drawing. Can you come have a look? It is in the living-room."

" Okay, all right," Calvin says. "I will have a look at it."

The oldest child does not look so good. He looks sad. His head is hanging and he gradually walks towards his dad.

" What's the matter with you, my child?"

" I bumped my head and lost the sports game."

" Oh, that doesn't sound like fun. Come here. Where does it hurt?" Calvin asks.

" Well, it's gone now. But I still dislike that it happened."

" That's life, son. I'm happy you see it. Bad things happen all the time. And losing? Just take a look at me. I have been trying to figure out a formula for the past week and I still do not understand it."

As he is saying it, he understands that he let it get to him. His discouragement got the best of him and he has given up too fast. Some things just take a long period of time anyhow, and if this is actually as big as he expects it to be, putting a little time into it is the least he can do. He sees himself as this little boy who is downtrodden since he is losing; or he lost. And this brand-new awareness has made him determined again. Tomorrow, he will go back and try again ... and again ... till he understands the correct mix.

" Don't stress, child," he finally says. "You may have lost the game, but you have not lost the league. And let's see if you can beat this tickle monster!"

Calvin leans over and begins tickling his kid. The other 2 get on his back and a rough rumble and jumping game begins. For several minutes, the fun with his children does not stop and thankfully, nobody gets hurt, which actually does happen sometimes.

" Dinner time!" Calvin's spouse shouts. "Come on, guys! Do not let it get cold."

" Hold on," Calvin says. "I still have to see our daughter's drawing."

After his daughter displays her skill and he happily pats her on the head, he thinks about what he said to his own son: He lost another game, another match ... by not having the ability to get the formula right; but the league is far from over. Tomorrow there is a new day and he might just get it this time. And if not, then in 5 days, or 10, or twenty.

This brand-new combination of fluids is going to be grand. It will have an extensive impact on cravings, the economy, and people's way of lives. It is worth fighting for.

On the other side of town, a corporal screams his lungs out.

" Forwaaaard! March! One-two, one-two, one-two! Keep moving, you lazy bedbugs!"

Corporal Johnny has handled numerous difficult circumstances. He is a man of honor. Always putting his best foot forward, he has acquired favor with the generals in the city's army. In numerous battles, he has combated threatening Black shades, skeletons, zombies, beasts, vampires, and other dangerous creatures from the deep and dark lands.

One time, he stood before numerous Black shades, who were already provoked by the staring soldiers in his army. At first, the coast appeared clear, but then Johnny saw a twinkle in their eyes, an upset sparkle originating from deep in their souls. They raged and were ready to attack.

" Draw back!" he yelled, but the noises of the storm they were in outweighed his voice. Thick clouds had already burst into loud thunder and terrifying lightning flashes had set the scene for a more significant war that was already raging. Rain was pouring on each and every soldier, soaking their outfits and muting the sounds of their voices.

They didn't listen.

They didn't pull back.

As one weapon, they marched forward to the threatened Black shades, who were in no other way willing to forgive or stand down what had just caught their attention.

" Return! Retreat!" Corporal Johnny kept shouting, but only a handful of the guys obeyed his orders. The others were too unconcerned of the fact that these Black shades would run into them and completely crush them with their numbers.

So they marched forward, not even seeing the few men that pulled back with Corporal Johnny. All they concentrated on were the beasts in front of them. The Black shades kept still, but inside, they were boiling with a raving fire that was about to blow up. Hundreds of Black shades were standing there ... in the odd chaos of heavy rain, weird trees, and a soaked field of moss and random blades of grass.

Corporal Johnny was overwhelmed. More than anything he wanted to save these men from the awful fate that was about to beset them, but he felt defenseless.

" Give me that bomb," he finally said to a nearby soldier. He nabbed the product from his hand and ran forward. Side by side, the majority of the guys were still marching towards their enemy, but Johnny was going to stop these creatures from damaging his valiant boys.

As quick as his legs could carry him, he ran in front of his whole army, with the bomb and several matches in his hand. A couple of hundred feet in front of them, he knelt down and lit one of the matches.

" Pssshhhh ..."

The fire from the match got quenched by the wetness of the weather.

" Dumb annoying matches ... Come on!" he said as he anxiously stroke the matches and lit them up one by one.

" There!" he said excitedly when he managed to illuminate a match and the fuse of the bomb. He stuck it in the ground and ran back.

" Go back! Get out of here!" he yelled to the men he was running to, waving his arms in the air.

They finally comprehended it. They had seen him place the bomb in the soil. Now the guys were sprinting back and panicking, moving into all different directions except for the one between them and the Black shades.

" You too! Get back!" Corporal Johnny yelled in another soldier's ear. "|Don't you see? It is about to explo ..."

Boooooom!

The blast burnt a hole in the ground, in a perimeter of a hundred feet, triggering the grass to catch fire, as well as a few poor trees next to the field. The sky lit up, the smoke covered the atmosphere. The Black shades hesitated. They despised the light and the fire. The previous provocation wasn't enough for them to strike back. The numerous dark creatures reacted by running in the opposite direction, never to be heard of again. The corporal had saved his men; he had prevented their damage. His courageous deed would be long remembered in the years to come.

Satisfied with his accomplishments, Johnny watched the men march, do push-ups, and struggle to get in shape and go through an obstacle course. The battle has become a cherished memory and the future looks bright.

Johnny is not scared of anything, or so it seems. He dislikes laziness and loves discipline. As a commander, he ranks above the most affordable soldiers in the army, which he doesn't take lightly. More than anything he has determined to take these slackers on and teach them what it means to be a man.

When someone disobeys his orders-- which has occurred before-- he knows how to control these weak souls into tougher tests, so they can grow up and develop their strengths. Some dislike him for it; others think it's a regrettable necessity to kick the softness out of their spoiled characters. It's for their own good, and they will see it later. Nobody develops character without hardship, and he knows it more than anything.

Some of that hardship came when his partner left him. They had been attempting to work out their relationship for many years, but the issues in their home were too confrontational, so they chose to separate. Nevertheless, seeing his kids only once per week brought him unhappiness. Since it took place ten years ago anyway, he has somewhat accepted the situation and made attempts to toughen up by telling himself it wasn't all his fault. The future for his family remains uncertain, but just to compensate, he has pushed himself to work hard at securing the future of the city by protecting it. That is his objective. It's the only thing he knows how to do right.

After training the cadets, he goes back to his office and finds his commander there, standing and looking at a few pictures.

" Have a seat, corporal," he says.

" What are you doing here, sir?"

" Sit down and we'll talk," he says in a friendly tone.

Corporal Johnny sits down and leans on his desk with one elbow. He is captivated. The last time the general came to his office was a year ago. He has been so busy since then that he barely saw him at the military terrain at all.

The general starts, "You might know some of the projects the army has supported in the past."

" Certainly, sir," Johnny says.

" Good. Recently, we began a project in cooperation with a lab, and we haven't even heard anything for weeks. In the meantime, the Professor there is draining our checking account by charging us the regular hour wage and not reporting any valuable actual results. Simply put, he is wasting our time and our cash. I want you to go to the laboratory and see how far the project has advanced. If nothing good has come out of it, I want you to shut it down. We do not have room for leeches who take advantage of the system."

" Yes, sir. I will leave very first thing in the early morning, sir."

" Thank you, corporal. I expected nothing less. That will be all."

It's early in the morning. Professor Calvin opens the front door of the lab. His key gets stuck for a few seconds, but after a while, he easily pulls it out. He switches on the lights, puts his bag on the floor, and takes a look at the failed experiment he disrupted yesterday because he got tired of it.

He sighs.

It already looks discouraging and he hasn't even done anything yet. Calvin thinks for a second and recognizes again how big this discovery could be. The effects could be magnificent. He has to pursue his dreams and move on with this formula.

He decides not to linger on these thoughts any longer and goes to work. He has barely begun blending compounds together and writing intricate computations on a notepad. He hears a knock on the door.

Knock knock!

" I'm coming!" Calvin yells. He finishes a few notes he was making.

Knock knock!

" Yes! I said I was coming! Patience, please!"

He walks to the door and opens up. Without any further ado, the corporal walks in and takes a peek. Then he turns around and reveals the reason of his visit.

" I am here to check if you are making any progress," he says in a stern voice.

" Oh yes," Calvin answers. "I have made tremendous progress, but we're just not there yet. I just need more time."

" I see," Johnny says. "But the officer ranking higher than me has advised me to shut this place down if you do not report any substantial changes. You have a due date, which is tonight. If your experiment does not have any results, we will close this place."

" Oh, no, don't do that," the professor begs. "I just need a bit longer. |Don't you see the effect this can have on society? I am creating a compound that can make plants and fruits grow faster. If I have success, starvation will be over all over the world. All we would need to do, is put it in the crops, and they'll grow 10 times much faster and larger. The economy would get an increase and everybody would succeed."

" I understand. I will stay with you today and help you any place I can, unless you do not want me to naturally. But no matter what we do, it has to end tonight."

" I will try to rush," Calvin says.

They work at it the whole day, blending this or that, writing solutions and reasoning and introductions. Clearly, Corporal Johnny has no clue what he is doing scientifically, but at least he gives Calvin some support and encouragement.

Eventually, late in the evening, Calvin says, "It is not totally done yet, but I just need one more day. That's all I need. Could you please give me another day?"

" Sorry," Johnny says. "I have my orders. Finish it now or shut it down."

" Can't you be a little more flexible?" Calvin asks.

" No, I cannot. Now hurry and do what you have to do."

" But it's not done yet!" Calvin lashes out.

" I do not care, professor! You have till midnight!" Johnny sneers back.

" Fine, I'll just try it out. But I may be wrong about this. And I don't want to be held accountable for the effects. You gave me this deadline."

" Do whatever you want. Just make sure you close this evening," Johnny says.

" Okay, here we go."
Calvin takes a tube and carefully pours it on a plant. They watch patiently and wait on the actual results.
Nothing.
" What? Why? Why isn't it working? I almost had it right!" the professor grumbles. "I'm going to try more."
" You better know what you're doing," Johnny says.
Calvin takes another tube and puts the entire content on the tomato plant. He goes back and waits.
Hey, what's that? Something is boiling. That's not the chain reaction he expected. He gets a little closer and observes the boiling soil.
" This is impossible," he says.
" What's impossible?" Johnny asks.
" This chemical reaction only happens when there is a Dark pearl involved."
" You put a Dark pearl beneath the plant?"
" Well, I didn't do that. It must have existed when the boy dug up the plant I asked him to bring me."
" And what does that mean?" Johnny asks.
" I don't know. It's reacting and I don't comprehend how. This is incredible."
It is incredible, but not in the way the 2 men hoped it would be. The Dark pearl keeps boiling and boiling. It's growing faster than they thought it would. Within seconds, the pearl has increased in size so much that it now looks as huge as a brick. And it does not stop there. It keeps growing and growing.
" I don't like the looks of this," Corporal Johnny admits.
" It's unbelievable, but I wonder if it will stop," Professor Calvin agrees.
It's not stopping. By now, it has grown as huge as the both of them and is leaning against the ceiling. Black Shade shapes are being formed by the pearl, creating a head, arms, and legs. Still in its infant state, the pearl continues to flexibly fill up the laboratory's space and exponentially push the 2 people out the door.
" We need to leave. Now!" Johnny shouts.
" No, we cannot desert it. I want to see how it develops. This has never happened before."
" You stubborn fool. Follow me out of here or I'll knock you out. This is leaving control!"

Professor Calvin feels miserable leaving his growing speculative pearl. His curiosity has taken over. But after a while, he sees the necessity of securing their lives by escaping too. They open the door and run out of the laboratory.

Crrrrrraaaasssssh!!!

In the nick of time they jump from the building onto the street. When they look upwards, they see the monstrous pearl break through the roofing. The pearl has now taken form and looks like a big, black man.

" You unclear, absentminded idiot! You truly had no clue what you were doing, did you?" Corporal Johnny screams as they run for their lives. "Remove your coat! It's slowing you down."

Professor Calvin drops his coat and looks back as he runs behind the corporal. He feels like he accomplished something, but now, it has become a catastrophe.

" Keep running!" the corporal commands. "Don't look back!"

But this only kindles Calvin's desire to look back a lot more. Now he truly wishes to know what has become of his monster. He stops running, catching his breath, and turns around. He cannot believe his eyes. The monster has grown to over a hundred feet high. Its limbs are long, its face is dark and scary, with radiant eyes and diabolic horns on its head. It takes a look at the 2 with a permeating stare as if it is attempting to say that it's going to chase after them.

" It's enormous!" the professor exclaims.

" My goodness," Johnny says as he glances back. "What have you done?"

They can't help but stand there and look at the roaring monstrosity. It's hard to believe what they are seeing. There is no time, though. They need to keep moving.

" Follow me to the base," Corporal Johnny suggests. "We can discuss how to defeat this thing there."

Shortly afterwards, the 2 get to the military base. They run in anxiously, disconcerting several soldiers that risk is on the way there. After a few turns, they go into the general's office.

" Excuse me, sir," Johnny says. "I'm sorry to intrude like this, but we have a serious issue."

Chapter 5: City Scape

" What is so important that you have to disrupt my meeting, corporal? I need an immediate explanation," the general says.

" Do you remember clinical task you sent me to? The one you were going to shut down? Well, it has backfired on us."

" What do you mean with 'backfired?'".

" Well, the professor and I were inside. And when we evaluated this liquid on a tomato plant, something began to grow. It ended up being substantial!"

" Would you explain it to me in more detail, please? What exactly grew so big?"

" That!" Calvin yells as he points at the monster through the window.

" Holy cow!" the general exclaims. "It's kind of like a Black Shade but bigger."

" Appears like an appropriate name for my development," Calvin mumbled with almost a little pride in his voice.

" I do not have time for this, corporal. I was going to head out when you came in. But upon my departure, I am giving you complete command of the troops in this region. Congratulations, major. You just got promoted ... temporarily ... depending upon the condition that you get rid of this thing. If you don't, you will be degraded to the rank of soldier. The outcome of your career is in your hands now. Best of luck."

With that, the general sticks the symbols of the said rank on Johnny's shoulder and vanishes out the back entrance, leaving Johnny with his brand-new rank behind, who has huge eyes and an open mouth, looking at the situation in amazement. He can't actually believe he just got promoted, but he recognizes too that he will lose his entire status if he doesn't blow this monster up. Suddenly, he snaps out of it and takes control. He marches outside and takes a look at the panicking soldiers in the camp.

" Men, gather your weapons! I am in command now! Get your muskets from the ammunition room. You two, go around the corner! Move, move, move!" Major Johnny yells as he claps in his hands to motivate the soldiers to take initiative.

" Professor Calvin, if there is anything you can do to help, do it. If not, get out of our way now. This is a military operation now."

" Yes, sir," Calvin says.

He can't come up with anything to stop the huge monster. And he does not want to be an annoyance. Additionally, he doesn't want to die here, so he chooses to return to the ruined lab they left behind.

Meanwhile, Major Johnny is commanding his soldiers and doing everything he can to stop the threat. The beast stomps on tents and barracks with its feet, swipes away trees and buildings with its arms, and breaks rocks with its fists. The soldiers have gotten their muskets and are lined up to fire at the beast.

" Ready ... aim... fire!" Major Johnny commands.

A dozen bullets fly through the air, only to drop dead on the floor after bouncing off the beast's hard skin.

" Again!" Major Johnny says. "Aim at its head this time. Reload ... all set ... aim ... fire!" The bullets hit the beast's head and repeat the exact same pattern. They drop on the floor like flies, all without results.

" Major," one of the soldiers says. "We cannot kill this thing. It's too strong. We need better devices and more powerful weapons."

" You're right," Johnny says. "Draw back! Let's get the bombs out."
The army retreats to the ammo storage and goes out all the bombs they can find.
Several soldiers carry them out while others stand all set with fire to light them. After
several minutes, 6 bombs are being thrown at the massive beast.
" Hide!" Johnny screams.
The soldiers drop to the floor on their stomachs and cover their heads.
Boooom!
A half lots bombs blow up at the exact same time, tearing the sky with their light, their
fire, and their excruciating sounds. Thick smoke emerges from the hit location, along
with many pieces of particles, grit, and dust. When the soldiers look up, they are
confident and expect the beast to be gone. But their expectations aren't being met.
Without a scratch, the black being steps out of the enormous damage effort. Impatiently,
it walks past the army with several giant steps, heading into the direction of the city.
" This is horrible, major! It will reach the city in no time," one of the soldiers says.
" Let's go after it," the major suggests. "We need to keep trying. It's gotta have a
vulnerable point."

In the meantime, Calvin unfortunately arrives at what is left of his laboratory, the place where it all started. He picks up several beakers and tubes that have been shattered by the growing beast and takes a look at them with a glum expression on his face.

What in the world has he done?

He has unleashed a beast, caused a disaster waiting to happen. His self-confidence is shot. His self-confidence is broken. All he wants now is to crawl under a rock and hide himself from the world.

He glances to the corner of his experiment and sees his notes on the table. After walking to the table, he puts his hand on the notebook he left behind and browses the pages. One by one, he finds the solutions he doodled in there, the signs, the equations, and the overview of lined up data that helped him produced the fluid.

If only he could reverse this disaster.

" Wait a minute," he says. "What if I turned 'X' around in this calculation? That would make sense. The most logical result of this formula is the reverse of the root divided by ..."

And so he goes on for several minutes. He begins taking notes on another page and gets excited about his new discovery. Completely concentrated on his possible solution, he isn't seeing the shaking ground brought on by the beast that has reached the city by now.

The monster stomps on the ground, crashing houses and overturning structures along the way. People all over Miner City go to all different directions in an attempt to evade the large catastrophe that has entered their town. Screams by girls and women are heard, in addition to afraid weeps of so-called brave young men and fathers who are horrified. Houses are burning, churches are become ruins, and small business are turned upside down by the frequent stomping and knocking of the upset monster.

Turmoil is in the air, desperate souls are attempting to save their own skin; useless attempts from the military consist of still shooting at the found hazard.

" Major, I'm so glad you are here!" Calvin exclaims. "I might have found the remedy. If it works, it will reverse the results of the development spurt."

" What are you saying? That you can reverse this mistake?" Johnny asks.

" That's precisely what I am saying."

" Then what are we waiting on? Let's give it to him."

" Well, there's an issue," Calvin says. "It has to be injected into the scalp, meaning someone has to climb on its head and put the injection needle in its brain. That's the only logical way. I am certain of it. The formulas all make good sense now."

" And how do you think we can do that, teacher? It appears almost impossible what you ask of us."

" Well," Calvin begins. "I made a strategy. I didn't expect this to be easy. The beast is so high that it would take a great effort to climb up all the way up there. It bends over often, but insufficient to time it perfectly. We just can't afford to gamble on this."

" Then what do you suggest?" Major Johnny asks curiously.

" Let's trip that thing. If we can extend a strong cord from one end to the other, we might be able to tangle its feet up and wrap the cord around its ankles, causing it to fall. And

that will give us a minute or two for somebody to climb on his head and inject the needle."
" That makes sense. Let's get to it."

Within minutes, Johnny manages to get a huge group of soldiers together and commands them to take some rope.
" The strongest and thickest you can find," he adds. "And the 5 of you over there, keep shooting to sidetrack the monster! We are going to set the trap on the other side of the town square. Set the clock at two minutes. After that, you'll run like your life depends on it to the predestined place. We will meet there and cover the ropes to trip it. Understood?"
" Affirmative."
" All clear, sir."
" Then move! Come on, teacher, you can come help set the trap."
Calvin runs after Johnny and gets to the town square. Not too much later, a group of soldiers brings a big rope.
" Is that all you could find?" Johnny asks.
" Sorry, sir. That's the best we could do."
" Fine, I think it will have to do for now. Let's hope it works. Hand me that needle, professor."
" You mean that you're going to jump on the monster's head?"
" Obviously. I'm not going to let one of my guys sacrifice himself. If you want something done right, do it yourself. Besides, if I screw up, at least I'll have nobody else to blame."
" Okay," Calvin says, "Good luck."
The beast is coming closer. The 2 minutes are over. The men in front of it are shooting in the air and screaming their lungs out, drawing the monster into the rope trap the major and his guys set. Without a doubt, the beast follows these supposed lunatics and roars madly at them while stomping behind them.
" Faster, quicker! Get over here!" Johnny shouts.
The running soldiers hide behind the wall of a nearby building and pant greatly.
" Now it's our turn, men," Johnny says.
The soldiers cover the rope. The beast comes closer, and closer, and trips over the rope, exactly as prepared.
Bam!
The monstrous giant falls on the town square, together with a number of poor, victimized houses.
Craaash!
Bits and pieces of the tiles, the roofing systems, and the monument are being bounced up from the crash. The beast is down, lying on its side, hardly knowledgeable about what just happened.
" It's just you and me now, ugly head," Johnny says before he runs towards the monster's head. He jumps over bricks and pieces of the damaged monument, grabs onto the beast and gets on its head. The beast grumbles and whacks at him with his hand.
Whoosh!
It almost got him, but since the major ducked, the hand missed him. Johnny uses the monster's horns to pull him around the head, takes a few steps to what he thinks is the center of its scalp, and injects the needle.

" Take that, you filthy monster!" he says with conviction, after which he slides off the beast's body.

In the beginning, it seems inefficient, but then, after about ten seconds, the beast begins to shrink. It gets smaller and smaller. The soldiers, the professor, and the major wait and watch as the beast gradually turns from a beast into a pathetic little pearl.

Chapter 8: Friendship

"Well, would you take a look at that," Professor Calvin says. "What a cute little Dark pearl we have here."
" Yeah, if I didn't know any better, I would damage it right now," Major Johnny adds. The soldiers get around the area where the monster vanished, finding it hard to believe their eyes. They take a look at the small pearl and stay speechless.
" Thank you for all you've done, major," Calvin says, holding his hand in front of him. Johnny shakes his hand.
" I'm sorry I got on you for your error, professor. You are an intelligent addition to this army and to the city. It was an honor to work with you. And thanks to you, I have progressed in my career. My high rank will stay, due to the fact that you created the remedy."
" Good. Now if you'll excuse me, I have to go home to my family. Are you married, major?"
" Separated," the major answers.
" I'm sorry to hear that. Why do not you come by for dinner some time, just to have some fun? In fact, how about you just follow me to my home right now? My better half is an expert at cooking casseroles. Trust me, they are the best."
" All right," Johnny says. "That seems like a great idea. I have to admit that the tomato plant a few hours ago already made me hungry. I don't know how you do it ... staying up so late and not even grabbing a snack or something. Do you think supper will still be warm? It's almost midnight."
" I'm certain it will be. And if not, we'll just warm it up. I've had many times when a heated up dinner tasted even better than before. Speaking of which, did I tell you about the time I developed food additive to improve the flavor of it? It's a long story. I'll tell you all about it on the way home."
The 2 new pals walk through the narrow alleys of the city, ready to eat a tasty meal.

THE END

Back in Time

Chapter 1: Out in Nature

This is Tyson. I am 19 years old ... well, I don't know how else to start a diary, or journal ... whatever. This is the first time. I just want to jot down what took place just recently. It was incredible, and by that I mean that it would be hard to believe unless I clarify every detail, and even then there might be doubters.

What I experienced with my good friends, surpasses the typical and the natural. It was supernatural; that was for sure. We actually didn't actually believe it ourselves initially. So let me just get to it, or I will just keep babbling about how amazing and strange it was.

Everything started when we chose to check out the environment. You see, our town is surrounded by gorgeous mountains, but we just never went there, partly as our mother and father were so busy and we didn't want to go by ourselves. My friends, Fred and Tjeerdo, were about the exact same age at that time and were happy that their father and mother finally consented to let them go off on their own, with me obviously. So we did. We planned an outdoor camping trip.

Initially, we packed our bags, the tent, and some cooking equipment. It was interesting. My dad took pride in me, since this would mean I would become more mature, being self-reliant and all. My mom was a little concerned, but she gave in and let me go. She knew that it would be safer it there were three of us.

It was a hot summer season day. We met in front of my home and took off after hitting each other on the shoulder (like guys do).

" What do you want to do initially?" Tjeerdo asked.

" I just want to go towards the mountains," I said. "When we arrive, we'll decide what to do first. If we do all sorts of things first, it may be dark already when we come to a good spot. So let's find a spot first. After that, we can have as much fun as we want."

" Seems like a strategy," Tjeerdo said.

" Perhaps we can eat some rabbits," Fred said.

We both looked at him. That comment was totally lost. Tjeerdo was a pretty clever kid, but Fred ...? Often we wondered what was up with him.

" Uhm ... yes, maybe," I said.

We were all quiet. For some reason, we just didn't have anything to add, so all of us kept packing our stuff.

We put our bags on our backs. We bid farewell to our families and began our journey. As we walked towards the mountains, we passed by lovely orchards, farmlands, and forests. At the foot of the mountain, we paused.

" That appears like a long way up there," Fred said.

" Not so," I said. "We're not going all the way up there, just midway. It will suffice. That's where we'll pitch our camping tents."

We began climbing up. We were lucky there was a clear course, but it was steep. Every once in a while, we rested, being seriously tired out after such a tough climb. But ultimately, after a few hours, we came to an area where the roadway wasn't so high any longer. We found a creek and some lush, green bushes and trees.

" Let's move up a bit more and then pitch our camping tent near the creek somewhere," I suggested.

My good friends concurred it was a good idea.

After another half hour, we selected a spot and pitched our camping tent. It was challenging, and we observed how much clear communication mattered when you're collaborating as a team. Fred was too clumsy to put the pins in the ground, Tjeerdo was grumbling about the wind, and I just couldn't find some of the tiny items that make a camping tent total. When we were done, we put our bags there, set out the sleeping bags, and took a look at the creek.

" I bet you can't beat my record," Tjeerdo said.

" What's your record?" I asked.

" I can skip a rock 27 times on the water."

" No chance!"

" It's true. So what do you say, Tyson? Are you up for a good challenge?"

" Bring it on." With that remark, I picked up some flat rocks and started skipping them on the water.

1 ... 2 ... 3 ... 4, 5, 6, 7, 8, 9, 10, 11, 12.

" Twelve!" I said. "That's not bad, is it?"

" But it's not 27," Tjeerdo said.

" Well, if you skip a rock 3 times 12, it will be 36," Fred added. "So all you need to do, is do it 2 more times and then you beat his record."

We both looked at one another and rolled our eyes while smiling.

" That's not how it works, Fred. It has to be with the exact same rock."

" Oh," Fred said. "Then maybe you could get the rock from the bottom of the creek and use it again. You know, like recycling."

We couldn't stop chuckling. Fred and his easy logic ... sometimes we actually learned something from his way of thinking. It made more sense than some of the complex matters grownups come up with.

" Sure, Fred," Tjeerdo finally said.

After some fun skipping rocks, we got our fishing equipment out. "Fishing is one of the most dull things in deep space," Tjeerdo said.

" I could not concur with you more," I said. "But I heard there is some good trout in this creek, so let's just give it a try."

We broke up. I stayed with the fishing rods and the other 2 went to get some wood for a campfire. When they came back, I proudly presented a huge trout I caught. They were satisfied. I was pretty happy to see they made themselves useful too.

" Let's get this fire going," I said.

It was great. We roasted fish and marshmallows and hotdogs. Fred kept burning the marshmallows, even after we tried to show him how far he should hold them from the fire.

" Have you guys ever wanted to perform some heroic deed?" Tjeerdo asked when we were just chilling at the fire.

" What are you focusing on?" I asked.

" Just ... you know, do something that you are proud of, something that means something to other individuals."

" Yes, I have," I said after a little thinking. "I once had a dream that I saved some girl. She was being assaulted by shades and monsters, but I came to nab her away and put her to a safe zone. And after that I combated the enemies one by one. It was a pretty spectacular dream, to be honest."

" Ha! And who was the girl? Olivia? Katherine? Sydney?" Tjeerdo asked.

" Oh, come on. Do I have to expose to you who I think is the most popular girl in our class?"

" Yes. Naturally."

" I sort of like Sydney," I confessed.

" Oooooow!" the 2 boys yelled with a grin on their faces, teasing me a little. "Tyson has a crush on Sydney!"

" Shhh ... I do not have a crush," I said.

" Sure. It's alright. No one can hear us here in the mountains."

" Well, what about you? I asked. Who do you like?"

Tjeerdo blushed a little but then he told me. We were just having discussions young guys have, about girls, about cool stuff, kids we despised, sports, etc. When we were not hungry anymore, especially with the scrumptious fish I caught, we entered into the tent and slept all night. It was tranquil, with the sound of the streaming water in the creek and the rustling leaves on the trees.

Chapter 3: Weird Things

The next day, we climbed some trees and prepared another meal. We all swam, regardless of the fact that the water was a little cold. And at night, we sat around another campfire.

Then I saw something.

" Hey, what's that?" I asked.

Tjeerdo and Fred came to look. It looked like another pebble, but it was purple. I had never seen a purple pebble before. I picked it up and held it in front of me.

" Unusual," Fred confessed.

" Perhaps it is a dark pearl," Tjeerdo said. "I have heard about those. They're always purple and glossy. They can be found in the mountains and they make you do strange things."

" Yeah, it appears like it," I said. "It's nearly like it is magical or something. Here, let me rub off the dirt."

I started getting it smooth by rubbing it with my T-shirt. Something took place. I do not know what. But before we understood it, we were at the campfire again. Everything looked the same.

" Have you ever wished to perform some heroic deed?" Tjeerdo asked when we were just cooling at the fire.

" Wait, what?" I asked.

" Just ... you know, do something that youyou are proud of, something that means something to other individuals."

" Hang on ... what did you say?"

" Didn't you hear me? It's just that ... I thought about how cool it would be to prevent some disaster, or to do something that would serve mankind."

" No. That's what I mean," I said. "I heard you, but it just does not make any sense. You already said what you said."

He raised one eyebrow. "You're the one who is not making any sense," he said.

I was puzzled. Didn't he already ask that specific same thing yesterday? Why would he ask that question again? And why did it appear like he was burning the exact same marshmallow in the same way as the day before?

" You asked me the same question yesterday," I insisted. "Have you forgotten that?"

" Okay, you're starting to freak me out, Tyson," Tjeerdo said. "I didn't even see you yesterday. So how could I have asked that question a day earlier?"

" What? But we were here, at the campfire! You were asking me this and then I told you that I liked Sydney, and we talked about other things."

" You like Sydney?" Fred asked. "Ha-ha-ha-ha!"

Tjeerdo smirked. "Well, thanks for telling us that, but we really weren't here yesterday. I think you're going a little nuts."

Then I looked at the dark pearl. Did I just return in time? Maybe the wonderful power of this odd pearl was to return in time. But how would I know for sure? I thought and thought while Fred and Tjeerdo were talking away.

Then I had it.

" What's today's date?" I asked.

" Huh? It's the 23rd, duh," Tjeerdo said.

There was my proof. I had returned a day. When I rubbed the pearl, it shoved me back in time for an entire day. Our discussion changed. We didn't talk so much about girls or sports anymore. I revealed them the dark pearl I had found uhm ... well the day after actually ... and we attempted to find out what it could do.

" Guys," I said in all severity, "This is a magical thing."

They both looked.

" Oh, I have heard of those. They're dark pearls," Tjeerdo said.

" Yes, and it sent me back in time."

" It did what?" Tjeerdo asked.

" It sent me back in ... stop! That hotdog is going to fall into the fire!" I warned Fred. But it was too late. The hotdog fell.

" Hey, how did you know it would fall?" Fred asked.

" That's what I have been trying to tell you. I went back in time."

" Oh yeah? Then what am I going to do now?" Tjeerdo asked.

" Well, I don't know every little thing that's going to happen," I clarified. "But I rubbed the pearl and returned a day."

" That's so cool," Fred said.

" Hang on. Hold on. Let's say you are right. What are we going to do with it?" Tjeerdo asked.

" Let me figure that out later. I am open to recommendations, but let me just say that we have a really powerful pearl here, something we can use to change lives, including our own."

" Time travel ..." Tjeerdo said while rubbing his chin.

We talked some more, among which things about some of the possibilities this newly found power could give us. Nevertheless, we didn't come up with a lot of ideas that were both ethical and useful. We were going to keep it and think of it later.

The next day, the 2 boys swam and climbed up some trees. I didn't truly just feel like joining them, since I felt I had already done those activities the day before. So I just sat there and considered the influence this dark pearl would have on our lives.

" We need to use this for something good," I said while my good friends were splashing water at each other.
" But what?" Tjeerdo asked.
" I don't know. Stop criminal offenses. Help those in need. Something like that."
" Nothing ever happens in this village anyhow."
" I know. So maybe we should just hide it away till something does."
" Sounds good to me," Tjeerdo said as he shrugged his shoulders.
" Just do not tell anyone, alright?" I said.
" Okay."
" Fred?"
" Tell what?" he asked.
" Never mind." I thought that if he didn't know, then he most likely would not tell anyone. I inquired to do something else, since watching them play in the water had become a little boring. We went to search for berries, so we just left the tent there with our equipment, considering it safe enough for the moment.
We took off and began searching. Tjeerdo said he had heard about blueberries being up here, but I aspired to find some raspberries. Those were my favorite. Fred wasn't clear about what he wanted. He put a pinecone in his mouth and even tried to eat a leaf. We both sort of chuckled about his silly experiments. He said he wanted to prove that you could eat leafs, which he did, but it didn't appear like he was enjoying it, and that's why we cracked up.
When we went up the mountain a bit more, Tjeerdo all of a sudden stopped me and said, "Do not ... move ... a muscle."
He was looking in the distance. I tried to see what he was looking at. Then I saw it. It was a bear! It was huge! I was as quiet as I could be. This bear was brown and looking mean. But it didn't see us. What was it doing?
" It's eating our berries !!!!" Fred said as if he heard my ideas somehow.
" Silent, you idiot," Tjeerdo sneered.
But it was too late. The bear had picked up the sound of Fred's voice and was quickly moving towards us, growling loudly and showing its teeth.
" Run!" I said.
We all tried to run downhill, which I have to mention is actually hard to do without tripping. I mean, I do not consider myself a very clumsy character, but this time, I just got my foot stuck behind a tree branch and fell forward. I saw the huge bear coming at me. It was getting closer. It swung at me with its sharp claws and ...

When we went up the mountain a bit more, Tjeerdo all of a sudden stopped me and said, "Do not ... move ... a muscle."
Huh? Is this where we were? In desperation, I had just rubbed the dark pearl a little, attempting to place us back in time so we could avoid being chased after by an unsafe

bear. The bear was staring at us. It was looking for berries, but I already knew that Fred was going to be silly enough to open his mouth. So I leapt towards him and covered his mouth with my hand. I held it there and ensured he couldn't say anything.

When I let go, he quietly said, "How did you know I was going to say something?"

" I've been telling you guys that I have returned in time yesterday. So that's what I just did."

" Wait, you returned in time tomorrow to tell me to be silent now, which is exactly yesterday for you?" he asked.

Fred was making things needlessly complex.

" No," I whispered. "I just went back to the time we were watching the bear since I was nearly becoming its lunch. Now, let's get out of here before the same thing happens all over again."

" That's strange, man," Fred said after thinking for a while.

My good friends and I left and returned to the camping tent, which was a lot farther away. Just to be safe, we left the mountains that day, because we didn't want the bear to find us.

We got back and our mother and father greeted us. They asked about our experiences in the mountains and we just told them about swimming, campfires, and berries, but not about the bear, since that would cause them to be worried. Nor did we tell them about the dark pearl with its magical powers. That would just puzzle them. Besides, I didn't know what I wanted to do with it yet. It sounded so powerful but so bad if it would fall into the wrong hands.

I would quickly find a way to use it though.

The next day, we met in school. As we were sitting there, the teacher asked everyone what they did last weekend.

" I went on a pony ride," one girl said. It sounded a little childish, but then she explained that she trained horses and that she learned a lot about guiding them by rewarding them with carrots and such.

" We worked on the farm," another kid said. He told us how they milked the cows, stacked the hay, and gathered the water from trenches and wells in the ground.

" We went outdoor camping," I said when it was my turn. I told the class about our hike up the mountain, our campfire, and climbing trees. Tjeerdo told a similar story, just adding bits and pieces to what I was already saying, from his perspective.

Then it was Fred's turn. "We found a magical stone that reverses time," he said bluntly. I buried my face in my hands.

" Oh, that sounds fascinating," the teacher said. "Please tell us more about that."

" Well," he started. "We were attacked by a bear and then Tyson told me to shut up as I was making way too much sound, but the bear didn't see me, so it was okay, and the stone looked purple. It was more like a pearl, a purple pearl. And at the campfire, Tyson anticipated the future as I dropped my hotdog and he knew it was going to happen, so that's when we chose to not tell anybody about it, but I just did ..."

He realized what he just said.

I expected the worst.

" Whoops," he whispered.

The whole class looked at me. How was I going to talk myself out of this one? Why could not he just keep his mouth shut about the dark pearl? I knew we could not trust him. He couldn't help it.

" Well?" the teacher said.

At first, I looked anxious, then sheepish, and after that confident. I was going to pretend to lie by telling part of the truth. My sarcasm had no limits; everybody knew that. So I would use it to my advantage.

" Oh, he is absolutely right," I said with an amusing tone in my voice. "We found this wonderful rock that helps us turn back time. We can even take a trip to the future and turn your nose into a pig's nose."

Everybody chuckled ... everybody except for Fred.

" It can do that too?" he asked with huge eyes.

" Yes, I just didn't want to tell you as I wanted to pull a prank on you. I was going to slip up on you in your sleep and give you a pig's nose, just for fun. But now that you discovered my secret ... oh, me and my big mouth. Sorry, I spoiled it. Maybe I could still do it to somebody who does not know about that unique function."

Fred looked happy. He was most likely relieved that I wasn't going to give him a pig's nose anymore. And the rest of the class didn't take me seriously at all. They thought it was all just a huge joke.

" That sounds uproarious, Tyson. I am certain you can make up a ton of stuff about all kinds of 'wonderful' items, but we are attempting to have a serious discussion about what we did in the weekends here."

" Sorry, instructor," I said.

" It's okay. Let's hear it from someone else."

After class, I didn't even snap at Fred. Like I said, I didn't think he could help himself. He was just a little different. Tjeerdo came to me and told me what a genius I was for talking my way out of that one.

" Thanks," I said. "Have you thought of what we could do with this yet?"

" We could win the lottery," he said.

" I guess so, but I don't know if that's what this was meant for. Let's think of it a little bit more. It's not like we frantically need money. Besides, that would be sort of deceitful, wouldn't it?"

" Only if you get caught," Tjeerdo said.

I chuckled. That Tjeerdo and his way of justifying everything. I knew he meant well, but sometimes, he crossed the ethical line a little in my eyes.

I got back and listened to my mom and dad having a conversation. They were pretty stressed, to say the least.

" Shades will attack the village," my dad said. "They have been identified outside the town terrain and some of them were especially hostile. They attacked a number of villager, and now the entire town is restless and upset."

" How many do you think there are?" mom asked.

" I don't know. Some have mentioned several, others lots, and one of the villagers even said he saw lots of them, hiding in the forest."

" What are they after?"

" Oh, you know. They are uncivilized, vicious monsters. They do not have to have a reason. They just want to ruin our town, I am certain."

My mom looked frightened, and my dad noticed he went a little overboard.

" But," he said quickly, trying to relieve my mother's mind, "I think that if we just leave them alone, they won't come any closer. Perhaps they just want to perform a few easy acts of violence and after that head back to where they originated from. Who knows? Besides, we live in the town's center. They will most likely attack the houses at the town borders first."

" I sure hope so," my mom said.

I couldn't sleep that night. I knew without a doubt that I had run into this mystical dark pearl for a reason, and now the town seemed to be in peril. I didn't know how at the time, but perhaps I could make myself beneficial in some way. If I could utilize the pearl's wonderful powers, I would be able to save lives.

They came one by one. It was hard to stop since it was so sporadic. The shades that assaulted the town were vicious and ruthless. A little fight here, a little killing there ... it was unstoppable.

One of the shades that attacked the town, was a small, sneaky one. The Burges family had been living on the town's borders for a long period of time, but now they were seriously thinking about moving. When the sneaky shades snuck into their home, it destroyed all the fruits in the basement and all the veggies in the shed. After that, it followed them.

" Dad! Dad!" the little girl shrieked. "Where are you?"

" Come on, honey," the mother told her while hanging on to their newborn baby. She came running from the house, attempting to protect her offspring but fearing for the life of her husband.

They left, looking back and seeing something happen on the window through the window. But they didn't have time to stay. The father would meet them at his brother's place, but he never made it.

The next day, there was a funeral service, but throughout the ceremony, an entire horde of shades made this moaning sound and attacked the attendants. Many were harmed, couple of were killed.

That same night, a giant Shade, at least 15 feet tall, got in the village and began slamming walls and hitting monoliths. When the town's people fought back with pitchforks and pickaxes, they were simply smashed to the ground. People were kicked numerous feet away by this massive monster; others were just stepped on or pinned to the wall of one of their homes. It was mayhem. It was horrible.

Reports from deaths by shades or losses through those assaulting enemies were all over the place. People were distressed. The town held a council meeting which my father participated in. He brought me along, just to observe what was going on, and perhaps since they were so desperate they could have used suggestions from anyone ready to add an insight of some sort, even teenagers.

" Our town is going crazy," the mayor said. "We have come together since we cannot hold back the shades any longer. Their random riots and assassinations have become way too much. This should have never occurred. If we do not do something, we will all be exterminated."

" Let's burn the forest," someone suggested.

" Then they will only be forced to come out and kill more of us," another disagreed.

" Perhaps we should attack them," my dad suggested. "They would never see it coming."

" Sounds like an idea," the mayor said. "But even if we could kill some of them, we wouldn't have the workforce or the combating abilities to eliminate them entirely. We have heard reports of numerous these terrible creatures, hiding underneath the shadows. How are we ever going to match that?"

" We should learn what they want," I said.

Everyone turned to me.

" Who is this?" the mayor asked.

" Uhm ... this is my son," my father said happily.

Then the mayor turned to me and asked, "And how are we going to do that, boy? They do not speak our language. They don't even talk. They simply come in and start pillaging our village. How do you suggest we find out about their intentions?"
I was silent.
" I don't know," I admitted. "But if we could somehow find that, they may leave us alone after that."
" We will keep it in mind," the mayor said. "Any other ideas?"

Chapter 8: Even Weirder

When we came home from the meeting that night, I was sad. I grieved just because of the families who had lost really loved ones. People who had been extremely killed by those revolting beasts ... it just wasn't fair. We didn't even know why they were attacking us. Usually, shades would leave us alone if we didn't look them in the eyes. We always had to make certain we didn't bother them, and they would not react. But this time it was different. They were upset. They were after something.

I sat there in the middle of the night, thinking about the causes of all these unusual events.

Then I thought of the only thing I could do, the only thing that made real sense: I was going to go back in time and learn about the origin of all this. If I could only get near to the shades and search for a motive, I may be able to stop all these tragedies.

I chose.

I was determined to resolve this.

This was the reason I found the dark pearl.

I took it out of my pocket and rubbed it. I rubbed it hard, just to ensure it would work.

Before I knew it, I was back in the living-room. It wasn't night any longer, but throughout the afternoon. My father and mother had a discussion. They were pretty worried, to say the least.

" shades are about to attack the village," my dad said. "They have been identified outside the town terrain and some of them were particularly hostile. They attacked a couple of villagers, and now the entire town is anxious and upset."

" How many do you think there are?" mother asked.

" I don't know. Some have mentioned several, others lots, and one of the villagers even said he saw hundreds of them, hiding in the forest."

I recognized this discussion, and it was before it actually all took place. No one had died yet, and I was going to make sure it would never happen. I told my mother and father I had to go outdoors and ran out. Then I went to Tjeerdo's home.

" Psst, Tjeerdo," I said while looking up.

He opened his bedroom window.

" What's going on?" he asked.

" Want to follow me into the forest? I have the gut feeling we can actually use this odd pearl we found."

" Sure. Give me a 2nd and I will be right there," he said.

A little later, he stood next to me in front of his home.

" So what have you learned?" he asked.

" These shades are going to kill villagers," I said. "It already took place ... well, in the future, I guess, but I went back in time, to the present time, to stop it."

" That is so remarkable!" Tjeerdo said. "So you are from the future?"

" Yes, well, I know what's going to happen. And now I want to make an effort to prevent a catastrophe from happening. Does that make sense?"

" Of course. Shall we get Fred too?"

" Let's leave Fred where he is," I said with a smile. "Let's just go together, just the two of us. I am certain we'll get to the bottom of this."

We ventured to the forest with the dark pearl. To be sincere, it was kind of spooky, with the fog and the spooky sounds we heard. We could not see much, so we remained near each other. The fog was so thick that we could only see about 15 feet in front of us, if that. As we gradually approached the open space in the middle of the forest, which was a place where I thought we had the biggest chance of encountering shades, we heard the sound of feet. Like I said, we could not see much, but we were certain that we were being followed. We turned around but saw nothing. When we turned around again ...

" Wraaah!" Tjeerdo and I yelled.

A creepy Shade was right in front of us, gazing in our eyes from only two feet away. Where did that one originated from suddenly? But he wasn't the only one catching us by surprise. Before we could say another word, we were surrounded by shades. They were all coming closer and looking at us.

Why weren't they attempting to kill us?

I didn't understand any of this.

" Quickly," Tjeerdo whispered. "Get the dark pearl. Perhaps we could go back to the time before they snuck up on us."

I took it out of my pocket, but that brought about a reaction I didn't expect. As soon as these mean-looking shades saw the dark pearl. They all kneeled down. What was happening? Were they worshipping this item or something?

One of the shades wasn't kneeling. It looked like their leader. He came forward and made a gesture as if he were to say, "Hand it over."

Then it clicked in my mind. Perhaps they lost this valuable pearl and were going to start their killing spree out of anger. Perhaps they were just trying to find it in their desperate attempts to scan the place. Perhaps giving it back to them would stop this rubbish before it even happened.

" What are you doing?" Tjeerdo asked. "Do not hand it to them. It's our only escape." But he really missed the point. He didn't get it, so I overlooked his recommendations and handed the dark pearl to the Shade. He gladly accepted my present. When he held it, he looked at it with happiness. The other shades were still kneeling. Then he held it up and expressed some strange noises I had never heard before; it was probably in their language, or so I figured.

When he was done talking, the shades stood up and followed him. They were headed into the direction of the mountains, far from the town.

We both gazed at the departing, black creatures, attempting to understand what had just occurred.

" This is amazing!" I finally said. "They are gone. GONE! They won't ever return. All they were doing, was looking for their pearl. It's so simple if you think of it."

" So that was it then?" Tjeerdo asked. "They just wanted their pearl back."

" Yes, and remember you said you wanted to perform a brave deed? Now you did! We just stopped the deaths of many villagers. We just stopped a war! Aren't you proud of yourself?"

" A little," Tjeerdo said. "I just pictured it to be different. You know, with sword battling and swinging and getting a beautiful girl to save her from the scourging flames of a fire, or to be carried on the villagers' shoulders and have an after-party."

" Oh, come on. You have to admit this was cool. It doesn't matter that nobody saw it. We know what we did, and that counts for something."
Tjeerdo was still a little upset when we walked home. He didn't get the exact same heroic feeling as I did. We talked some more, going over the events that had been happening since we found that strange pearl.
Then, suddenly out of the blue, he said, practically weeping, "But we could have won the lottery!

THE END

The Zombie Experience

Chapter 1: Suffering

Dear diary ...
No, no, no ... that's not how I should begin. I am a tough guy for crying out loud! Let's begin over, as it might be journal but that does not mean I have to sound like a wimp. These are hard times, so let's put it in a way that will get the adrenaline in your blood going.
Look, we had just barely reached the dumb barn, but as soon as we arrived, the zombies were already pounding at the doors. They just would not go away. A continuous howling, gnashing of teeth, and wailing were heard. Their noises were renting the air, as it were, and the reeking smell of corpses entered our senses every day we got away.
There were lots of them ... COUNTLESS of them. I lost count of how many I already killed. Two of my friends were keeping the score though. I think one of them already reached number 765 or something. It was a cool pastime if you ask me; something to keep them busy and help them concentrate on other things.
Not me though. Such minor activities didn't inhabit my mind. I was only obsessed with just one thing: Finding civilization. I knew for some reason there were others out there like us. Others who had endured the disaster and were now waiting for a rescue or were building up their society the way it used to be.
But listen to me rambling about this or that. I am sure that you get the picture. We were stuck in a barn, surrounded by zombies, thinking that we would be safe but discovering that quite the reverse held true. Let me introduce myself and my group to you.

There were 4 of us:
First there was me.
My name is Mike. I am 25 years of age. I had been fighting zombies for an entire year and it was practically as if I did nothing else in life. Naturally, I was just a student when the entire thing came falling apart down on us and panic emerged, but that's another story. Let me assure you that my preferred weapon was a golden sword. Do not ask me how I found it. I just did; and besides, that too, is another story.
Then there was Patrick. He was 24. He still had a difficult time adapting to the situation, and he displayed everything all the time as his hormonal agents went up and down throughout the day. The fact that there were 2 girls and two men made him go a little crazy in some cases, and he definitely liked the brunette. Either way, they flirted back and forth all the time, which put me and the other girl in an awkward position. Patrick's preferred weapon was an iron axe. He got it from a barn just like this one, and he never parted with it since.
The third member of our little fabricated group was Chelsey. She was only 19 years of age and had just finished high school when the zombies assaulted. Her brown hair and blue eyes made her a target for many flirty men in school, and the fact that she had been a cheerleader all that time made it worse. All she ever discussed, was make-up, hair, outfits, and nails. She wore short skirts and tight t-shirts all day, and I doubt that she ever got good grades in school, because I've seen her handwriting and spelling ... Awful ... Like I said, she flirted a lot with Patrick-- the only person in the area that would show interest in her-- but I often questioned if she was actually into him or if she simply

liked the attention. By the way, she typically used a shovel to defend herself. Often, I caught her throwing a bottle of fragrance or nail polish remover in a zombie's face. Ten points for creativity whenever.

The last one in our group was Lanea. In my eyes, she was a lot smarter than the brunette, and contrary to the popular viewpoint about her hair color, this blond was a bright, strong survivor. With her pickaxe, she would bust the heads of numerous zombies and take out her weapon within seconds each time as if she had been combating all her life. It was always a satisfaction to watch her from the corner of my eyes, especially when her hips swung one way and her arms the other ... it was just amazing how she ... well ... anyhow, I am daydreaming here. Lanea was 21 and she had an adorable face, but she didn't put a ton of effort into beautifying herself. She was in survival mode, and she just had a way to get things done quickly, dealing with solutions and fast ideas to get us to the next place.

So there we were, discussing what to do and where to go. It was a predicament, as we thought we had lost them, and now we had to move again.

" How far is the town?" Lanea asked.

" If I am correct, it should be about 10 minutes from here," I said.

" Let's go then," she said.

" But how?" Patrick asked.

" Through there," she said, pointing at a crack in the back of the barn.

" Do you think there are any zombies there?" Chelsey asked.

" I do not know," Lanea confessed. "But I hear noises from all sides of the barn. All the doors are being smothered while it appears like that opening might actually help us sneak out. It's our only chance."

All of us agreed that it would be the best way to get out of there, so we rushed towards the fracture. It was at the bottom, so we had to lie on our stomachs and crawl through it. Lanea was the first one. She lay flat on her stomach and began crawling through. All of us waited and then we heard a whisper, "Guys, it's safe. Just keep quiet and follow me." I went 2nd. I crawled through and securely made it outside. There I noticed Lanea hiding in the bushes and signaling with one hand to go to her. Patrick was after me and soon joined us in the bushes, gone from the barn with zombies. Chelsey was the last one to crawl through, but when she stuck her head through the crack, a zombie appeared and shouted in her face.

" Wraaaaah!"

Chelsey quickly pulled back and shouted, "Eeeeeh!"

" She didn't make it," I said, burying my face in my hand.

" Well, don't just stand there! Let's go get her!" Lanea said.

She rushed towards the barn and smashed the zombie in the head with her pickaxe. His screech alarmed the zombies on the other side, who came running at us within seconds. Lanea helped Chelsey crawl through while the 2 of us were fending off several zombies with our weapons.

" Let's go! Let's go!" I screamed.

We all ran as fast as we could. I discovered immediately who was out of shape and who wasn't, as there I was, running and observing Lanea's backside, who was way ahead of everyone, sprinting her lungs out and reaching the town long before we did. Impressive. What woman!

Chelsey kept up with me, but it was sad to see that Patrick, the one who flaunted so much, could not truly support his mouth by running fast. He fell behind, though still ahead of the zombies, and I actually made a smile when I saw him panting greatly and showing up late.

" Ugh ... ooof ... owowow ... Heeesh ... hey, men. What's the rush?" Patrick said. "It's not like those zombies are the fastest in the world or something."

" Sshhh ..." Lanea said, "... there may be zombies in this town too. I say we head for the church tower. A lot of those towers have hatches that lock. If we can make it there, the zombies will eventually quit, or we can come down with this rope from my bag and slide down by means of the roofing."

" That sounds like an exceptional idea," I said.

No sooner said than done, we tiptoed to the church and went inside.

No zombies.

Good.

Our next move was to climb the stairs to the belfry and hide there. We even found some food hidden in one of the spaces in that building. When we came, it was beginning to get dark. We closed the hatch and all fell asleep. It had been a long day.

It was all a huge accident. At least, that's what we heard. Not too far from one of the bigger villages in the country, there was a speculative lab. I didn't think our scientific research had advanced this far yet, since all of us lived under reasonably primitive scenarios, but apparently, they knew how to produce mysterious compounds.

One of those compounds was the Y412, a chemical green slush that was supposed to cure clients from certain illnesses. Instead, it did the opposite. When they tested it on rats, it didn't appear to do anything, so the biggest mistake they made, was presuming that it would be safe for humans too.

And then it occurred.

The man lying down on the bed was injected with the Y412.

Instantly, he occurred and assaulted one of the scientists. The client leapt at him and began choking him while the others were kicking and punching him, attempting to prevent a murder.

But this made it worse.

It stirred the aggressiveness in the client's brain. He became a lot more wild and relentless than before. His nails became claws and his teeth into fangs within seconds. As the drool from his mouth hit the floor, the newly-bred monster attacked the other researchers as well, biting and scratching each of them.

Before they knew it, they were all the exact same: It only took seconds before they developed into zombies themselves and began wrecking the place. They broke out and intimidated the town the scientific center was at.

There was a soldier there, Benjamin, a retired hero who heard about the outbreak. He didn't wait any longer and got his silver sword. Then he stormed out of his house and opened his mouth in wonder. Dozens of zombies were quickly going through the streets, breaking homes and biting victims along the way. He had never seen anything like this.

" Let's fight back!" Benjamin yelled. "Resist! We cannot let them take the village."

He banged his sword on the doors of those who were still uninformed of the circumstances. The civilians gradually came out and looked at the continuous mayhem.

" Get your weapons!" Benjamin shouted. "Let's kill these guys!"

Some of the villagers grabbed pitchforks and shovels. Others equipped their children and wives with hammers and knives, but most of them ran away in panic.

" Come on!" Benjamin yelled as he stabbed one of the zombies in the stomach. "We can win this!"

He stabbed and yelled and slashed. He fought back with all his might, but the zombies were becoming too numerous; they were growing exponentially. They were dashing through windows and turning everybody in their way into zombies. Panic was all over.

" We can beat these beasts!" Benjamin kept yelling. "We can beat ... ".

THUD!

Some zombie punched him in the face. It knocked him out and left him there, being stepped on by various zombies but allowing him to stay human. Who knows what occurred after that ...?

I heard it didn't take long before the whole town became zombies and dead people. From there, the disease spread across the country. This was the beginning.

Chapter 3: The Note

I woke up by the noise of snoring. Patrick was lying on his back and seemed like a saw cutting through a log. It wasn't the best way to get up, but I saw the sun rose anyhow, so it made a lot of sense to begin taking a look around.

Lanea was concealed with a blanket, and so was Chelsey. They were so tired from the day before that they kept sleeping, despite the incoming rays from the sun.

I just sat there for an hour. I was going to leave them there, because I knew they needed it. Besides, I took pleasure in watching Lanea sleep. She was so pretty. I wondered if she even knew that I was so amazed by her. Most likely not.

Chelsey awakened.

" Whe-where am I?" she asked.

" We're in a church tower," I replied. "We're safe here. No zombies."

I guess the word "zombies" woke Lanea up, since she immediately rose from her sleeping position and reached for her weapon. "Zombies? Where?" she said.

" Do not worry about it," I said. "We locked the hatch, remember?"

" Oh yeah," she said as she rubbed her eyes and yawned. "So what is the plan?"

" We should try to find any clues to find a colony of survivors," I said. "There is only so much we can do by ourselves, but if we join others, we can stand up to all the zombies."

" Well, how about awakening this drowsy head?" Lanea said, pointing at the snoring Patrick.

" Sure," I said. "Hey, Patrick, time to wake up."

No response.

" Patrick!" I yelled. "Wake up! It's time to wake up!"

Nothing.

" I can poke him with my pickaxe," Lanea said.

" Amateurs," Chelsey commented. "Let me show you how it's done."

She leaned over and softly whispered something in his ear. It appeared to penetrate through his brain immediately, because his eyes opened and he stood up, looking at Chelsey with big eyes.

" What?" he asked.

" Oh, nothing," Chelsey said.

" What did you tell him?" Lanea and I inquired.

" Do not worry about it. Isn't the most crucial thing that he is up?" she said.

" I guess so," I said.

Patrick was attempting to get his hair straight. "What now?" he asked.

" Let's go downstairs," I suggested. "We'll search the houses for any indicator that people left and gathered somewhere. We can't stay here for long. We need to find others."

After thoroughly opening the hatch, we went down the stairs and searched the church. Thankfully, we didn't need to look anywhere else, because on one of the benches, there was a note that read, "Meet us at Utopia. Turn left at the Elephant Rock."

When I picked it up, we all looked at it for a while.

" Man, that's incredible," Patrick said.

" Where is Elephant Rock?" Chelsey asked.

" It's on the other side of the country," Lanea said a little dissatisfied. "It's not that amazing. All we have, is a note and some vague directions. And it's far. It will take at least several days to walk there, if I'm not incorrect."
" But it's a chance," I said. "Before this, we had nothing. Now we have a goal."

We took the note and searched for other supplies. None of the zombies in the area were alarmed by our sneaking around the village. Thankfully, they were all gone or hiding from the light.

Something that I had been seeing before, was that the zombies seldom came out throughout the day. They were immune to light and in some cases they did appear in the daytime, but most of them disliked the light. They remained in the shadows until the sun would set.

This would give us a long time to pack up on stuff. So we did. We found food, water, and blankets; and we packed every little thing that worked.

Then we left town.

On our way to the presumed group that we hoped would exist.

The plains were dangerous. If there would be any zombies there, they would have seen us by that time, but there weren't. I was just hoping none of them would be clever enough to take a peek there.

And since there was nothing else to do, Patrick got into boasting mode, like always.

" You know, Chelsey," he said. "It's good we returned for you or you would have been bitten and turned into a zombie."

" Yeah, that would have been terrible," Chelsey admitted. "Thank you for saving me."

" Of course, if you had gone first, then one of us would have been in danger. It was just a coincidence," Lanea said.

" Still," Chelsey said. "Patrick was brave to come back."

" No, he wasn't," I said. "He just came back since Lanea told us to go back."

" But I would have gone anyhow, whether she said it or not," Patrick firmly insisted.

" Sure," I said. "I still think you should be thanking Lanea instead of Patrick, Chelsey."

After that, it was silent. All of us noticed it. Chelsey was just searching for a reason to flirt with Patrick and Patrick was just boasting again, although he was the last to come in the town because of his sluggish speed.

Lanea and I exchanged some looks. It was sort of like teaming up against the weirdos in the group or something. By having two people to tease, it was as if we connected better. We both smiled and shook our heads.

" So where did you get that golden blade?" Lanea asked.

" Well, let me tell you," I began.

This is the story of how I found the golden sword. The easy truth is, I had been looking for a weapon for days after the outbreak. My father and mother tried to protect me, telling me to hide in the basement when the zombies assaulted. When the noises had vanished, I came out of my hiding place and found an empty home. After all that time, I still didn't know what had happened to them. Perhaps they had developed into zombies, or maybe they had just died. Nonetheless, I still had an unclear hope of finding them in the group, which was why I was so determined to find it.
I truly hoped my father and mother were still alive somewhere.
Anyway, I climbed up out of that basement and found the entire town to be empty. I knew there were zombies hiding underneath the corners of the houses, so I rushed to a neighboring castle.
The castle was owned by some wealthy lord who had settled in this village, and some of the townspeople had worked at this place to make a living. I knew that if I wanted to find an important weapon someplace, it was going to be in that building.
When I came there, corpses were all over the floor. It was dreadful. The sight of it was horrifying. And I think I even got a little nauseous when I saw them. I stepped over them and went into the castle. The bridge was large open, and so was the gate. I took a look around and tried to determine where the best place would be to find a weapon to defend myself.
I went downstairs and looked some more until I found the armory. Racks with axes, spears, and bows were leaning against the walls, making my dream come true.
" Oooh, nice," I said when I picked up an axe with accessories and a shiny surface area. I put it down and looked for the perfect weapon to wield. I was going to be extremely choosy, as I knew I could not take all of them with me.
But then I heard something. The door opened up and a creepy zombie stood in front of me. It was the very first time I had seen a zombie. It was a scary experience. I need to admit that I wasn't completely prepared for this. It was a woman, and the flesh on her face and arms was hanging loose. It was super gross and it was the least appealing picture of lady I would ever see. And now it was out to kill me. She came right at me.
" Creeaaaah!" she screamed, holding her arms and claws in my direction.
She knocked me over.
I fell back.
The female zombie was on top of me, attempting to bite me, but then I managed to get my feet up and push her in the stomach, away from me, so that she would fall backwards. Before I could blink my eyes, I saw a blade from the armory impale her. She had fallen onto it and had now become a dead zombie.
I stood and brushed off the dust from my body. Then I looked at the weapon that had killed my enemy.
It was a golden sword.
It was beautiful.
I didn't know why I hadn't observed this blade earlier, but now that I had, I fell in love with it. It would become my main weapon, particularly since it had inadvertently saved my life. I put the sheath on my back and looked a lot like a real warrior. I practiced pulling it out and putting it back in for several minutes and went outside.

And then I saw her ... the total reverse from the monstrous monster I had just destroyed. The classy girl standing in front of me was the supreme beauty. Her long, blonde hair was waving in the wind and she was leaning on one hip with a pickaxe in her hand, and it was dripping with blood. She looked at me, and I knew at that moment that the extreme ugliness I had experienced in the castle was hell before paradise. Wow! Could there be any creature on the face of the world who looked more beautiful than this girl?

" My name is Lanea," she calmly said. "Nice sword. Where did you get it?"

" At the armory," I said. "There are more weapons if you want any."

" I'm good," she said. "Thanks though. I have just become pretty good with this pickaxe, and I am starting to like it."

She looked down at a zombie that was trying to get up, moaning heavily.

" I told you to stay down and die!" she screamed as she thrust her pickaxe in the zombie's neck.

After that, he made no more noises. I was surprised. For a girl this adorable she definitely had experience when it came to eliminating zombies.

" You're pretty harsh," I said laughingly.

" Yeah? Well, I've been doing it for a while. In case you haven't seen, they are everywhere."

" I have actually, but I just made my first kill."

She laughed a little. I wasn't certain if she was being sarcastic or friendly, but it was kind of funny. "Congratulations," she said. "Prepare yourself to kill more of them. There is no shortage of these horrible monsters."

" Sounds about right," I said. "By the way, where are you going? If you want, we could travel together."

" Sure," she said. "But you better not get in my way. And if you become a zombie, I won't waver to chop your head off. Nothing really personal."

" Oh, I comprehend. Well, I am looking for a colony of survivors."

" Good idea," she said. "You never know if someone else may be out there."

And that's the moment the other 2 showed up.

" Oh my, did you just kill those zombies?" Chelsey asked when she walked towards us.

" Some of them, yes," was Lanea's response.

" Are-are you guys warriors?" Chelsey asked.

" I have been training a lot since the outbreak," Lanea said. "But he just got his first kill."

" Good," Patrick said. "I started eliminating some yesterday. It's an excitement, and I don't even feel guilty about it."

" I do not want to kill," Chelsey said. "Why is this happening?"

" Well, honey, you'll need to, whether you like or not," Lanea said. "If you don't kill them, they will kill you. It's as basic as that. Here, take a shovel. Then you'll at least be able to take them out when they run at you."

Unwillingly, Chelsey accepted the weapon Lanea handed her. Patrick stood beside her and put his arm around her shoulder. "Do not stress, girl. I will take care of you. I have an axe and it's mad."

From that moment on, I already knew our whole trip was going to be like this. And that's pretty much how we met one another.

Back to the plains. We were walking and walking ... it took forever. We hid under a huge rock, taking turns standing guard in the evening. And we did the exact same thing the next day and the next day. We had enough water to get through these empty landscapes, but in the end, we had to economize, because our resources were running out.

Eventually, we saw something though: The shape of a village.

" Good," I said. "Finally. Maybe we can fill up on water and food there."

" I'm tired. I long for a bed," Chelsey said.

I could tell that Patrick was exhausted too by the way he was walking, but he tried to look tough and walk up straight in order to impress Chelsey. Still, he was slouching a little. It was funny.

When we came to the village, it was awfully quiet.

" I do not like it," Lanea said. "Something's wrong."

" It's not that unusual for it to be quiet," I said. "We've been to many deserted towns. How is this one any different?"

" I do not know. It's a feeling. Call it female instinct if you will, but there is something fishy going on here. Just be prepared for anything."

" I do not feel anything," Chelsey said.

We didn't comment on that. We let it go and got our weapons ready. When we looked up, we saw it.

Zombies were all gathered on the rooftops, lying in wait to assault us. They were all over ... hundreds of them, and they all climbed up on the houses to ambush us. When they discovered that we saw them, they all jumped off immediately.

" It's raining zombies!" I shouted.

" Let's get out of here!" Patrick yelled.

" To the opposite side of the town. Hurry!" Lanea said.

We ran and ran, and evaded zombies that were falling out of the sky. Some of them hit us a little, making us differ from our straight course, but most of them missed.

" Ouch!" I said when a zombie scratched me with its claws.

" Take that!" Lanea said, cutting him open like a fish.

" Thanks," I said.

" Do not mention it. Now, let's keep going!"

We kept running. I saw Chelsey and Patrick kill a few zombies behind us, and Lanea was blazing a trail, attempting to direct us through to leave this evil snare.

" In there!" she shouted. She pointed at an airtight home without any windows and a steel door. We followed her inside and held the door shut. "Check if there is any way to get in upstairs," she commanded. We went upstairs, but every little thing was sealed, as if somebody was attempting to be a hermit or something.

" Good house," I said. "I wouldn't want to live here though."

The others concurred.

We could hear the eerie noises made by the zombies outside the door. We put a beam halfway the door, just to lock it more securely. We heard the zombies scratch and bite, but none of them could come in.

" Just how long are we going to be here?" Chelsey asked.

" Till they leave," I said. "And seeing how excited they are to get to us, that could be a looooong time."

We sat there for hours, thinking about methods to get out of the home unnoticed to bypass the zombie crowd. But we couldn't find a way. Even Lanea sat down and rested her arms on the pickaxe. She sighed. It was hopeless, and she knew it in addition to everyone else.

We just looked in front of us, not saying a word. This went on for a while.

Then unexpectedly, when it began to become dark outside, we heard another noise.

" Blasted zombies! You won't go away from me so quickly!"

It was a harsh voice. It had to be a man. But we didn't know who. All we knew, was that when we took a quick peek, we saw zombies being thrown up in the air and blood spraying all over the place.

" Let's help him out," Lanea suggested.

We all stood and began fighting the zombies. When we slashed through a few of those monstrous creatures, we saw a guy with a sword.

" The name's Benjamin," he said. "Those wicked rascals thought they had me, but I pretended to be dead and got my revenge. Now, let's get out of here, before their little friends will leap off the roofings again."

It was obvious that not all zombies had been hanging out at the front door, and that some of them had left. This gave us the chance to run out of town.

" Do we know where we are going?" I asked.

" I have a respectable idea," Benjamin said. "Follow me!"

He ran towards the other side of the village and revealed us the rock in front of us.

It was Elephant Rock!

Ha!

It looked precisely like an elephant. Odd.

" We have to turn left," Lanea said. "That's where they said the colony would be."

" Well, how do you know it's on the left side? I see a course causing the other side," the retired soldier said.

" We found a piece of paper that said they would be there," Lanea insisted. "So we have to go left."

" But what if they meant a left turn coming from the opposite side?" I asked.

She scratched her head. I guessed she had not thought of that before. She sought to the left. There was a vast, empty desert with more rocks in sight. Then she sought to the right. Trees had popped out of the ground, there was a little creek, and a course leading through the trees to an even greener area.

" I have determined we should go right instead," she said sheepishly.

" Good decision," we all agreed.

We went left and looked back sometimes. The zombies were still after us. How were we going to endure this? Sooner or later, they would catch up.

But suddenly, we saw little homes made out of wood. Villagers from the houses ran towards us and safeguarded us.

" Are you all right?" one of them asked.

" We are fine, but the zombies are chasing us," I said.

When he looked, he ordered all capable guys to get their weapons and march forward. I watched in wonder as an army of villagers took their rakes, pitchforks, shovels, machetes, swords, and axes, and beat those pathetic zombies down. Our opponents didn't stand a chance against these strong guys. It was only a matter of minutes before the last zombie was slashed by a brave man from the village.

" It's good to have you here," one of them said as they came back.

But I didn't pay much attention. I saw some familiar faces. Could it be true? No. Impossible. After all that hoping and battling and running ...

" M-mom?" I said.

One of the villagers turned around.

It was mother!

" Mother!" I exclaimed.

" Mike!" she said as she welcomed me.

Soon after, my dad came towards us.

" I take pride in you, boy. You have grown up a lot, and I don't just mean physically. I can tell."

" Thanks dad," I said.

Chelsey and Patrick had already vanished. Perhaps they found some other villagers they knew, or maybe they just ran to kiss or something. I didn't need to know. I figured I would see them later.

But Lanea was still there. She looked a little jealous when she saw me hugging my parents. She was quiet. I had never seen her this shy before.

" Mother, father," I said. "Meet Lanea. She is my friend and she saved my life."

" So great to meet you," my father and mother said. "And thank you for all you've done."

" Oh, it was nothing," she said.

" Can we take her in till she finds her family?" I asked.

" Sure," my dad said. "If she wants to. Is that what you want, Lanea? Or do you have some better place to go?"

" No, I don't," she said. "Thank you for your hospitality. I would really love to stay."

It was like a dream come true. The most gorgeous girl in my house. Could you imagine?

" Thanks, dad," I said.

" No," Lanea said quietly. "Thank you, Mike."

With those words, she kissed me on the cheek. I melted away.

THE END

The Ghost Fanatic

Chapter 1: My Personal Path

I guess I wasn't always the most popular girl in class. And when my dad died, I became much more to myself. The years went by and I ended up being older, and a lot of people said I was beautiful, but I just didn't do much with it. At the time I changed, I was nine years of age. It was that age where most kids in school are trying to put you down so they can climb higher on the social ladder. I wasn't going to play that stupid game, so I usually pulled away to my own areas.

I disliked school. It was very boring. And even though I was more of an introvert, books bored me too. I was searching for some enjoyment by myself, so sometimes, I just went to the fields or the woods by myself, just to sniff the fresh air of nature and take a look around me. It was always interesting, as I found new things and new life.

I mean, the time I helped a fox out of its hole or the time when I went after some fish in the river ... those were the times I completely felt alive. One time, I even saw a big worm. Yuck! I've got to tell you that those are pretty odd creatures. I do not even know if you can call them animals, but hey, they live out there, and I saw one.

The only thing I dislike is the spiders. And I'm not talking about the tiny ones you can splat with your shoe ... No, I'm talking about substantial spiders the size of human beings. I found one just recently. It was on the other side of a waterfall and some rocks. I hid behind the tree as I didn't want it to identify me. Uuuugly! Fortunately it didn't, but I wanted to keep away from those as much as I could.

Oh, by the way, my name is Helga. I completely forgot to introduce myself in this diary. Ha-ha! I just thought that ... oh well ... it does not matter. Yep, Helga. That's my name. Anyhow, I was talking about all the creatures I had met, and the animals I had seen in the forest. My mother was always okay with it. She didn't think it would be harmful to head out there, but she always insisted I would get home before dark. And this is where it ended up being so frustrating.

It was winter season, and the sun set early every day, so early that I barely had time to get out of school, change into something else, and go out in nature for an hour or more. It would get dark quickly, and I would be stuck inside playing with our cat or doing some boring research. Not fun.

Little did I know that my life would change that one day I got lost.

You see, I went to the forest and walked on the usual routes till I saw a path I had not seen before.

" Hey, this must be intriguing," I said.

So I chose to take a calculated risk, to differ from my typical course, and to tell you the truth, I had no idea I was going so far away. I didn't know where I was going, but curiosity had taken control of me. I walked and walked until I saw flames.

" Odd," I thought. "In this cold weather, how could there be fire?"

I came closer and saw a tiny being, flying in the air.

" Wow!" I said.

It was a ghost. I had learned about those at school. I was told they were mean and hostile. They emphasized how vicious and hateful they were, and that they never thought twice to attack. But this one wasn't that way at all. It was just flying around, just cooling, just enjoying ... till it saw me.

It looked at me, and I felt sad. Why? Since it looked a lot like the poor little thing was sobbing.

" Is something wrong?" I asked.

No response. I figured they weren't able to talk. I came closer and touched it. What had all that rubbish had to do with instantly assaulting people? This one was as harmless as a cow. It flew around, almost as if it was attempting to show me what it could do. Was this a child ghost or something?

Then it hit a tree.

Thud!

It fell, but just before it hit the earth, I caught it.

I looked at it.

It looked back at me.

It was a serene moment.

Then I saw some other ghosts appear.

" Are you this little pal's family?"

They came closer and nodded. They understood me! Okay, they could not talk, but I was certain that this meant a "yes." Wow. Nice. Ghosts could speak our language! And here we always thought they were just harsh predators. We were so wong! Or was it just me?

I waved at them, just to say "hi." They twirled in the air, as if they were waving back. I blew in the air. They blew a fireball. So cool. I was sold. I loved these creatures more than any of the other animals I had seen. These ghosts were my favorites.

Chapter 2: Ghosts Are Amazing

Did you know ghosts are totally legit?! They rock! I became best friends with them. I headed out to the forest every day to see them. They showed me all kinds of tricks, like how they could spit fireballs and fly around. They were able to bounce off a tree and make an unusual noise when they did.

I revealed them some stuff too. They all gathered around and watched me start a fire with sticks and matches, climb up a tree, and swim in the river. We had a blast, despite the cold weather.

Summertime came. The weather had finally turned around, which meant I could stay at the woods longer. Yippee!

Nobody had ever discovered the ghosts, except for my mother. We had a conversation about it once, and initially, she wasn't convinced I was being safe, but ultimately, she accepted it.

" Are you going back to those weird flying ghosts again?" she asked me one day.

" Yes, I am going back. Why not?"

" Well, don't you think it would be wiser to hang out with some other kids from your class? Perhaps there are some good girls that would want to chitchat or shop for clothes."

" Mother, all the girls dislike me. They think I'm weird."

" Well, what about the boys? Are they interested in being with you?"

" Are you kidding? They're so immature! They burp and fart on purpose and after that they laugh about their own jokes."

" Are you serious? All of them?" my mother asked.

" All of them, Mom."

She smirked and came closer, looking straight at me. I tried to look away, as I knew what she was doing. She knew I was hiding something, and she was determined to get it out of me. "All of them?" she asked again.

I could not stop smiling and I looked up, to the right, and to the left. "Okay," I said shyly. "There is one boy who ..."

" Aha! I knew it!" Mother said. "Tell me all about him."

" His name is Raiden, but he does not pay attention to me, not that I observed at least."

" Well, why won't you just go talk to him? Find out what he's like?"

" Mohooom, stop pestering me. Are you crazy? I can't do that. Then he will think I like him."

" Which is very true, isn't it?"

" Yes, but I can't let him know that."

My mother started seeing a little annoyance in my posture and chose it wasn't time to push my buttons. I wasn't prepared for such a move, and she would leave it at that. Thank goodness.

After the afternoon snack, I went to the forest again. There were more ghosts than before. I didn't remember seeing all of these.

" Where did the new ones originate from?" I asked, practically hoping to get a verbal answer.

One   osts flew midway into a circle in the direction of the mountain, as if to
          rection they came from. I thought for a moment and presumed there was

a ton of lava in that mountain, and that's most likely where they came from. But it was paradoxical and fascinating to see that so many of them had gathered here in the forest to see me. I felt popular, even though it wasn't amongst my own kind. Now there were about 30 ghosts flying between the trees, surrounding me with their presence.

" Hey, you know what?" I said. "I think I know a game. How does that noise? It will be wonderful. Are you in or are you out?"

The ghosts nodded, which meant they wanted to play.

" Okay," I said. "Here is what we're going to do ..."

" There is barrel in the area. I know exactly where it is. The barrel has oil. And do you know what oil does?"
One of the ghosts ended up being truly thrilled and flew up and down in the air.
" Right! It burns like crazy! And you guys like burning, don't you? So who is up for the contest?"
All the ghosts flew in circles. They almost produced a tiny tornado of some sort. I could tell they were passionate about the idea, and I immediately revealed them the way. I ran down the course, down another path, and took a faster way through the trees. I looked back and saw a whole troop of ghosts flying behind me. They trusted me and they would go anywhere I would. It felt great.
Finally, after some running and flying around, we got to the designated area. The barrel was there. It was on the borders of the town, and I didn't think we would bother anyone with our contest.
" Stay here," I said.
I ran towards the barrel, which was next to a barn with hay, and checked if the coast was clear. No one was there. It was safe. I put the barrel in front of the barn, far enough from it, or so I assumed, and ran back towards the 30 ghosts that were lined up and waiting on my command.
" Whoever strikes the barrel first, wins," I said happily. "Ready? Objective ... FIRE!!!"
All the ghosts were spitting fireballs to their best capability. Most of them really missed, since the barrel was so far away, and some of them, like the baby ghosts, didn't even make it that far.
" Okay, all right," I said after a while. "The little ones can come closer. I really believe that would be fair." And so they did.

Chapter 4: Accidents

Something took place though, something I had not foreseen. Later, when I looked back, I thought of my stupidity and my carelessness. It was bound to happen. It was a destruction waiting to happen.
One of the ghosts hit the barrel.
Whoosh!
The barrel instantly ignited. I cheered and celebrated with the other ghosts. Some ghosts made loops in the air. Others dropped to the ground and jumped up again. It was like a party.
But then I looked at the barrel.
Whoops.
That wasn't meant to go wrong. This was terrible! The barrel had tipped over and the oil was spreading out. It was slowly flowing to the barn ... the barn loaded with hay.
" Noooo!" I screamed, running towards the barn. But I was too late. The barn caught fire as well. The flames spread within seconds to other sides of the barn and the entire structure was being incinerated, all starting with the dripping oil.
I dropped on my knees, feeling desperate and afraid. What if someone discovered? How was I going to replace a huge barn like that? What would I do? What would I say? I couldn't bear to watch any longer, so I turned to the ghosts and told them to follow me into the forest. Maybe if I pretended to be oblivious of the matter, no one would blame me. But was that actually the right thing to do?
I was quickly about to learn, since the structure wasn't the only thing the fireball had kindled ...

Obviously, a few hotheads (pun intended) who resided in that location ... farmers from the beyond the town, had seen every little thing. They ran at me and the ghosts and waved their hands in the air. One of them was holding a pitchfork and the other a shovel.
" What are you doing there, girl?" one of the farmers said.
" Are you nuts?! You destroyed every little thing, you stupid, little ..."
" I'm sorry!" I shouted back.
One of them came actually close and threatened me with his weapon. He was raving. I had never seen anyone so furious before. The farmer was wearing a blue outfit and a pair of black boots. His hat was scruffy and the ends of his pitchfork were incredibly sharp.
" Why are you with these beasts?" he asked. "Look at what you've done. You are a disgrace to the village."
But then I got protective. "They are NOT beasts," I said. "They are nice creatures that are just misunderstood. You have not the slightest idea how smart and gifted they are. They can a lot more than you think."
" I don't care what you say, girl. I am going to tell the whole town, and when they hear of this, they will penalize you. And don't count on a light penalty. It will be harsh."
" Fine. Then I will not go back," I said. "Come on, friends. We run out here."
That surprised the farmer. He looked at me with big eyes ... speechless just because of my last remark. The other farmer, who was really out shape, finally caught up and asked while panting, "Hey ... wha-what's going ... on?"
" She says she will not come back to the town," the farmer said. "I do not know if she means it or if she is just bluffing. In either case, we'll be rid of her. Do I look like I care?"
The other farmer disagreed. I heard it from a distance, although I was already far away. He argued that I was only a teen and that my mother would be looking for me. But neither of them wanted to follow me and discover where I was going. Perhaps that was for the very best. I despised the villagers. They never accepted me. I had finally found my home: With the ghosts in the forest.
And that's where I remained, at least for the time being. I wasn't going back that night, and I didn't care. I looked at the ghosts. Some of them wept. They sympathized with me.

That night, I didn't leave the forest. I crawled under a bush and put my jacket over my body. I had never stood still at the fact that ghosts needed their sleep too. I had never seen them sleep. I watched as some of them went to sleep on branches and others behind rocks.

The baby ghost was still my favorite. It was charming to see it coming towards me and giving me a hug.

" I love you too, pal," I said with a smile, closing my eyes while welcoming it.

I didn't sleep much that night. I heard all kinds of odd sounds. I was afraid. This was my opening night in the forest. I heard an owl fly by, and I am pretty sure something unusual or dangerous was making the leafs rustle in that bush in the corner. I shivered. I didn't like this. I thought I undervalued how homesick I would become if I stayed away from home in an unidentified place ... well, unidentified at night. I had been coming here every day during the day.

One of the ghosts observed my worry and came closer. The ghosts were glowing a little in the dark and having them near me made me feel more secure. The ghost stayed awake and hovered above the ground by my side, waiting on me to go to sleep.

Ultimately, I fell asleep. The fatigue had conquered me.

But in the middle of the night, I woke up. I looked around me. All the ghosts were asleep. They were glowing a little, but besides that, it was pitch black. No streetlights in the forest ... that was obvious.

I heard something. Something was coming closer. I crawled back and wound up under the bush I was hiding under. Then I saw it. Eight red eyes were shining in the unknown blackness of the night. It looked dreadful. No ... wa-was it one of those enormous spiders? Wou-would it try to eat me?

I worried and got up the ghost beside me, elbowing it in the face. The ghost emerged with a jolt and looked at me with a mean face, nearly not recognizing me at first. Then its facial expression changed when it saw that it was me. But the ghost was also knowledgeable about the fact that there was something wrong with me. I was frightened and I looked at the red eyes which appeared from the shadowy corner of a tree trunk. Trembling while gazing at it, I gradually lifted my arm and pointed at it.

The ghost turned around and instantly discovered what was going on. I could see the anger in its eyes. How dare this spider threaten me, the ghost girl? Without doubt, the ghost spat a fireball at the disgusting beast. The burning ball hit the eight-legged animal in the face, and not too long after that, it vanished from our sights.

What a fantastic ghost! It had safeguarded me and saved my life. I gave it a kiss, even though it felt sort of funny.

The next day, I woke up by chirping birds. The sun came up and a bright new early morning was going to have lots of surprises. The first surprise was somebody calling my name.

" Helga! Helgaaaaa!"

Was that my mom? The ghosts were all awake now, and they were surrounding me like a protective guard.

" It's all right," I said. "I think it's my mother. Moooom!"

" Oh, Helga. I am so glad you're alright. I have been trying to find you for hours. Why did you run away from home?"

" Well, I mistakenly burned down the farmers' barn, and since a ton of people do not accept me in that town anyhow, I thought I would just keep away. It made more sense to me. Nothing really personal towards you. I just don't know what to do."

She embraced me and held me tight to her chest. "It's good nothing happened to you. |Don't you think it's a little dangerous to be in the forest by yourself?"

" By myself? Who says I am here by myself?"

My mom looked around her. The 30 ghosts had increased, or so it seemed. More of them had arrived from the volcanic mountain. I had not discovered it before either, but when my mom gazed at the flying fire creatures, I quietly counted them and came to the number of 58. Wow. More and more were joining our little get-together.

" D-don' t they attack you at all?" Mother asked.

" Obviously not," I said. "They are perfectly harmless ... well, around me at least, and it seems like they feel quite comfortable around you as well."

" Fantastic."

We looked at the ghosts a bit longer. Some of them were flying in circles, others were spitting fireballs at the river, and the closest one to us, the baby, began flying around my mom, observing her with all the interest that a baby has.

" Anyhow," my mom continued. "You cannot stay here. Please get back with me. I will explain to them that it was just an accident, and I am certain they will leave you alone."

In the beginning, I refused, but I wasn't stubborn enough, and Mom was proficient at convincing. She did that thing again where she looked me in the eyes and pled me to come along. Ultimately, I gave in and followed her to the town.

But it wasn't how it used to be. Even my mother didn't know about this. When we reached the village, big spiders were all over ... tons of them. They were crawling on roofs and breaking doors. They were getting on lights and rolling through windows. It was mayhem ... total chaos.

" Aaaaarhg!" we heard from one corner.

" Eeeeeeh!" we heard woman scream.

Everybody was panicking. Spiders were pursuing villagers, guys were battling them off with silver swords and iron pickaxes, and ladies and kids were hiding behind the walls, hoping not to be seen by these hairy devils.

My mother and I didn't say a word. We could hardly actually believe our eyes. The harmful scene before our eyes was the material of problems.

When I came to my senses, I tapped my mother on the shoulder. "I am going to get the ghosts," I said.

She stared at me for a second and then said, "Go! You are our only hope!"

I didn't wait any longer. I ran off to the forest, turning left and right in an attempt to find the best faster ways to the river area where the ghosts were. When I came, I had to catch my breath.

" Ughh ... heeheee ... The village ... pfew ... is ... under ... attack," I said, trying to speak but struggling to find the air to do it.

The ghosts gathered around me. They were all there. I stopped briefly for a moment and told them the rest. "Spiders are all over the village. I know the villagers don't like you, but this is your chance to prove them wrong. If you can go there without burning any other structures, or worse, people's homes, then follow me and kill these spiders at last!"

The ghosts moved sporadically in excitement, understanding totally what needed to be done. I took nerve, shook my head, and sprinted back to the village. Fortunately, the damage was down to a minimum, but if I had waited any longer, it could have been devastating.

The ghosts flew in. It was war. They spread all over the village and spat fireballs at the spiders, aiming to their best capability and killing many.

I was there. I commanded ghosts to go here or there, and I kind of felt like a supreme woman, controlling and ordering the forces of nature around me. The little baby ghost was there too. I watched as it quickly cremated a massive spider in front of me.

" Good going, pal!" I cheered. "That was super remarkable!"

The child ghost almost blushed a little. It was so adorable!

" Good job! Keep going!" I said, encouraging it a little.

One spider was going to pounce on a little girl when a ghost appeared in front of it and burned its face with an incredibly hot flame. Other ghosts were flying above the roofs, searching for the spiders that were closest to the villagers or knocking some tarantulas to the ground. The massacre was in our favor. Spider corpses were piling up on the streets and the remainder fearfully scurried away, leaving the town and never looking back.

Success was ours! The ghosts had saved the city!

Chapter 8: Better Acceptance

When all the spiders were either gotten rid of or killed, chased away or roasted like a barbecue, the ghosts were surrounding me. Gradually but certainly, all the villagers came to the main square, curious to see what had just occurred.
They saw me.
More than fifty ghosts were flying around me in circles, alert to the fact that anyone might still threaten me. I was their friend, their relied on partner ... their supreme leader.
I watched several villagers come closer. The farmer was in advance ... the same farmer who had been scolding me near the barn. He took off his hat and asked forgiveness.
" I am sorry for mistrusting you and your friends," he said. "You saved my family and my house from those horrible spiders. I owe you thanks."
" Oh, it was nothing," I said. "Always happy to help. I'm sorry I burned your barn to the ground. It was never my intention to do so."
" I totally understand," he said. "Consider us even."
" Sounds good to me," I said.
Mother came too. She gave me a hug after kicking away a dead spider in front of her feet. The trash man took a snow shovel and dragged some other carcasses away. It was pretty horrible, but everybody really felt like celebrating, and later I was told that there had been no dead casualties.
The other villagers approached me, thoroughly treading the location where the dozens of ghosts were still circling in the air. But something that stuck out ... somebody who moved forward out of the crowd, caught my attention: A pretty face I instantaneously recognized.
It was Raiden.
" That was really cool, Helga," he said.
I was amazed he even knew my name. The butterflies in my stomach got wilder and wilder. He was so handsome. Wow!
" Maybe we can go do something fun. How about tomorrow?"
" I 'd like that," I said. "Any ideas?"
" Well, I thought of heading to the forest, and after that you can show me what else these ghosts can do. I kind of like them."
I smiled. The boy of my dreams was asking me on a date, I had just saved the village and had been accepted by lots of the people there. The ghosts were still my good friends and I felt more positive than ever. This was the best day of my life!

THE END

The Town Ghosts

There is a story, an ancient story ... one about 2 ghosts that safeguard the town of Sprang Village. Everybody in town has heard about them, others have seen them, or at least one of them; but nobody understands what occurred and how these ghosts have become their guardians. What everyone does know, however, is that since these ghosts have been showing up, opponents have stayed out and the village people have become safer ...

Mason is in his house. He has barely finished cooking and has set the plates on the table. He sits down and smells his meal. "Aaah ... nice ... cauliflower, meatloaf, and potatoes. This is going to be scrumptious."
He begins eating and is stopped by a gush of wind.
" Huh?" Mason says. "What was that?"
He looks to the left and notices the door is open.
" I thought I closed the door. Am I going crazy here?"
He gets up and closes the door again. That was weird. Oh well, he isn't going to let it spoil his dinner. But then it happens again, this time more powerful. The door swings open and the wind blows away one of his napkins.
Whoosh!
How did this happen? It doesn't make any sense. Just an hour ago, the wind wasn't so strong and now it's blowing over his stuff. Mason gets up again and closes the outside door. Everything appears calm. Nothing going on.
But unexpectedly, he hears a soft, groaning sound, "Boooooh!"
" How is there?" Mason asks.
No answer.
" If you think this is funny, then come laugh over here! Since I think it's a sick joke!" Mason yells.
Again, no response.
" Oh well," Mason thinks. "If it is just one of those frustrating kids from across the street, I will learn ultimately."
He reads a book and goes to sleep. That evening, there are no more disturbances.
The next morning, he awakens by the noise of birds chirping. The wind is gone. It's all quiet, except for the birds. He stands and puts on his clothes, after which he heads to the main town castle. When he walks through the gate and passes the guards there, he welcomes his exceptional and reports the tasks from the previous day.
Mason is a town guard, a knight that secures his home town from attacking enemies like zombies. Some of them are actually dangerous and frightening. He has had times that he barely survived and thought he shouldn't have lived. But hey, it pays the bills and he is a daring type anyhow. He doesn't mind it. Besides, he is not scared to die. He has nothing to lose. Most of his relatives are gone or deceased, and he isn't even married. That's not to say he doesn't consider his life valuable, but he is more than happy to sacrifice it for the wellbeing of others, if needed. So why would he care?
" Prepared to go, sir," he says.
His exceptional, Mark, is a tough man. He has a strong chin and some big muscles. He has been a guard been as long as Mason, but his extra courses and training helped him

battle his way up the profession ladder and become a commander. He is wearing a red t-shirt and always carries his sword behind his back.

" Get your sword, Mason," he says. "We have reports being available in from the northern borders. Dark shades are attacking the farmers there. I need you to go and stop them. Do not come back until they are defeated."

" How many are we talking about, sir?" Mason asks.

" Oh, just a handful I think."

" Well, sir. I will go immediately."

Mason salutes Mark, turns around and runs out the castle gate. When he reaches the designated area about 20 minutes later, he sees what the officer means. Immediately, he is faced with a few dark shades beating up a villager behind a farm.

" Hey you! Stop that!" Mason screams. And with those remarks, he dashes forward to eliminate the dark shades. The villager quickly hides behind a wall, watching the brave guard put his life in danger to secure his.

Mason slashes with his sword and decapitates a dark shade. The other leaps back and attacks Mason quickly later on. He misses and Mason counters his moves by stabbing the dark shade in the chest.

" Die, evil beast!" Mason exclaims.

And with that, the battle is over. The last dark shade leaves into the forest from whence it came. Mason helps the villager up by reaching out. The villager grabs his hand and thanks him elaborately.

" Come have some tea," the farmer says.

" Oh, no thank you. I need to be on my way," Mason answers.

" No, really ... just sit down with me for a few minutes. It will be my satisfaction."

" Okay, I think a few minutes would not hurt," Mason says.

He follows the farmer to his home, where he gets a cup of hot, steaming tea. The farmer sits right across from him and says, "You should take care out there. One of these days, you're not going to make it. Have you thought about that?"

" It comes with the job," Mason says. "I do not care actually."

" You do not fear death?"

" Nope. It's all just a phase. I actually believe in the eternal worlds. My spirit will proceed when I die."

" Well, that's good to know. I am terrified of death. What if there is nothing after this life?"

" Then I better make the most of it," Mason answers. "Now, if you will excuse me, I need to report to my commander. Thanks for the tea."

" You're welcome."

Mason returns to the castle and reports defeating the dark shades. "Absolutely no deaths on our side," the report includes. Mark takes pride in him. He lets Mason choose the rest of the day.

" Nice," Mason thinks. "All this free time for myself." Satisfied with his accomplishment, he walks home and rests on his bed. He closes his eyes. Time for a nap.

Mason sleeps and sleeps. The combating has made him worn out. Initially, all is serene, but when time expires, he is awakened by the same gush of wind.

Woooosh!

The door swings open again.

" What is up with that door?" he asks himself. He walks over to close it, and after that sees a weird animal in the distance with green eyes, hovering above the ground.

" What the ...?" But before he can finish his sentence, the creature flies at him and knocks him to the ground.

" Ouch!" Mason says.

He gets up and goes to get his sword. He grabs it and holds it in front of him, looking around and wondering where the creature is at.

" Are you a ghost?!" Mason screams. "I am not afraid of you! What do you want from me ?!"

The ghost flies at him again, but this time, Mason averts its attack. "Come face me like a man!" Mason screams.

" Booooooh!" the ghost answers.

" Booh? Is that all you need to say? Can you even talk?" Mason asks.

" Obviously, I can talk," he hears.

Huh? A talking ghost? He didn't expect that one.

" Come here and I'll impale you with my sword, you coward," Mason says.

" You wouldn't have the ability to, even if you wanted to," the ghost says. "You would stab right through me. I am a ghost, remember?"

" Then what do you want with me?" Mason asks again.

" Oh, I just wanted to have some fun. I am extremely bored, you know."

" Well, if you want fun, then just come speak to me. What's the point of haunting me?"

" Sure," the ghost says, and he flies over to Mason. Finally, Mason gets to take a closer, longer take a look at the ghost. It's incredible that he can translucent him, yet still he sees him.

" What's your name?" Mason asks.

" I am Uria. I used to be a guard, until I died ... and I've been flying around as a ghost since. It's pretty cool actually. No one can do anything to me, but I can do something to others. That's how I think it works at least."

" So now what?" Mason asks. "Are you going to use your powers for good or are you just going to bully me and others around with your spooky sounds?"

" Well, since you are a guard, perhaps we can team up and defeat enemies together," the ghost says.

Mason thinks for a few seconds. Then he takes a look at Uria and says, "As long as you stay out of the castle. If they find out I brought a ghost to do my dirty work for me, I do not think they will like it."

" Fine. I will stay out of the castle. Anything else?"

" Yeah. I would like to know how you died precisely. Perhaps I can gain from your experience."

" I died trying to defend the village," Uria says. "I was surrounded by three-headed skeletons, but I was winning. It was a piece of cake. I butchered them one by one, and the dead skeletons accumulated in front of me. Quickly I would have defeated the entire army, but my pride got in the way. I celebrated in my mind before I was there. In the meantime, dozens of skeletons were slain by the slashing moves of my sword. But then, when I finally thought I had beat most of them, one of the skeletons stood in front of me."

" What was so unique about it?"

" I had never seen anything like it," Uria says. "It was enormous, twice as big as the other skeletons. It was wearing some insane armor, with signs and symbols all over it. I was frightened. The skeleton intimidated me. I didn't know what to do, so I stressed. I stabbed another skeleton and ran. He chased after me and swung his giant sword, missing the first time but hitting me the second time. That was it for me. I struggled with breath, and I died within minutes. If only I had had the courage to stand up against it, I could have been triumphant. I still feel awful about it."

" Where is this three-headed skeleton?" Mason asks.

" I believe he is wandering around on the western border, but if I were you, I would stay away from it. I had my chance, and I died. Don't let that happen to you."

" I will not, but I just feel like it's my duty to avenge you," Mason says.

" You don't have to ... I mean ... it was my mistake. You still have a whole life ahead of you. Don't risk it."

" What if you come with me? You could sidetrack it, and I could kill it."

Uria has to think of that one. "Maybe," he says.

Mason and Uria talk all night. Mason learns more about Uria's former life, gets the verification that there is life after death, and tells the ghost about some of the adventures he has experienced safeguarding Sprang Village. They are having lots of fun, until Mason tells Uria he has to go to sleep. Ghosts don't sleep, so Uria decides to fly away until the morning.

The next day, Uria is standing beside Mason's bed when he awakens.

" Waaaah! You frightened me to death!" Mason says.

" No, as you're still alive," Uria replies.

" It's an expression, you weirdo. And by the way, you need to wait till I am done eating, because I am not going to protect the town on an empty stomach."

" Fine. No problem."

Uria watches Mason eat some sausages, eggs, and bacon, but it doesn't do much with him because he doesn't have a nose anyway. When they go out the door and arrive at the castle, Mason tells Uria to stay outside so he won't scare anybody. Then Mason goes to Mark and asks him where he is needed.

" At the westside of the city" is the response.

" Wow. What a coincidence," Mason thinks. "Who knows ...? I may come across that big three-headed skeleton that killed my ghost friend."

Mason runs towards the west side of the village, near the edge of the woods. And there they are: An army of skeletons, prepared to assault the village, found by some of the best spies from the castle. Ready to attack ... yes ... but he is going to stop them.

" Shall we?" Uria asks while drifting next to him.

" This ends now!" Mason says in a low voice.

He takes his sword and storms at the skeleton army, dashing and slashing, eliminating lots of zombies. His buddy, the ghost, flies along and punches some skeletons in their faces, making it easier for Mason to stab them with his weapon. It goes on like this for a while. A huge fight occurs on the plains in front of the forest border, but then they both hear a loud stomping.

" Wha-what was that?" Mason asks.

" I do not know," Uria says.

Suddenly, it jumps in front of them.

Baaaaang!

The ground shakes and Mason and his ghost buddy are looking up at a huge skeleton, a monstrous figure with armor, a guard, and a substantial sword, bigger than Mason's own height.

" That's him!" Uria yells. "That's the skeleton who killed me! Do not just stand there, just ..."

But it's already far too late. The three-headed skeleton impales Mason with his sword. Mason coughs and falls to the ground. After several convulsions, his body remains still and blood streams from the injury, soaking the ground and turning it red.

" Oh no, Mason! I tried to caution you!" Uria screams. "What's going to happen now?!"

Then he hears a voice behind him, something he didn't expect. "What is the grumbling really all about? Grow up and do not be a dumb moron."

Uria turns around and is looking at another ghost, one that looks comparable but has blue glowing eyes instead of green. Is it ...? No, it can't be!

" Mason?" Uria asks thoroughly.

" The one and only," Mason says. "Now, let's get this jerk and take him with us to the other world."

Mason has become a ghost ... a ghost with many advantages: He can't be stabbed or hit or thrown around. He has become invincible and effective. He enjoys his new form of life, well ... death actually, but life however.

" Do that again, you idiot!" Mason says to the giant skeleton.

The three-headed skeleton swings his sword at Mason, but as he tries to kill him, the weapon goes right through him. The skeleton tries it again ... and again ... but without results.

Mason chuckles. This skeleton can't do anything to him. When he is done, Mason says, "Now it's my turn, ugly head!" and he punches the skeleton in the face.

Bam!

The skeleton falls over. Mason flies around him like an annoying little fly. The skeleton becomes disappointed and tries to hit him.

" That's what you get for killing me and my good friend here," Mason says. "Let's finish this!"

He flies towards the skeleton's sword and pulls it out of his hand. Then he aims and stabs the skeleton between the ribs. Death! The skeleton dies quickly with an agonizing cry ripping the air in half.

" Great," Uria says when he flies over. "What are your strategies now?"

" Now that I avenged you and died myself, I can still do my job," Mason says. "I do not need to live to do it. I am simply going to fly around this town and make certain it's safe. And any enemy that ever comes near it, will have to solution to me."

" Can I join you?" Uria asks.

" Obviously you can," Mason says. "How about you stay on one side and I stay on another side? Then we can turn off and stand guard."

" Sounds like a great strategy," Uria says.

And so, ever since that time, the town has been safe. Dark shades, skeletons, and zombies all kept away. Nobody dared go into Sprang Village without permission of these 2 undetectable guardians ...

THE END

They were being in a wagon ... they both loved it there. Their mom had already stepped out, prepared to move into their brand-new home. Angie ran to the horse and wagon. "Are you coming or what?" she asked.
The two girls stepped out of the wagon and avoided the muddy puddle in front of them by leaping over it.
" Mindful," the mom urged them. "The house is over there. Let's not lose way too much time and arrive before it starts drizzling again."
" Mom, Rose pushed me," one of the girls said.
" But Mary was saying that I looked amusing with the bow in my hair," the other said.
" I don't want to hear it," Angie said. "Move along now. Come on."
Before they knew it, it started drizzling again. They reached the house in time before they got soaked. Your home was enormous. It had ten different bedrooms, 5 hallways, and two sets of winding staircases. Its classy decors reminded Angie of the Victorian period, the "good old days." Now she was going to reclaim the home that was already hers. Her husband had left it to her. He had died a very long time ago, and Angie was raising her two daughters by herself.
Now they were standing there, dealing with an empty home with more space they could have ever dreamt of. Angie looked at her two girls and told them to swipe off the moisture on their coats.
" But we will be the only ones there," Mary objected. "It does not matter if we are wet or not."
" This house is going to be clean and tidy," her mom answered. "I will not have you abandon your good manners because we have no guests."
The three went inside.
" Whoa," Rose exclaimed. "This is big, Mother."
" I know, Rose. I acquired it a long time ago. We moved away before you 2 were born."
" I like it," Rose said.
" It looks a little scary," Mary disagreed.
" Well, you'll get used to it," Angie said as she walked to the windows and started aligning the drapes.
" What is that painting on the wall?" Rose asked.
" That? Oh, that's a taking off beast. I don't know why anyone painted that. Let's eliminate it. It looks hideous."
" Didn't Father used to eliminate those things?" Mary asked.
" Yes, he did," Angie said. "Your father was a brave man."
Angie walked to the horrendous-looking painting and stared at it. Somebody had painted a green beast with ugly teeth and mean eyes. The shadows behind it were even eerier than the animal in the foreground. It gave Angie the shivers, so she took it off the wall and tossed it out the door. The girls looked in amazement when they saw their mom's sudden display screen of assertiveness. The painting and the frame were being flooded by the rain in the mud to be forgotten and thrown away.
" Don't look. We don't want it, right? So there is no problem, is there?"
" No, Mother," her two daughters said.

That night, they were sleeping in the exact same room. All 3 wanted to stay together, just because of the dark, scary house they were in. It was roomy, but it didn't put them at ease. They all slept ...

All, other than for Mary ...

She was large awake, and she would not go to sleep anytime quickly. "Such an inheritance," she thought. "Simply because this place is huge, doesn't mean I need to like it. Look at the walls ... they're black, and the curtains are an ugly brownish color. I need to go to the bathroom."

She got up and went out of the bed room. Her mom and older sister were still sleeping. They didn't see anything. Mary tiptoed to the opposite side of the corridor, where the bathroom was. The corridor was long and high, and the shadows of the trees were giving it a gloomy atmosphere through the leaded glass windows on her right. Fortunately, she found the light switch in the restroom and turned on the light. She looked in the mirror. There were big bags under her eyes. She was dead tired. Then she raised the toilet seat.

Thud! Thud!

Huh? What was that? "Is anyone there?" she asked.

Silence.

" Hello?"

Still no sound. Then suddenly ...

Thud! Thud!

This scared Mary so much that she didn't take a chance and ran back. "Aaaaaah!" she screamed. "Mommy! There is somebody in the bathroom!"

Angie awakened. "What? What is it?"

" I do not know, but there is someone there. I swear," Mary answered while crying.

" Oh, don't be so ridiculous," Rose said. "It's not like there are ghosts in this home or something. Ghosts don't exist."

" Be nice to your sister, Rose," Angie said. "I will go check it out. Can you stay here?"

" Sure," Mary said. "I'm not going back there."

Her mom checked. After being away for a few minutes, she came back and shook her head. "I found nothing," she said. "Sorry. It must have been your imagination."

" But I heard something," Mary firmly insisted. "I don't know what it was, but there was certainly something there."

" Well, whatever it was, it's gone now," her mom said. "Please return to sleep."

So she did.

That was the first encounter ...

The next day, Mary and Rose were playing.

" I am the magnificent princess who defeats the dark monsters in the underworld," Rose said.

" Then I am the sweet princess who gets saved by the hero," Mary said.

" Or I could save you," Rose countered.

" No, I will be rescued by a good-looking prince," Mary said.

" A prince would not want to marry you, because you're too afraid. You're a wimp."

" I am not a wimp!"

" You are always making things up and begin being afraid of them," Rose declared.

" That's not true! I did hear something last night."
" Oh yeah? Then how come Mother didn't see anything?"
But before Mary could answer, they both heard a thud, once repeated.
Thud! Thud!
" Wha-what was that?" Rose asked.
" I do not know, but it's the same sound I heard last night," Mary said.
" Haha! Most likely just a rat or a foolish cat," Rose said. "Let's go see what it is. It could be fun."
" Nooooo, don't go over there. It might be a beast or something."
" Ughh ... such nonsense, I do not know where you get all these ideas."
But when they heard another thud, Rose became a little nervous too. They both went to the opposite side of the room and opened up the door. It was dark in the other room. The drapes were closed. They could not see anything, and the only light switch was near the other door.
" Stay here," Rose said. "I'll go turn on the light."
" Do not leave me," Mary said.
" It's fine. I will just be a few seconds."
Rose walked through the darkness to the opposite side of the room.
" Aaaah!" Mary yelled when she saw a white, see-through figure standing in the room. Now she was certain the house was haunted. She just saw a ghost, a little girl like herself ... drifting above the floor, in a white gown.
Rose turned the light on and the figure vanished.
" Now what?" Rose asked. "Why are you yelling?"
" You didn't see it? There was a ghost right there!" Mary said.
" Then how come I didn't see it? I think you're just making it up again."
" I'm not! I really saw a ghost, Rose."
" Yeah, sure. There is always something. Let's just return to the room and play again."
This was the second encounter ...

That night, the sky was dark, but the rain had stopped. The ground was still soggy but a round, clear, the moon shone through the clouds. Angie had spoken with her daughter that day and ensured her there was nothing going on, but Mary firmly insisted. The three members of the family were in white sleeping gowns. Again, Rose and Angie were fully asleep. They didn't seem to worry. But Mary was shaking greatly. She knew there was a ghost, but she questioned why. What did the little ghost girl want from them? Was she trying to frighten them? Kick them out of the home? What was happening here?
The anxiety caused her bladder to fill quickly. She felt it ... she needed to go to the restroom again, but she didn't want to. She was exceptionally restless for the ghost to show up.
" But the ghost hasn't assaulted me so far," she reasoned.
It took her several minutes of withstanding her bodily urges before she gave in and got up. She walked through the large corridor and saw the moon through the window. Then she turned on the restroom light and searched in the mirror.
She gasped for air. She wanted to scream, but something was telling her not to ... something ... or somebody! There she was, the little ghost girl. She was holding her finger in front of her mouth regarding tell Mary to be quiet. Mary nearly peed right there,

but she held it in. She was awfully scared. She looked behind her. The ghost was gone. The only place she saw her, was in the mirror.

" What do you want?" she finally asked, wanting to communicate with this spirit from the other realm.

The ghost girl waved to the right, telling her to follow her.

" I need to go first," Mary said, so she sat down and went.

After she flushed, the ghost girl appeared in front of her, indicating Mary to follow her again. Mary obeyed blindly. She knew something was wrong, but the little ghost girl didn't look so scary any longer. She was just like her, except for the fact that she was a ghost.

They walked through the corridor, with the ghost girl blazing a trail. When they were in the bed room, she signaled to wake up her mother and sister.

" Why?" Mary asked.

The ghost girl came closer and was right in her face, giving her a rebuking look, as if she was saying, "Just do it already."

It shocked Mary, but that was precisely what the ghost girl wanted. So Mary said, "Mom! Rose! Wake up!"

They both got up and saw the ghost.

" Whoa! What is that thing?" Rose asked. "Is that a ghost?"

" Dear, please stay away from that thing," Angie said. "Come here."

" No, Mom," Mary answered. "I think she is attempting to tell us something. Let's just follow her."

" Are-are you sure?" Angie asked. "How do you know we can trust this ... uhm ... ghost ... this girl?"

" I just do. Trust me. Initially, I was frightened too, but I know now that she is showing me things, so it must be all right."

" Fine. Let's see what she will show us" was the response.

All in their sleeping gowns, the mother and two daughters followed the ghost girl, who was flying quicker and quicker through the long hallways of the giant home. Ultimately, she flew down the stairs to the front door.

Panting a little, Angie asked, "What is it already? My curiosity has been stimulated."

" Let's open the front door," Rose said. "That's where it must be ... the thing she wants to show us."

They unlocked the front door and walked outside. It was cold, specifically on their bare feet, but it was manageable. The ghost flew in front of them and hovered above the ground for a minute, pointing at the mud. Angie and her 2 girls looked stunned.

" Is it the painting?" Mary asked.

The ghost girl nodded.

They came closer, and the mom dug into the mud to get the ugly beast painting and its frame. She brushed off the mud and after that she saw it.

" Oh no," she said.

" What is it, Mom?" Rose demanded to know.

" We are doomed. This painting meant something. Look!"

She showed the back of the painting to her daughters. It read the following:

Wherever this painting will be, the next explosions will be. One hundred exploding monsters in the dark of the night, only illuminated under the full moon. Beware the curse. Vengeance will be theirs.

" What does that mean, Mommy?" Mary asked.
" It means we get out of here ... fast!" she replied.
They looked at the ghost girl one last time. "Thank you," Angie said. "Thank you for warning us. Quickly, girls, do not worry about our things. The majority of them are still at the other home anyhow. We just need to run. Let's go! Let's go!"
She grabbed her daughters' hands and ran downhill with them, from the house. When she felt she was far enough, she took a look around and looked at her inherited home. The ghost girl was still there, waving at them. Then she sought to the right and saw numerous of those green evildoers dash up the hill and run at the house. Some of them tripped, others jumped over rocks and moved quicker, but all of them were speeding into the exact same direction. When they arrived, the house exploded into dozens of different places.
Booooooooooom!!!!
" Mother!" Mary and Rose both screamed. Angie knelt down and put her arms around her daughters, just protecting their ears from the sound and their sight from the bright light the fire emanated.
Boom! Boom! Boom! Boom!
It didn't pick up another five minutes. Exploding monsters were still assaulting the house and committing suicide doing it. When it was over, Angie let go of her daughters. They all watched their newly acquired house burn to the ground.
" Why did this happen, Mother?" Rose asked. "I do not understand."
" When your father died," Angie clarified, "he often spoke about the monsters he battled at the borders of our land. He must have killed thousands of them before he died in battle. He also mentioned a little girl he tried to save but could not. The regret was strong. It was as if he had failed completely. I still remember him talking about it over and over again."
" But why did the green monsters attack our house?" Rose asked.
" They wanted payback. They finally found our address and wanted to avenge the deaths of other monsters. All of it makes a lot of sense to me. The girl who died, probably presumed it and came to this home to warn us."
" So where will we live now?" Mary asked.
" Oh, do not worry. We still have our other house. We will return there. The only thing that's a disappointment, is that this home was a lot larger. It was huge! I type of liked it."
The three of them started to walk to the village from whence they came a few days earlier.
" Mom," Mary said after a while.
" Yes, dear. Go ahead. What is it?"
" If it's any alleviation to you ... I didn't like that home anyway. It was black and huge and ugly."
Angie chuckled.
" Thanks, Mary. I'll keep that in mind."

THE END

Confused

My name is Skeltorian. I am uhm ... well, that's just it; I don't think I have an age any longer. I am dead. I died. I think it was an accident at work. I was working in building, and I know the guys cautioned me, but for some reason, I ignored their voices of care and kept doing what I did.

I was in my own world. I have always been a little odd. Somebody in the area had detected me earlier with an impairment called schizoph ... I do not know. I forgot the word, but in any case, the physician told me I had to beware whom to listen to. A lot of wrong messages were in my head that didn't accompany reality.

And so, it happened that I wasn't paying attention. A big, steel bar was coming my way, and my coworkers were shouting that I should duck to avoid it.

I didn't.

BAM!!!

The metal bar hit me in the head, exactly at a spot where it caused my immediate death. I didn't feel anything after that. I was gone. But I had always learned that my spirit or soul would go to the afterlife. I don't know why it didn't. It was as if I was stuck or something. Maybe I had some incomplete business. Maybe I still had an objective, a mission to accomplish before I would proceed.

I had lived a hard life. My parents had broken up, my brain wouldn't leave me alone, with all the contrasting ideas that participated in it, and I had been a social outcast for many years. I was just feeling fortunate enough to work in construction. In my free time, I would go searching, not just to have some additional food on the table but also because I loved weapons.

I had been searching for many years. My precision knew no boundaries. Whenever I would see something to contend, I would just aim, release the bow, and watch the arrow hit the specific location I was pointing at, to the inches. It was a rare talent I had come to value throughout the years, although to this day, I still do not know if there was some higher purpose to it. Maybe that is another reason I would not carry on: I didn't know what to do with my archery skills. I had never felt the fulfilment I was trying to find. Sure, I had won competitions and added hunting trophies to the walls in my home, but it still didn't just feel like it sufficed.

When I died on that building and construction site, I felt as if I was still there. It was weird. And when they brought my body to my tomb, I still kind of felt like I was in it, despite the fact that I could not really do anything.

It took another month before I occurred from the tomb, kind of like having actually slept for a whole month. When I stood up, I looked at myself. The flesh on my bones had decomposed. It had decayed away typically. All that was left of me, was a simple skeleton. It was fascinating and brand-new. I decided there and then that I would find my purpose, that I would take my weapon and look for some type of sense to my undead life, if you know what I mean.

So there you have it. I am dead, but not truly; I am undead. I am a skeleton, trying to find purpose and prepared to move on to the next phase of death, but only if I find what I am trying to find first.

The voices are irritating. I have had them since I was a teen. They were always there ever since. They are voices that tell me I deserve nothing, that I should harm myself, sometimes even that I should kill myself. Because it's so hard to tell the difference between a real voice and the voices in my head, I usually wind up doing things I am sorry for later.

I do not know where they come from. Maybe it's just how I am wired. But then, if they are all related to the brain, are they still there? I do not have a brain any longer! I am a skeleton!

It does not make any sense to me, but I need to deal with them nonetheless. The biggest difficulty is to differentiate between the real and the fake ones. I am not always proficient at it. One time, I heard a voice that I swear was my dad's voice, but when it told me to just kill a colleague, I knew it was just something that was in my head. At those moments, I understand that I do have some control over them and that I do recognize the madness of all of it when I am faced with something that is made up in my mind.

Another time-- I will tell you an amusing youth story-- I "unintentionally" did something bad, because one of the voices told me to do it.

It was a teacher. His name was Mr. Dull. Go figure. Was that his real name? Yes, it was. I still do not know why you would make education your profession with a name like that, but he did, and man, was he DULL!!!

He would talk our ears off with his various stream of facts, the random dull stuff that came out of his mouth, the words that went into one ear and out another. It wasn't a pleasure to listen to him, particularly with that intonation. And that's a huge understatement.

But that day was different than few days ago. He had become so dull that he went to sleep throughout his own class. Maybe he hadn't had enough sleep that night. He had huge bags under his eyes, so he was probably tired to start with. If you ask me, he should have just called in sick, but he didn't. He was determined to finish the lesson. Poor teacher. He didn't deserve what I tried to do to him.

There he was, having his head on his arms behind his desk. His lecture was halfway over, and most of the kids either stopped taking notes or simply started talking about after-school stuff.

Then came the voice in my head. "Get your lunchbox," it said.

" Okay," I said, not understanding what to do with it.

" Now, open it up," the voice said.

I opened it up.

" Now, take the pieces of cucumber and place them on Mr. Dull's eyes. It will be hilarious when he wakes up."

I blindly obeyed, thinking that this was what had to be done. I took the pieces of cucumber and walked towards the instructor's desk. I was silent, but the other kids in class were really noisy. When I leaned over and tried to put the cucumber on his eyes, he woke up before I could.

" What are you doing?" the teacher asked. "Go back to your seat instantly!"

I ran back and dropped the cucumber pieces on the floor by mishap. One of the girls, who had just returned from sharpening her pencil, stepped on it and slipped.
Thud!
She landed on the floor.
" Whaaaah!" she wept.
I don't know if I should go deeper into this story, but let me just keep it at the bottom line: I had to stay for a very long time after school. Detention had become more regular anyhow, but this time, I had to clarify myself to the instructor, write 100 words on the blackboard, and do 300 math problems. He didn't actually believe me when I told him about the voices.
It took hours for me to finish what he made me do.

I dislike the voices. They're not my good friends. They tell me to do evil things and reach into the bottom of my soul to find corruption and wickedness. But I can't eliminate them. Hatred, aggravation, and doubt are the consequences of these voices, so hopefully, I will live on without those.

Chapter 3: Stolen

One of the first things I did as a skeleton, now that I got my body of bones, is leaving the graveyard and walking to town. But then I hear the voices again. One of them is more powerful and louder than all the other ones. It pierces through the marrow in my bones. I can't overlook it. It's just like a loud trumpet that blasts through my thick skull.

" Get cash," the voice says. "You need cash, a lot of it."

It makes a lot of sense. I mean, how else am I going to eat? I have no cash, since I just came from the grave. So I give in. I listen to the evil voice within me.

" Where do I find cash?" I ask.

" At the mayor's house," the voice claims. "He is loaded. He does not care if he misses a few bucks."

" That's right," I say. "He most likely earns the most in the whole village. I will go there and steal some of his cash. Then I can eat."

With that being said, I sneak through town, in the dark, and head towards the mayor's home. There is a back door, and I break it open, easily. I think it's better that the villagers don't see me. I think a skeleton would terrify them off, no matter what I do.

I sneak into the back room and come across a little vault.

" Try the different combos," the voice in my head says.

So there I go: 3-5-7-9. Wrong

Okay, perhaps 4-6-8-9. Wrong.

Then maybe it's 1-2-3-5. Wrong again.

What am I going to do to discover which code to use? Let's see, maybe if I listen to it very closely. I put my head beside the vault, only to discover that I have no ears. Oh yes, I forgot.

Then I just decide to quit. I can't figure out the code anyhow. I hit the small vault in aggravation.

Thud!

Hey, wait a minute. It moved.

I pull with all my might and rip out the box. I put it under my arm and leave the home. Good. No one sees me.

I walk back through the streets and go to my home. It's still the way it was before. Apparently, no one has even touched it or tried to sell it. And till they do, I am just going to live here.

I open the front door and look inside. Everything is still in place. The only difference is that all products and surface areas have gathered some dust. I sit down and try to burst the little vault. But then something strikes me. I can't eat! I am a skeleton. Why did I even do this? To get money? I don't need money, because I don't need food! Ughh ... maybe I'll take it back sometime.

Chapter 4: Damage

I sit there, dissatisfied that I did something wrong when I didn't even need it. The voices; they aren't stopping. They are still telling me what to do.

" Aaaarrgghh! Go away!" I shout, feeling helpless to silence them.

They will not disappear. They are in my head. I shout out in mental strong pain, but I still hear them everywhere.

" What do you want?!" I scream.

" It's not what we want. It's what you want," a spooky voice tells me, controling the others.

I stop shouting and I sit still, listening intently. Perhaps this time, the voice is right, so I better hear it out.

" Do you know the wall around the town? Everyone dislikes that wall. It just blocks out the sunlight and the simple methods to get in and out of town. How about you take that vault you have, the heavy, steel vault, and throw it against the weak points in the wall to crack it? Then it will be safer and simpler to leave town."

" That sounds like a reasonable suggestion," I say out loud.

" Well, what are you waiting on then? Take the vault and let's go!" the voice says.

" Okay, fine, I'll go."

That night, I go to the walls around the town, which are supposed to protect them from hostile trespassers. I take the vault box and tell myself, "Okay, here I go."

BAM!

I toss the vault against the wall. It fractures it a little, but it isn't efficient enough. I grumble a little in myself as it didn't work. It's frustrating. I can't get it to break. I try again.

Nothing.

Then I sit down and ponder what needs to be done. How am I going to break this wall? I have to admit that thinking without a brain is a lot harder. It takes me a very long time to come up with another idea again.

All of a sudden, I hear the same voice in my head again.

" The coalminers," the voice says.

" Coalminers? What about them?"

"They have dynamite, you idiot," the voice answers.

"Now, hold on a minute. Let's not start calling each other names," I say.

Again, I am glad no one sees me here speaking with myself, but it's in the middle of the night, so everybody in town is asleep. It looks like a good, sensible solution though.

Instantly, I betake myself to the mines, where it does not take me long to find some dynamite. I grab some sticks of dynamite and shove them between my ribs. Then I head back and light the sticks in front of the village wall. I escape and hide behind a building. I cover my ears and count down.

Three, two, one ... here we go.

BOOOOOOOM!!!!!!!!

The wall blows up. The rocks and granite dust are all over the place. Smoke evaporates from the scene. I wave the smoke away a bit and watch the results.

Great. The wall is broken. The villagers will be pleased. Now they can leave town more quickly, and not just through one gate.

Chapter 5: The Wicked Plan

I watch from the shadows as the villagers come to look at the loud sound. The explosions definitely woke them up, and they are eager to find out what just took place. I see them gather around the damaged wall, holding torches and searching in awe at the destroyed structure, or what is left of it at least.

" This is horrible," one of the female villagers says. "We cannot protect ourselves against enemies this way. How are we going to repair this?"

" We will be killed by the creatures from the Underworld!" a man shouts in panic.

" Our kids won't be safe," woman says.

I do not comprehend. I thought I was helping these people by blowing up their wall. The voice in my head said that they would appreciate it, but they don't. Did I just make life harder on them? Oh, why did I listen to that voice in the first place?

I don't know what to do, so I return home and go sit on a chair. I take a look at a glass of water but realize that it would just go through me if I try to drink it. Being a skeleton is a unique obstacle, but belonging to the undead also has some advantages. Like I said, I don't need to eat or drink to stay alive, and that night, I cannot sleep at all. I don't have to sleep, so that's most likely why.

Then the voice comes back. "Well done, Skeltorian. Now you will be ready to join me and my army in the invasion against the town."

" What?" I ask. "Who are you anyway? You appear in my head and I never asked who I am talking with. Who is this, and how did you get in of my head?"

" Ah, let me introduce myself. My name is Keesa. I am the chief of the army of the undead. I am able to enter your head as I am sending a signal only skeletons can hear. You, my good friend, have the privilege to prepare the way for my undead soldiers to take over; and by exploding the wall and taking the mayor's money to purchase fixing it, you have removed their last resistance. I will attack at dawn in two days. Be ready and help me wipe out these disgusting villagers."

I am stunned. I didn't expect this. I thought the voices in my head were all there just because of schizophrenia or something, but it seemed weird to me anyway, since I do not have a brain any longer. But now I recognize it was that skeleton leader the whole time. He plotted a plan against the villagers, and now he just used me to meet his goals. I feel dreadful. What have I done? Why did I listen to that evil skeleton?

" |Don't you worry, Skeltorian," Keesa says. "Every little thing will be great. We will kill the villagers and use whatever we find in there. We will chase them out of their houses and make them suffer. Hahahahahaaa!"

" Aaaarghhh!" I scream. "Are you still there? Get out of my head!"

" Hahaha! Fine. I will leave you alone. At my command, all the skeletons in this area will be prompted to do something about it and go to battle. You will see what happens, whether you like it or not. Goodnight."

I am upset. I rage. This Keesa person is going to crush this town and murder these good people, and I helped him do it.

But this has to stop.

The next day, I figure out a trick. I don't want to be viewed as a skeleton. No one should recognize me as that or they will go nuts. I just know it. So I take some outfits and wrap them around my bony body, ensuring that everything gets concealed. I even conceal my head totally, with a little room for the eye sockets. I kind of appear like a ninja, but at least I won't look like a skeleton.

I wait until the evening falls. It has to be dark, or this won't work. But this time, I don't wait till the middle of the night. As soon as the sun sets, I take the small vault I stole from the mayor and drag it to his home. The weather is chilly. It's a great night, with a cool breeze. The lights of the mayor's home are dimmed. I am barely noticeable. The outfits cover every inch of me, and my eyes (or lack of them) aren't clear beneath the hoody.

I knock on the door and wait.

After a while, the mayor opens up.

" And who might you be?" he asks, a little hesitant.

" My name does not matter right now," I said. "I am here to provide a message. I have learned that an entire army of skeletons is on their way to ruin this village. Gather all your guys and stand prepared to face them."

" How do I know I can trust you? And how do you know all this?"

" You'll just have to believe me," I say. "I have my resources."

" When will they come?" the mayor asks. "Just how long do I have?"

" At dawn. They will come at dawn, and they will barge in through the wall I destr ... I mean ... someone ruined last night."

" You want me to gather all the readily available men by tomorrow? Are you ridiculous?"

" Don't ever tell me I am outrageous!" I sneer. "Everyone has mental issues. Why should I be any different?"

" Okay, alright. I will see what I can do," the mayor guarantees me. "Anything else?"

" Yes," I say, as I reach into my bag and pull out the vault. "I found this somewhere. I actually believe it comes from you. It had a little note on it that said, 'I am sorry.' Undoubtedly, the one who took it, shows remorse and regrets what she or he did. Please take it."

" Wow. Thank you. You are right. I was trying to find this. I am happy I got it back."

" You're welcome. Good luck, Mr. Mayor. You will need it. Farewell for now."

With those words, I turn around and vanish into the distance. I don't look back. It's up to him now. All I can do, the next day, is help. It will be a massacre, but the question is: One which side?

I can only hope for the best.

The stillness of the early morning scene enables a tranquil start of the new day. Birds call one to another; the night dew sticks to the leaves and trees and makes the plants shine like crystals. Sweet vapors rise from the ground, and the sun hasn't shone its hot rays upon the predestined villagers yet. It's still early, and the bunnies hop around on the soon-to-be battleground as if it is yet another morning of tranquil nature.

But they couldn't be more wrong about this day, the day a potential trouble will result into the massacre of innocent villagers trying to protect their homes and families.

I am already awake, seeing that I haven't slept at all. Why would I? I am a skeleton, and I need to be alert for what is about to happen.

I stand in front of the town, concealed in rags and outfits. It's silent. No one is there. Then, all of a sudden, like a gush of wind, a whole army of men appears on the horizon. They have come together in desperation, wanting to survive the anticipated skeleton attack.

I wait on them and greet them.

" Who are you?" they ask.

" And why are you hiding behind a mask?" someone asks.

" Never mind that. I am here to help you combat the battle. Is that fine?"

" Sure. No issue, we need a ton of help, so yes, you're welcome here."

" Okay, so shall we forget the name and the mask and just kick these skeletons out of our hometown when they come?"

They do not have anything to say after that. They just continue lining up. It's an army, but an army of villagers who clearly lack some battle abilities. I look at them and shake my head when I see only a handful of them carrying swords, and others pitchforks, pickaxes, and shovels. They appear like a lot of farmers who don't know what they're doing. It's not soothing, since the skeleton army will soon be coming at us with everything they have got. Personally, I still like the weapon.

We hear sounds. Screeches from afar enter our audible senses. The piercing war weeps of an undead army, ready to kill and damage. We are standing on top of the hill and ignore another hill that appears a few miles away. Behind that hill, gradually but definitely, an army of skeletons emerges.

" Prepare yourself, men!" a huge guy with a beard begins. "We are here to protect our wives, our kids, and our really survival! Do not get frightened by their grave, ferocious appearance. They are dead, and they shall die again. Now, join me in the ranks against the forces of damage and set all your fears aside. This is the moment of nerve. This is the moment we say 'no' to evil!"

He raises his voice during the last couple of words and all the men cheer. They hold up their weapons and scream as loudly as possible.

But then they look at the other hill. The skeletons are overwhelming. Their numbers are excellent. When I do the math in my head, I see a legion, a vast militia counting thousands of skeletons with swords and shields. I look at the men on my side. They are scared. They didn't expect the army to be this huge.

" Do not fear!" the leader screams. "They are but bones and skulls! We have the sacred blood of our predecessors! Get ready to protect yourselves and everything you love!"

The time for fight has come. The bloodshed can start. The army of skeletons runs down the hill. I shoot an arrow, and another one, and another one. I kill several, but they are approaching within seconds. It will not be long now till the individual battles will start. Swords are banging and clanging. Male and skeletons are shouting. I put effort into fighting some of my own, but I am searching for a permanent solution.

Then I understand what has to be done. The leader! He is the source behind all of this! Where would he be? Oh, that was easy.

I see a skeleton on a horse. It's the only skeleton who has a horse. He is wearing a red cape and a war helmet, screaming commands at the other skeletons and pointing his sword into our direction.

" Keesa," I say in a low voice. "You're gonna die."

But I still do not know how. I will have to break through numerous skeletons to reach him, and a battle may not even be the best way to end this. Maybe I could shoot an arrow at him?

No, meaningless.

If I miss, he will just know where to find me. I have to find something better, something that will not only eliminate him from the scene, but also give the villagers an advantage. I need something ... something ... explosive! Yes, that's it! I am getting more of those sticks of dynamite from the mine.

I do not wait. I rush to the mine, leaving the fate of the civilians behind me. I run inside, look for the sticks, and find them at the specific place where I saw them last. I stuff them into my backpack and run back to the battleground.

" There," I say.

I find a way to navigate past a lot of skeletons and quickly, I find myself within a hundred feet of Keesa. I hit a skeleton on the head, punch another in the ribs, and stand in front of the malicious beast.

" YOU !!!" I say.

He steps off his horse.

" Hahaha!" he laughs. "Skeltorian, is that you? Take off that outrageous disguise. It does not matter any longer."

" Why not?" I say. "I would rather look like one of them than like you or your dumb, brainless skeletons."

" You're just like us," Keesa says. "|Don't you understand you are mocking yourself?"

" I do not care," I say. "This ends now. You lost your right to live by planning an assault on innocent people."

" Bring it on," he says, holding his sword prepared.

" I don't want to fight you. I just wanted to get near you. Any last words?"

" Huh? What are you talking about?" he asks.

" Funny. I would have said something else," I say. "Oh well, I guess your ending isn't going to be extremely poetic then."

I secure a stick of dynamite and attach it to an arrow. I aim, shoot, and hit the arrow in his skull.

"Nooooooo !!!!!" Keesa yells.

But it is too late. The explosions of the one stick activate the other ones to blow up too in my backpack, and the total battleground becomes a large, enormous ocean of fire, swiping through the majority of the skeleton army.

Chapter 8: A Lot More Dead

Needless to say, that I die here as well. My spirit drifts up as it looks down upon my body. I, my spirit, glance around and watch with satisfaction. I just blew up about 90% of the countless skeletons in the direct vicinity. They are piled up on and scattered right across the battlefield. In the distance, I see some villagers kill the rest of the wicked army.

I take a look at my own body. It has broken into a thousand pieces, intermingled with the dead body of the offender, Keesa. He didn't even stand a chance. I sacrificed myself, but I don't care. I just wanted to help these town's people live a good life. My life is over anyway.

I hear a voice in my head. It's not Keesa's voice. It's a soft, relaxing voice, like a colorful, forgiving wind that reaches the depth of my extremely being. It's strong and dominant but not powerful. It relieves my ideas and tranquilizes my mind. I drift and I feel greater than ever.

"Well done," the voice says.

I have not a single clue who says it. I have not the slightest idea who is speaking with me. But one thing I do know: My work here is done. This is why I stayed: To rescue this town from the horrible fate that would have befallen them if I wouldn't have existed. Now that I look back, I am glad I heard those voices. I could only predict the skeleton army's attack by hearing the voice of that awful leader. It was essential. My weakness had become a gift.

But I was there. I exploded the wicked undead and am now leaving this life with contentment.

Life is over. I am pretty happy. Whatever will happen now, I am ready.

THE END

Rogue Rabbit

Chapter 1: Chickens

It wasn't pretty. The mess was all over the chicken pen. Chickens were torn in half, and plumes were all over. The chickens that were still alive, walked around it as if nothing had occurred. They completely overlooked the victims in the middle of the pen.

Frits took his hat off and walked over to Johnny. Johnny looked at him and felt his pain.

" Extremely unfortunate," Johnny said. "I hope we'll be able to find out what triggered this."

" I hope so too," Frits concurred. "I do not think any predators have been spotted around the town. It's a big mystery. What sort of animal would rip chickens in half like that and not eat them?"

" I don't know, man, but just one thing I do know: This is screwed up!"

" Well, yeah. I have never seen anything like this. I'll go get the gloves and start cleaning it up, I think."

Frits left and Johnny went after him. "I will help you," he said. "We'll have this resolved in no time. Do not stress."

They tidied up the dead chickens and went back into the home. Frits offered Johnny some tea and a cookie. Johnny observed the flatware and the china on the shelves beside him. He flattered Frits on his home, saying that it was pleasant and comfortable.

" You actually worked hard to make this place relaxing and welcoming, didn't you?" Johnny asked.

" I started from scratch, Johnny," Frits said. "I value every little thing I have, but especially my animals, and if something or someone is disturbing their peace, it bothers me, and not just for monetary reasons."

" I understand," Johnny said while taking a sip from his tea. "What type of tea is this anyhow? I really love it."

" It's peppermint tea," Frits said. "I grow the leaves in my backyard. It's great. It gives you that little spike while relaxing the mind with its heat."

" That's deep, man," Johnny said. "You're a thinker. I do not think that much. And something is telling me that you stress way too much as well. Am I right?"

" Yes, you are. I dislike it, but it keeps me going," Frits said.

They talked some more and Johnny completed his tea. He left the house and walked home. He wasn't worried at all, unlike Frits. According to Johnny, the chickens were most likely just killed by some wolf or ocelot that had broken in.

" Good old Frits," he said as he got back and kissed his spouse.

" What happened this time?" she asked.

" He is devastated over a few chickens," Johnny said. "But I am sure we'll capture the predator soon. It must be a bear or a fox or something, or perhaps an ocelot or a wolf. Who knows, right? But then again, who cares? We have had attacks from those animals before, and we took care of them."

" Yes, we did. No problem."

" Exactly."

That night, Johnny was sleeping. His wife was up; she despised it when her husband snored. She tried to cover her ears with her pillow, but it wasn't effective enough. Johnny was loud, and there was nothing she could do about it. She sat there all frustrated, just wondering if she should just poke him or slap him and tell him to shut up. But she was too nice. She wouldn't do that to him.

But then she heard even louder sounds from outside. "Finally," she thought. "I have an excuse to wake my husband up."

She leaned over and shook him a little. "Johnny ... Johnny," she said. "I heard something outside."

" Mmm ... mwhah-what is it?" Johnny mumbled.

" I heard a strange sound. Could you please check what is going on?"

" Oh, okay. Sure," Johnny said. He got up and put on some clothes, and then he went outside. Now he heard it too. The chickens were panicking. He got a machete from the shed and ran towards the chicken cages. The moon was shining intensely, so that he didn't need to take anything to light his way.

When he arrived at the chicken cages, he could not actually believe what he saw.

" Oh no," he sighed.

He buried his head in his hands and gazed at the mess, nearly the exact same mess as his friend had encountered. Several chickens were ripped apart, and at least five more had been a little hurt, but enough that it was lethal. Ten chickens had been killed. As he stepped into the blood running away from the carcasses, he got disgusted and a little sick by seeing this dreadful slaughter.

But the danger was gone. Whatever or whoever did it, had left. Johnny took a look around, but in spite of the moonlight, he couldn't see anything or anybody that looked suspicious.

" Is that all you have got?!!" he shouted. "Come and show yourself, stupid animal!"

It was dead silent, so after a while, Johnny went back and reported the dreadful news. The predator had struck again.

Chapter 2: Seeing It

The next morning, half the town came to watch Johnny's poor dead chickens. Frits appeared and saw a big crowd loafing in Johnny's garden. They were taking a look at the body parts that were spread across the chicken coops. Johnny had gathered everybody to take a look and examine the criminal activity. The conversation had just begun when Frits showed up.

" Does anyone have an idea who or what may have done this?" Johnny asked.

" Well, I can tell you just one thing," a young man says, "this ain't no ocelot, nor a wolf. They don't attack anything unless they eat what they kill."

" If it isn't a routine predator, as you are saying, then what is it?" Johnny asked.

" What if someone in the village did it, just to get people upset?" lady suggested.

" That could be real," Johnny said. "But I can't come up with anyone who would do such a thing."

Frits was listening intently, since his chickens had become the victims of this heinous crime 2 nights ago. The people thought of ideas, suggestions, and even some allegations, but none comprehended the nature of the crime, nor the motive anyone or any animal could have to just kill chickens and after that leave them there. Everyone was shocked, and after some more meaningless arguments, they all became quiet. All of a sudden, a voice from the back of the crowd broke the silence.

" I've been telling you," it said. "I have been telling you for several years."

Everyone stepped aside and turned to the man who claimed to know more. He was wearing a hoody and was leaning on a walking stick. And although his face was rather hidden below the hoody, his eyes were piercing and intense.

" What have you been telling us?" woman wished to know.

" I told you about the killer bunnies," he said. "But no one listened. And now it struck again."

Everyone looked at one another for a 2nd, and when the time out was over, they all break out laughing. Some were cracking up so badly that they practically tipped over.

" A killer bunny?" somebody asked.

" Bunnies do not kill, old man. They eat carrots and lettuce. Have you ever seen this so-called killer bunny?"

" I have seen it," the old man confirms. "But I wouldn't try to find it if I were you. It's dangerous."

" Ha-ha-ha!"

The crowd scolded him. It sounded like an outrageous concept. Predator bunnies were unprecedented, but the man firmly insisted that he knew what he saw.

" Mark my words," the old man warned. "It will not be the last time it will kill. It will be back."

" Then we'll just kill it," Frits said. "Where do we find it?"

" Oh, I wouldn't do that if I were you," the old man said. "You cannot battle this monster. Its teeth and claws are sharp, and it has a bloodlust you are not acquainted with. My best recommendations: Stay inside and put better fences around your animals. Maybe even set some traps, but I question the killer bunny will be dumb enough to step into them."

" Thanks," Frits said, a little dissatisfied that he could not get more information out of him.

Frits returned home. He knew everyone was making fun of the old man with the hoody, but for some reason, he strongly believed him. What an unreasonable idea! A killer bunny? Who had ever heard about such a thing? But what if the man was right? What if it was true? He could not come up with any other carnivore that would murder his and his good friend's chickens that way.

A killer bunny? Seriously?

He poured himself a cup of tea again and sat there, thinking about what to do. "Those are my chickens," he said in a low voice. "I need to protect them."

That night, Frits set right outside the chicken pen. His axe was beside him, so he could easily grab it if he had to. The sun was setting and it was nearly dark. Crickets were chirping, the wind blew, and an eerie fog came by the farmlands. But Frits was prepared.

" Let come what may," he said.

He waited and waited. The moonlight illuminated some of the ground, yet Frits remained in the shade, hidden from any trespassers that could come that night. The waiting made him tired. He yawned and rubbed his eyes. He got comfortable and lay back, with his head leaning sideways.

He went to sleep.

The hours went by, and nothing happened.

Nothing for hours and hours ...

Unexpectedly, Frits heard a noise. It was a chicken. He grabbed his axe and ran towards the pen, but he was too late.

One of the chickens was dead, slashed through by some predator. Frits's heart started beating faster. He knew the predator was still around. He wanted to the right and to the left, he ran into the field, despite the misty air, and scanned the horizon.

There!

In the distance, there were too glimmering eyes, looking straight at him. Frits ran towards the animal and stopped. In front of him was a white bunny with red, glowing eyes. Its facial expression was wild and vicious. Its claws were long and sharp, and the bunny was showing its teeth and roaring a little.

" Whoa," Frits said. He had never seen anything like it before. He stared at it, and it stared back. Then Frits ran at the bunny with his axe, but as soon as the bunny saw him coming, it hopped into the bushes. Frits kept looking.

" Come back, you coward! Afraid of an axe?!" he yelled.

But there was nothing else he could do. Frits looked a little bit longer and after that gave up. The killer bunny was gone.

When Frits went to Johnny the next day, his good friend could hardly really believe it.
"So the old man was right then?" Johnny asked.
" Yes, he was. I saw it with my own eyes."
" Wow. Who would have thought that those things existed? Anyhow, what are we going to do now?"
" Kill it, of course," Frits said.
" I agree, but how?"
" I don't know; just bring a weapon and enough supplies for our trip. The old man would not tell me where to find the bunny, but perhaps he can give us a general direction."
" Sure, but how do we find the old man?" Johnny asked.
" You do not have to. He found you," a voice said.
They turned around and saw the man with the walking cane. A little shocked that he would appear like this, out of the blue, they asked him where to look for the killer bunny.
" Don't say I didn't alert you," he said. "I am certain you will die if you go try to find it, but if you want, I can still tell you where I think it hides."
" That would be really handy," Frits said.
" I've heard they live at the foot of the mountains. That way," the man said, pointing in a certain direction.
" They?" Frits asked. "What do you mean? Are there more than one?"
" Oh, I don't know that," the old man said. "Maybe not, but I can't ensure that there is only one. Who knows how many of those monsters there are?"
" Okay, thanks," Frits said. "Come on, Johnny. Let's get going. We will find the killer bunnies and make them regret what they did."
Johnny followed Frits to his home. They got as much equipment together as they could carry, but they still tried to keep their bags light. Johnny brought a net to drag the bunny back when they would catch it, and he put some food in his backpack as well. Frits packed a bow and arrows, matches, and his axe.
They took off, walking through the forest into the mountain areas. At first, everything seemed peachy. There was no danger, there were no wild animals, and a course led them to the foot of the biggest mountain in that area.
" What did it appear like?" Johnny asked after a while. "You got a take a look at the killer bunny, right? What did it look like?"
" White with red eyes," Frits replied. "It was as if the devil himself had seized that bunny's body. When it looked at me, it was as if it was looking right through me with those hollow, red eyes that glowed in the dark. Weird, I tell ya."
" The more reason to get rid of it," Johnny said. "I don't want such wicked things around my house, even if they do not kill any chickens."
" It should not be too far," Frits assumed. "The old man said the bunny went into the mountains. Sure, that may be so, but I do not think it went too far away, only to make a long trip to the farms each time."
" I think you're right," Johnny said. "We must keep our eyes open. Its home could be anywhere near here."
They kept walking, and the wind ended up being stronger. Some branches were already flying by and the soft breeze developed into heavy gusts of wind, pulling bushes out of

the ground and making the environment unsafe. A storm was coming, and it wasn't going to be fun.

" This is just going to get worse," Frits said. "Do you see the clouds? We need to find some shelter."

" Well, we're practically at the foot of the mountain," Johnny said.

" Perhaps there is a spot or a cavern where we can hide. Some rocks, some ledge, or something else ... what do you think?"

" I think that's an outstanding idea. Let's keep moving!"

The 2 of them headed into the direction of the mountain and found a cave in the mountain. It took them a while to find it, but with the strong wind, they figured they had no time to lose, so they hurried and went inside as quick as they could.

There they were, sitting and watching the storm do all sorts of things to the trees, the bushes, and the sand at the bottom. The two friends weren't certain if they could call this a "hurricane," but it sure came close to it. They had never seen a wind as strong as this, and Johnny said that if he didn't know any better, he would have seen it as a bad sign.

" Shall we go inside the cavern?" Johnny asked after a few minutes.

" Let's just hide behind this rock," Frits suggested. "There is only a small chance something will blow our way, and the cavern is pitch black."

" Then just light a match and make a torch," Johnny said.

" I would rather wait until the storm is gone," Frits said. "The wind could burn out the fire."

" I guess so."

They waited and waited. It took several hours, and the farmers ate a little treat. Just for fun, Johnny told some jokes he had heard from his kids, who had heard them from good friends at school.

The storm was nearly over. Quickly, they would go inside the cavern.

Chapter 5: Bunnies Don't Do This

" Now, can we light a torch and go inside the cavern? I am extremely curious," Johnny said.

" Obviously," Frits said.

He took the matches out of his pocket and used some dry branches to light a torch. When he was done, he held the torch up and handed it to Johnny.

Frits put the matches back and took his weapon. "You never know what's in this cavern," he said. "Go on and light the way. I'll be prepared if there is a bear or a cougar or something in this cave."

They snuck further and farther into the unfamiliar cave. They felt the rocky ground beneath their feet. Sometimes they looked at one another, and Johnny moved the torch around a lot. He was a little nervous.

Suddenly, he stepped on something. "What is that?" he asked.

He moved the torch to the ground. It was a pig skeleton.

" Whoa!" Johnny said as he stepped back. When he held the torch in front of him, at a low level, he saw that this was only the tip of the iceberg. Frits' and Johnny's mouths fell open when they saw a huge stack of animal bones and skulls, scattered all over the cavern. There were horse skulls, bones from wolves, and cat cadavers.

" There must be tons of them," Frits said. "Have you ever seen such a thing?"

" Never," Johnny said. "This is stunning. Bunnies do not do this. What prompted these adorable, fluffy animals to become huge murder creatures? It's a massacre. Look at all these skeletons!"

" There is only one thing that could have made them this way," Frits said. "It's pure evil, that's what it is."

" Let's get out of here," Johnny said. "I don't feel comfortable staying here. I am happy we found their hideout, but I am a little reluctant to combat this bunny after seeing this."

" You still think it's only one killer bunny?" Frits asked.

" There must be more of them. This is outrageous!" Johnny exclaimed.

They returned to the entryway of the cavern, intending to get out of there alive. But when they left the cave, they stood face to face with something frightening ...

Chapter 6: The Killer Rabbits

The two farmers couldn't believe their eyes. It was like they were waiting on them ... waiting ... to ruin!

In front of the duo were about twenty bunnies, all with glowing, red eyes, sharp claws, and grinding teeth. Their appearance was sloppy and wild. The malicious look in their eyes was both chilling and disturbing at the same time. Bloodthirst was apparent in their temperament, and they were prepared to attack.

But none were white.

They were all brown, black, and grey.

" These are not the ones I saw," Frits said while leaning over to his friend.

" What do you mean?"

" I mean that I saw a white bunny, remember? There must be another one."

" Oh come on," Johnny said. "You must have seen it wrong. It was dark. It was foggy. You said so yourself."

" I know what I saw. There is another one."

" Well, I do not see it now," Johnny said, "so let's just concentrate on these, shall we?"

" You got it," Frits said as he put an arrow on his bow and extended it back. Johnny took the axe and was all set for battle too. There they were, standing face to face with more than a dozen killer bunnies who were drooling and gnashing their teeth, expecting to feast on some flesh.

" Come on!" Frits all of a sudden shouted. "Come on, if you dare!"

He shot an arrow and killed one of the ruthless bunnies. The other bunnies didn't wait and hopped towards the two farmers. Frits kept stepping back and shooting more arrows, and Johnny swung the axe he was holding at the monstrous rabbits.

" Take that! And that! And that!" he said each time he killed another bunny.

Some of the bunnies came too close and scratched the 2 heroes, causing them to bleed. They tried to overlook their wounds and finish the predators off. Hacking and slashing, shooting and kicking, the 2 managed to kill the majority of the bunnies. There were only three left.

" Duck!" Frits said.

Johnny ducked and evaded Frits' arrow that way. After that, Johnny swung back his axe and made it land in the other 2 bunnies.

" That was that," Johnny said. "We're done here."

" Do not be so quick to celebrate," Frits said. "I told you there was another one. But where is it?"

They took a look around for a minute.

" There!" Johnny all of a sudden screamed.

Johnny was pointing at the white bunny, which leapt from one of the rocks that belonged to the mountain. Before it landed on the ground, next to Frits, it scratched him with his claws.

" Ouch!" Frits said, dropping his bow and arrow.

" Frits!" Johnny shouted. "Dumb bunny. You're going to pay for that!"

" Go get him, Johnny!" his partner shouted. He was injured, but he was alright, only bleeding a little from his shoulder.

Johnny held his axe in front of him. The white killer bunny was larger than the other ones. It looked at Johnny, aware of the weapon he was holding. Then it leapt at him, trying to cut him open with its claws.

Johnny ducked again, but this time, he thought of the idea of doing so himself. He watched the bunny jump over him and swung his axe at him.

Tsyaaaaaack!

It hit the bunny, which died quickly. Johnny had killed the killer bunny.

" That's revolting," Frits said when he looked at the dead bunny on the ground.

" Yes, but it's dead," Johnny said.

" Certainly, it is," Frits said. "Well, what now?"

" Have you forgotten why I took the net with me?" Johnny asked.

" Oh yeah, why did you take that net anyhow?"

" In contrast to the bunnies' bloodlust, I don't mind eating the victims I kill," Johnny said.

" Ha-ha-ha! Good one! You're going to eat these bunnies? What if they have some evil force in them that made them the way they are?"

" I want to take that danger. You?"

Frits thought for a moment. Although he had no clue why these bunnies had become so wicked and ferocious, he wasn't superstitious enough to think that there was an actual wicked force in them. So he shrugged and said, "Sure. Let's get them into the web. We'll cook them at home."

They gathered all the bunny lifeless bodies and put them into the web. After they were done, they headed home.

" Hey, Johnny," Frits said. "Do you know any rabbit dishes?"

" I am sure my marriage partner will know some," he said. "We haven't had bunny for dinner in years. By the way, I heard it matches peppermint leafs, so you should be fine. The question is: Who is going to take the big, white one home? That one has the most meat on it, doesn't it?"

" Ha-ha!" Frits laughed. "You can have it."

" Thanks. I appreciate that."

THE END

Competition

" AMM Corporation. This is Jennifer speaking. How can I help you?"
This is what I said every day, about a hundred times per day; perhaps even more. I was a secretary, a good one. I was a multitasker, and I didn't hide it. When I applied for this job, they gave me a testing day. They observed me as I answered the phone, organized documents, and replied e-mails at the same time. I was like a centipede. I could do it all at once.
" You're in," they said after seeing me being busy.
I was delighted. I was incredibly happy. I knew I would succeed at this company. However, what I didn't see coming-- which is always the case-- was that interacting with colleagues and coworkers would be one of the most important things. You see, there are a lot of people who do what they really love but hate their job since they can't work well with other workers. At the same time, there are those who don't perform their favorite jobs but love the comradery at work, which makes all the distinction to them.
In my case, I was at a job with all guys. It was a competitive company, and all they did, was take any risks, exchange stocks, and a lot of other complicated stuff.
All they needed me for, was to answer the phone and make consultations and such. I didn't know anything about the business, and in some cases, I had the gut feeling they looked down on me because of that.
All of it began on a Thursday. I would have the next day of rest, so my weekend would be long. It was afternoon and one of those guys, whom I believed to be a big bully in high school when he was young, came by my desk and told me to get him some hot chocolate.
" Uhm ... I am sort of busy right now," I said. "The machine is right there."
" I know," he said, "but I think you should get it. You do not do anything essential here anyway, and my time is far more valuable. Besides, you're lady."
I could not believe my ears. Unexpectedly, the rest of the world was gone from my concentration. My senses shut out all other noises, smells, and images. All I heard was "you're woman."
I stood and put the phone on hold. Then I looked him in the eyes and said, "Excuse me? I am lady? What does that relate to anything?"
" Well, it's your job to get me what I want," the guy said.
I swallowed some words I wanted to say to him and took a deep breath. This conceited loser was going to get it.
" Listen to me, Devil ..." I said.
" Devin," he said, remedying me.
" Whatever. Maybe if you wanted to lose some weight, you would drag your own fat body over to that device and get yourself some hazardous, sweet drink. But then again, I don't think you could withstand the temptation of an addictive substance, because you're just lazy. I hope you don't treat your marriage partner the exact same way."
" I'm not married," Devin said.
" That does not surprise me. Now, if you'll excuse me. I got work to do, things a multitasker like myself, lady, is proficient at."
" Oh, I acknowledge that," Devin insisted. "You, women, are proficient at those sorts of things."

I raged. This man was so pleased with himself. He truly believed that ladies were only proficient at certain things, and I was going to prove him wrong.

" Say something guys are normally better at than ladies, and I will defeat you," I said, being a little too confident.

" Oh, there are so many things. There is math, sports, building work, driving ..."

" What? How would you ...? Never mind. I think it's worthless to convince you of anything. Tell me the time and the place, and I will be there."

And after that it took place. The matches had begun. He contacted some of his coworkers, all guys of course, who would come to watch me fail.

Me and my big mouth ...

Before I knew it, a group of 5 guys came to my desk, including Devin, and required my attention.

" Yes?" I said sheepishly.

" I brought some of my coworkers," Devin said. "If you want to back up what you said, then accept the challenges of these four men. One of them is a math specialist; he does all the finances for our company. His name is Victor."

I looked at the nerdy character in front of me and understood I was going to get smoked instantly. But I didn't know what to say.

" Then we have Hakeem over here. He has played college basketball. He is challenging you to a basketball one-on-one match. That's Ivo. He works in construction. He says you will not last a day there. And then there is Carson. He is a driving instructor, actually. You said you could beat everybody at what we're proficient at? Go on and show it. I am waiting. Do you accept these challenges?"

I looked at them and sighed, "Sure. I do."

" Good," Devin said. "Then I will see you here tomorrow."

He left it at that, and I watched as he and his pals left the room. I put my head into my hands. What did I get myself into?

I was worried that night. When I went to sleep, I knew I was going to flop. I wasn't an expert at any of those things. Math? Basketball? Building and construction work? Well, at least I could drive. That would not be a problem, would it? I thought I would stand a chance at that, however, driving instructors are pretty strict, so even that would most likely be tough.

When I came to the workplace the next day, Devin was standing there with Victor. They welcomed me and went inside, beckoning me to follow. I knew I could not expect them to open the door for me and use the "ladies first" rule, but oh well.

After we sat down, Devin said, "You can still back off and reclaim what you said. Guys are just better at math. It's a tested fact. So, are you still in?"

" Yes I am," I said, hoping that I would get some things right.

" Suit yourself," he said. "Victor?"

" We are going to resolve 100 math problem on the computer system," Victor began. "Because it is a computer, we cannot cheat. You simply look at the problem and find out the response. It's multiple choice, so even if you have no clue what you're doing, you could still get some answers right by thinking, but your portion would be low, so I encourage you to just use your brain and those mathematics abilities you say you have. The problems are random, so there was no way for me to cheat by knowing the answers in advance. Are you ready?"

Great, this person was a complete geek and was still pleased with himself. But what else was I going to do? I accepted the challenge and we went to work.

" Ready," I said.

The first formula appeared in front of me. Was I supposed to solve this? Whoa.

I already knew that I was going to blow this. I remembered some stuff from high school, and that the instructors in my class always made it sound easier than it seemed to me. I remembered some equations and tricks, but most of them had left my memory.

" I guess I'll just guess," I thought. Hopefully, the response was D, which was what I filled out. The entire test became multiple-guess instead of multiple-choice, since I didn't know what I was doing. In the end, I probably got several questions right by actually knowing for sure what the answer was.

When the test was over, the results were horrible: I replied 54 questions out of the 200 properly. Victor, on the other hand, had a rating of 187 out of 200. It was obvious that he was better at mathematics.

" What do you need to say for yourself?" Devin asked after seeing the results, crossing his arms and gazing at me.

" Pffft ..." I said. "Simply because he is better at mathematics, does not mean all men are better at mathematics."

I could tell that he secretly concurred with my reasoning, but he still had to defend his ego.

" Well, you said you could do better and you didn't," was all he said. Then they both walked away.

I lost.

Chapter 3: Basketball

That exact same afternoon, we met at a little basketball court outside. The weather was great, and the sun was shining. It was a perfect day to shoot some hoops ... that is ... if you're good at it, which I wasn't.

Again, I questioned why I had not just shut my big mouth when Devin challenged me, but I could not back out now. It was too late for that. I had to show them that I was at least happy to try it, and I also strongly believed I had a chance of winning.

And that's where I was wrong.

Hakeem was there with Devin. The rules were simple. We didn't need discussing. When Devin tried to tell me how basketball worked, I told him I already knew that as I had played some basketball in my youth myself.

" Fine," he said. "Best of luck. You'll need it."

We started to play. I had the ball and looked at the basket. Too far, particularly with a 6 foot 6 inches high person in front of me, holding up his arm.

So I decided to dribble past him. Luckily, I was pretty fast, and I went up for the lay-in. Bang!

I got blocked, and he even managed to pursue the ball and keep it inside the court lines. Then he shot the three. Swoosh!

Ball game was 3-0. I got the ball and tried to shoot, but I really missed. Hakeem got the rebound, went to the three-point line, and came back to dunk it over me. Ball game was 5-0. This person was just too big and athletic. There was nothing I could do. He had probably been practicing every day as part of his routine. I didn't stand a chance.

Do you think I made at least 2 points?

I didn't. We went until 21, and it ended up being precisely that: 21-0.

Hakeem won, and I my ego was broken again. He was just better than I was.

" Not too easy, is it?" Devin said with a smile on his face.

I looked at Hakeem. He didn't reveal any feelings. He just stood there as if nothing had happened. I figured he didn't care and he didn't consider me a threat in the first place. He knew he was proficient at basketball and most likely didn't even think he 'd lose.

" Well, he is so much taller than I am," I said in my defense.

" Oh, come on," Devin said. "If you would have hit more shots, you totally would have beaten him. It's not all about being high. You know that. Some of the world's best expert basketball gamers are as tall as you are."

" I still didn't think it was fair," I said as I watched them walk off.

The next early morning, we had agreed to give me a day at the building site, just to know what it really felt like. Ivo was there, and he ensured I wouldn't be able to take a break.

He was wearing a dark sweater and had a stern look on his face. He welcomed me and told me where to begin. At first, we just put some screws into a wooden board and attached some nails to a rain gutter, but then the heavy stuff showed up.

" Okay," Ivo said. "This truck has lots of cement products and bricks. Whatever you do, don't hurt your back. We have tools for those sorts of things. But what you carry on your own, will be valued."

It was tiring. The other guys were carrying large rocks and products with their bare hands. I observed that a lot of time, I was just in the way, and that they had to wait on me to move or step aside before they could get the next rock.

" Stop," Ivo said after a while. "I think it would be better if you worked somewhere else. Follow me."

He led me to a part of the construction site that was further away from where the men brought in heavy materials. He handed me a shovel and said, "Start digging."

" Digging for what?" I asked.

" Nothing in specific," he said. "We just need a hole in the garden here. It should keep you busy for a while."

I began digging. I went on and on for hours. I didn't like it, because it hurt my back. I wasn't produced for these kinds of tasks. I rather remained inside, at the computer system or something, not outside carrying out all this physical labor. It was hard and tiring.

Towards the evening, as I was standing in the huge hole I had dug up until now, I suddenly heard a voice behind me.

" Not so easy, is it?" Devin said mockingly.

" Well, I wish to see you digging for about 4 hours. It gets you pretty tired."

" No, not me. I would be okay with it, as ..."

" ... as what?" I asked. "Due to the fact that you're a man? Get out of here! Such rubbish."

" You said it, not me," he said, and after that he walked away.

Oh, that arrogant, arrogant, contented jerk! I could have hit him with my shovel right there and after that, but I knew that would not help me get anywhere. If there was something I should be better at, it was controlling my feelings.

I stopped digging. I figured I had lost this one too, since I was in the way of the building and construction workers and even had a tough time digging a hole. Ivo came and told me I did a good job. He paid me and let me go home. I knew he wasn't entirely satisfied with my work, but at least he was a decent person, not like that Victor or even Devin.

I went home and feared the next day, which would most likely be another difficulty I could not overcome.

It was the last day of the weekend, and I was about to compete with one of the best driving instructors in the area. Carson and Devin saw me coming when they were at the huge parking lot. I looked at what they had done. Cones were all over, put down in a certain order to direct a circling and zigzagging car.

" I'll go first," Carson said when I showed up.

He got into a beige Volvo and started the engine. Then he took off. Devin was keeping an eye on his time. Carson swirled around every cone with sophisticated and fast moves, not hitting any of them. Then he took a sharp turn, drove a bit longer and stopped next to us.

" 5 Minutes and 34 seconds," Devin said, showing his stop-watch. "See if you can beat that."

" And if I hit a cone?" I asked.

" Then we'll add 20 seconds."

" What? That much?! You're kidding me!" I said.

" Bumping into surrounding items is a serious thing," Carson said. "It's not only about timing, but also about precision."

I couldn't argue with him. He was the driving instructor, and not only did he know what he was talking about, but obviously, he was excellent at driving too. This wasn't going to be simple.

I opened the car door and sat down behind the wheel. I despised myself for glancing at Devin and seeing a wicked laugh on his face. Boy, was I going to prove him wrong!

" 3, two, one ..." he said, "... go!"

I hit the gas pedal and swerved around some of the cones, but this car wasn't that easy to control. I have to admit that I was more used to my Chevrolet, my own car, and that the wheel in this one was annoying. And even though it wasn't fair that I was not familiar with this car and Carson wasn't, I still beat myself up for overturning some cones and making a few wrong moves.

It took way longer than Carson's perfect little drive, and when I came to the two men, I looked back and saw I had knocked over more than 10 cones.

Devin looked at his stop-watch and chuckled. "13 Minutes and 55 seconds," he said.

I was discouraged. "Fine. You win," I said as I shook Carson's hand. Then I left.

" I told you that guys were better at driving!" I heard Devin scream in the distance.

Again, I didn't think it was fair, and just that this qualified driving trainer was better than I was, didn't necessarily have anything to do with our genders. It was silly.

They were making fun of me, all of them. They worked at the same business, and still they thought they were better than I was, and some of them attributed their skills to the fact that they were guys. How ridiculous!

Oh well, if they wanted to play that game, then bring it on! I had some tricks up my sleeve too, and I knew how to use my womanhood to my benefit. I saw them at work, and I put the phone on hold. For this, I would take a little break. It was definitely worth it.

" Hey men," I said as they walked in.

The 5 of them turned their heads and looked at me.

" I have an idea," I said. "Do you like dancing?"

They all shook their heads. None of them enjoyed that stuff. Yes! I finally found something I was probably better at.

" Then I challenge you to a dancing contest tonight at the Jumper, which is the club on the other side of town."

" We know where it is," Devin said. "But why would we go along with such a dumb difficulty?"

I chuckled. "The five of you have become professionals at math, basketball, building and construction work, and driving, but I bet you a hundred dollars that you cannot beat me at dancing."

" How do you choose who is better though?" Hakeem asked.

" Oh, they have judges there. Do not stress. I have existed enough to know that they always have a difficulty night with experienced judges. So what do you say, boys? Will you do it, or are you to scaaaaaared?"

" We are not scared!" Devin said as he put his hands in his side and lifted up his head.

" That's right," Victor said. "We'll take the challenge."

" Good," I said. "Then I will see you there at 9. Have a good time today, boys."

I was in my component. I replied every phone call with a bigger smile that day. By the way, did I mention I had been a street dancing champion in college? I was the best! I had typically danced at the club and showed off. People loved me there. And even though I wasn't in a strong relationship at the moment, I knew a lot of men at the club who were looking at me whenever I danced.

That night, I appeared at the disco. I didn't dress up in a provocative way but attractive enough to be discovered. I had put on some extra make-up and came with complete confidence. The guys not so much. I picked up that they weren't convinced of their own dancing abilities, and I was liking it. Some of their outfits looked sloppy and baggy.

" Night, boys," I said. "Shall we?"

We went inside and danced around a little bit. I kept back, since the contest hadn't begun yet. Another 20 minutes and after that the fun could start. I went to the table of the judges and signed the 6 of us up.

And after that it began ... the crowd had formed a circle. The judges announced the entrants.

" Our first dancer is Victor!" they shouted through the microphone.

Victor stepped forward. He was insecure and shy. His moves were stiff, worse than a damaged robotic. He tried to do a few dance moves, but they all looked rusty. People snickered. They thought he was an awful dancer. It was apparent. The judges held up their numbers. A 6, a 5, a 4, and a 2 out of 10. Horrible.

Next was Devin. He strove, since he had such a huge ego; nevertheless, the more he tried, the more ludicrous he looked. The rolls of fat underneath his t-shirt were showing, and he was sweating like a pig. One time, he even tipped over. When he was done, the judges rolled their eyes and gave him an even lower grade than Victor.

Hakeem was the next candidate. I need to admit that he wasn't all bad. His athletic body helped him make a few moves that nearly impressed some of the ladies, and the judges gave him an average of 6.8. Not bad.

Ivo the construction worker just looked odd. He was making an attempt to breakdance, but in the meantime, he hurt his back and had to leave the dancefloor a little earlier. Disqualified. Ha! My chances became bigger.

The last one before me was Carson. He did these odd little hops and tried moves that only look good when a girl does it, if you know what I mean. People were a little shut off by it and searched in disgust as the judges tried to consider what to say about it. His average was a 5.3. Not outstanding, and that's an understatement.

And after that it was my turn. The music started. I enjoyed it. I went all crazy, with all the moves I had learned in the previous years. I shook my hips and tossed my hair into the air. As I kept doing expensive, cool street moves, I noticed the crowd got into it. After a while, everybody was clapping and cheering me on. My shoulders, my waist ... every little thing swung to the music perfectly. All of it came naturally. When I was done, I ducked and ended with a freeze ... with some attitude! The judges didn't need to concentrate about this one. I got all 9s and 10s.

I walked towards the five men who had been buffooning me in the previous days and said, "You know what the said thing is, boys? I will not even ascribe my marvelous success to the fact that I am woman. Sure, no man can move their hips and shake their torso or hair in the same way a girl does, but I have to admit that it was simply because I guess well ... practiced. It wasn't as I am lady. So maybe you should think about that tonight when you try to build up your egos again."

They didn't say anything back. I blew them a kiss and left the club with style. They looked at me.

" I need to admit she is type of attractive when she is dancing," Victor said.

" Oh, shut up," Devin said. "Let's get out of here."

The next day, I appeared at work with a smile, but my smile quickly vanished when I heard an awful noise. I turned around the corner and saw some of my coworkers lined up against the glass of the next office room.

" What are you all taking a look at?" I asked. "What's happening?"

" The CEO's daughter," one of them said. "She went nuts. Look."

The noise that tossed me off guard was the shrieking of a 7-year-old girl who was tossing a tantrum in the office. Some things had been knocked off the desks, and she was stomping and clenching her fists, banging them on the office carpet.

" She went crazy," Ivo said. "I do not comprehend, but her father isn't here and we do not know how to deal with it."

" I tried to give her candy," Hakeem said. "But she would not even accept that. What kid does not want candy?"

" I told her that her father would be very upset at her if he saw this," Devin said. "It didn't help."

I chuckled. Of course that didn't help. These men didn't know what they were doing. 10 men hesitated of a little girl. That was a very first. Ha-ha! Her tantrum was so wild and devastating that none of them had a clue of how to deal with her.

Punishments, bribery ... this girl just needed some empathy. I looked at my coworkers and asked, "Do you mind if I try?"

They all looked at me and said, "By all means, if you think you can do better, go ahead."

When I opened up the door, my coworkers all withdrawed a little, fearing what seemed to be a dreadful brat in the office room. They watched as I approached the little girl and asked what was wrong. When she saw me, she unexpectedly stopped shouting and banging her fists. This was my one chance.

" Please tell me," I said in a soft voice. "I won't penalize you for it. You can tell me anything. What can I do for you?"

" I-I just ..." she began.

" Yes, go ahead."

" I just want my daddy. He said he would not leave me and now he disposed me into this boring workplace. He is always busy."

" Oh, is it that?" I asked as I sat beside her on the floor and put my arm around her. She leaned against me and stopped sobbing.

" There, there, just cool down," I said. "It's fine. I comprehend that you want him back, and that he is taking way too long. Often I, too, think that he works too hard. Hey, I have an idea. How about you help me answer the phone and organize my desk? Then you can be my little assistant."

She sobbed and thought of it. "Okay," she said quietly.

" And you know what?" I continued. "We can have some fun. The office chairs have wheels; I can push you around on them, we can take a look at some of my family photos on the computer, and you can use some of my printing paper to make a drawing. How does that sound?"

" I think that could be fun," she confessed.

" What's your name?" I asked.

" Eveline," she said.

" That's a gorgeous name. My name is Jennifer, but you can call me Jen."

I saw a twinkle in her eyes. She got delighted about playing around in my office, and I didn't even have to assure her a treat. All she needed, I figured, was a listening ear, a hug, and maybe even a solution, but none of those insensitive guys at the window had thought of that.

I got her hand and took her to my workplace. When I opened the door and let her walk through, I looked at Devin and a few of the others and stood out my tongue as if to say, "See? There are some things women can do better than men."

I didn't say it, since I wasn't going to honestly generalize like that, but I need to admit that I thought it. And I think they knew it too.

Eveline played in my office room that day. It was a lot of fun. We had a fake tea ceremony, threw notepads at one another, and did amusing voices on the phone when clients could not hear us when being put on hold. When her dad returned, he thanked me elaborately and gave me a monetary bonus offer. It was just one of the best days at work I had had up until now.

The days after that went efficiently. No one bothered me any longer. They knew I possessed qualities that they didn't, and whether or not that was because I was lady, I didn't care. I revealed them I was good at something. But about a week later, something happened that nobody had expected.

The siren went off. It was audible throughout the city. A voice was heard through some speakers in the streets. All of us tuned in and listened to what it had to say.

Ladies and gentlemen of the city. We have some dreadful news. Zombies have gotten in the facilities. Stay in your homes and buildings and hide. The authorities will do all in their power to remove the risk as quickly as possible. Thank you for your cooperation.

" Everybody hide below your desks!" my company motivated his personnel.

We did what we were told. I discovered all my coworkers hide, but I knew where to find a weapon, just in case. Since it wasn't all safe, I was going to make certain nothing would happen to us. I knew of people who had died when hiding from the zombies. They always came all of a sudden, and after that the crowd would just sweep through the city and try to kill whomever would be in their course. They never remained for long, but they did a ton of damage every time they appeared.

But I was prepared, because I had a GIGANTIC SWORD in my hands !!!

Who would have a sword in their office, you ask? Well, I did, because these were some of my other hidden skills: Sword combating and fencing. I had a papa who was in the army. He had taught me to shoot guns and use swords.

It was quiet, and it remained quiet for a long period of time. We heard some noises from the city, but those were all outside the walls of our office building.

The zombies were in the city, and they were wandering the empty streets. Usually, they would not get in a ton of homes and buildings, but it wasn't impossible for them to do so. And it didn't take long before they just happened to get into our building.

Craaack! Clash! Caling! Clang!

They busted through the glass of our lobby and started to search for possible victims.

The CEO of our business got up and screamed, "Change of plans! Everyone get to their guns! Now!"

As quickly as they could, the staff members in the building ran towards the gun racks and armed themselves with gatling gun and shotguns. The zombies came closer. The staff members were lined up, ready to follow their company's orders.

" Ready?" he said. "Fire!"

Boom! Boom! Takadakadak!

The weapons were firing numerous bullets at the zombies. Some of the zombies fell and got up again. Others just jerked a little at the effect of the bullets but kept walking forward.

" Keep shooting!" the CEO shouted.

It was useless. The zombies were unsusceptible to bullets. It didn't do anything to them. And although it was holding them back, the workers were just stalling by shooting them and postponing their own deaths.

But then I ran downstairs and leapt behind the workers.

" Cease fire!" I shouted.

They all looked at me for a second. "|Don't you see? You can't kill them this way," I said.

" But what are we going to do then?" my employer asked.

" Haven't you heard?" I asked. "There is only one way to kill zombies: by slicing off their heads."

I didn't want to lose anymore words on discussing myself. I was a little stunned they even tried to use weapons against these zombies. I had always learned that you could only use swords, axes, pickaxes, or other sharp things against them. And I was right. My father had taught me well.

I dashed forward and swung my sword into the direction of one of the zombies. Tsyaaack!

I sliced his avoid in one move. I didn't look back to see my colleagues' reactions; I just kept slashing the zombies with my remarkable blade. Head after head fell on the floor of our lobby. It was a massacre.

My colleagues withdrawed a little and let me do my thing. They could not actually believe someone like me can such actions and skills. Up until now, they always looked down on me, thinking that I was this shy, weak person. Imagine what was going through their heads now! Several dozen men grouped together, watching woman kill numerous zombies in front of them by chopping their heads off.

It was priceless!

When I was done and there were no more zombies in our area, I leaned on my sword, a little worn out but pretending to be just fine. I smirked and saw their faces radiant with astonishment. They were speechless.

I stopped leaning on my sword and picked it up. With the blood leaking from the end of the blade, I put it on my shoulder and walked past them.

" Excuse me, boys," I said. "I still have some documents to do."

I do not think I have to tell you that I got a raise that extremely exact same day, and that all the men at the office complex were more respectful towards me after that incredible display of guts and fighting abilities.

I do not think I need to tell you that males and females have different abilities, but that the possibilities are practically endless, and that you never need to worry about somebody else being a sexist about it.

And I don't think I need to tell you that I was asked on dates every weekend after that, either by men working at the company or by other men who found out about me. It was a lot of fun being so popular.

And lastly: I don't think I need to tell you that you just have to really believe in yourself, that you don't need to be the best at everything, but that you should find what you have a natural talent for and continue to make that grow.

That's what I did.

THE END

Zombies and Couple Trouble

Cay gets up. His wife is still asleep. It's early in the morning, but he has plans. He has been married to his beautiful girl for 3 years now, and he wants to make it something unique. Today is the day before their anniversary. It's the day before they got married ... 3 years ago. He puts on his favorite sweater and slips out of the home with some golden coins in his pocket.

The neighborhood is silent, especially now. And despite the fact that they live in a medieval-like farmer's village, none of its occupants like to get up early. The only ones that do, are the real farmers on the borders of town.

Almost tripping over a few chickens, Cay makes his way to a house about ten blocks away. He takes a look around him. There is nobody there.

Then he knocks on the door and waits.

A young woman opens up.

" Ah, Cay," she says with a big smile. "I am glad you could make it. I know it's early, but you were determined to do this without your spouse knowing about it, weren't you?"

" Exactly, Nana," Cay says. "She has never been an early riser anyway, so I knew I could escape. I don't even think she discovered that my snoring stopped when I woke up."

" Ha-ha-ha!" Nana chuckles. "Well, come in. I will show you what I have."

She opens the door a little wider and Cay walks in.

" Great place you got here," he says.

" I know, right? I decorated it myself."

Cay looks around and observes the vibrant, framed paintings on the wall, the ornamental pendants and chimes hanging on the ceiling, and the stylish statues on the little tables in every corner of the room. Nana has some taste in art, that's obvious. She knows how to cheer up the place. She is wearing a green and red necklace herself, with a little skull and unicorn sign in the middle of it. It practically appears like she is attempting to be eccentric with her own random style.

" Intriguing taste in lighting and style," Cay mentions as he watches the red-green shades in front of the candles and the necklace Nana is wearing.

" Yes, I normally do not go with the flow. I do my own thing, even if other villagers think it's weird."

" No, it's good. I like it," Cay assures her. "Anyhow, are you prepared to show me it?"

" Yes. Here it is. See? I can take this board and jot down the text. Then I can go over it with this paint. Excuse me ... it's over there. Okay, and after that I can patch it up with color, add a little bit of this, and take all day dealing with the details. I have a board like it, but with a different engraving. Do you want me to show you?"

" Of course. If it's going to be like the other one, then I want to see what the results will be."

" Makes sense," Nana says. "I'll get it. Just a minute. It's in the shed."

Nana goes outside and turns around the corner of her open shed. She grabs the board she was talking about, but her white gown gets caught by a nail standing out in a beam. Riiiiip!

" Ow ... hey! What the ...?" she says.

The ripped dress reveals part of her upper legs, and as the whole thing is about to break down, her shoulders are bare. The dress is gradually falling off, and the annoyed Nana tries to hold the board with one hand and lift up the straps of her gown with the other. She walks to the front door in an awkward little circle, practically like a drunk person, and glances around.

" At least no one saw that," she says. "That would have been humiliating."

She puts the embellished board down after she heads inside; then she goes straight up the stairs. "Could you just wait a little while?!" she yells downstairs. "I have to get changed!"

" No issue!" Cay shouts back.

Nana takes her dress off and takes a look at it. "Oh well," she says. "It was a little worn anyway, and it didn't cost much."

She throws the dress on the floor and takes another one out of her closet. After dressing up, she returns downstairs, picks up the board, and walks into the living room, where she puts the board on the table in front of Cay.

" What took place?" Cay asks.

" You do not would like to know. Believe me. Now, let's focus on the board. See what I did there? I painted these colors here and added some decors there."

" Oh, wow! I really love that!" Cay exclaims. "That's exactly what I wanted!"

" Ha-ha! Good. Then that's what we will do."

She puts the board in the corner of the room and says, "That will be four pieces of gold."

" No problem. It's going to be great," Cay says.

They talk a little longer and Cay goes back home. He whistles on the way there, happy that he finally found something worth his cash. But when he gets home, his wife is standing in front of the door, awaiting him with her arms folded.

" What was that all about?" she asks.

" What?"

" Where did you go?" Cindy wants to know.

" I just headed out. You wouldn't want to know," Cay says.

" Oh, believe me. I do," Cindy sneers. "You have some explaining to do."

" Well, I will tell you later," Cay says. "Now is not the time."

" Why not? What happened?"

" Come on, honey. I just do not want to say anything about it at this time. Is that all right?"

" No, it's not alright! I want to know!"

Cay shrugs. He doesn't want to ruin the surprise. He feels no responsibility to tell his wife where he invested the last half hour. He goes inside and tackles his business. Cindy watches him enter their home and feels disappointed.

That night, they do not talk. They do not kiss one another goodnight. Cindy blows out the candle on their nightstand, and they go to sleep. Cay is happy. He knows she will love it once it's done. With a smile on his face, he drops off to sleep.

Cindy gets up. She was used to the noise of him snoring, but she notices instantly when it stops as well. She keeps her eyes closed, thinking he is just going to the bathroom. But then he gets dressed and she gets curious.

" What is he doing?" she thinks. "He doesn't generally get up till in an hour."

Then he exits the house and Cindy gets ACTUALLY curious.

" I need to know what he is really up to," she tells herself, and she puts on some pink t-shirt and red skirt. She goes out the door and sees her husband turn around the corner. Cindy keeps her distance and follows her really loved one to the home where he knocks on the door.

When a young, appealing lady opens up, Cindy gets suspicious. "Who is that girl?" she asks herself. "I have never seen her before. And how does she know my husband?"

She listens thoroughly. She can't make up what they're saying, but when she sees the young woman laugh about something Cay said, Cindy is boiling up inside. Is she flirting with him?

" That mean, horrible, wench!" Cindy thinks. "How dare she steal my spouse from me?"

They're taking too long. It's driving Cindy crazy. What on earth are they doing in there? Then a bird captures her eye. It's singing loudly, right next to her.

" Ssshhh ..." Cindy whispers. "I am attempting to spy on my partner here."

Cindy turns her head to the house again and is in shock.

" What?!!!" she thinks. "That woman is only half-dressed! You can see her legs and shoulders, and her gown is nearly falling off! And what is that thing she is keeping in her hand? Appears like a wood board or something. Look at the way she walks! She looks intoxicated! I have to know more about this."

Cindy tiptoes to the front door and starts eavesdropping.

" Oh, wow! I really love that!" she hears Cay say. "That's exactly what I wanted!"

" Ha-ha! Good. Then that's what we will do."

" Huh? Do what?" Cindy thinks. "What was exactly what he wanted? This is getting weird."

Then she hears the young woman say, "That will be 4 pieces of gold."

" No problem. It's going to be great," Cay says.

" Whaaaaat ?!" Cindy thinks. Her brain is going nuts. She always thought about Cay as a good guy, but what is he spending money on now? As she captures herself become more psychological, Cindy chooses it's time to leave. She doesn't want to know anything else about this. Her man better has a good explanation for all of this.

Troubled by what she heard and saw, she walks home and holds back her tears. Oh, if only she could trust him, but now she isn't even sure of that anymore. Where has she gone wrong? Was it her fault? Why did Cay let himself fall for another woman? Was their marriage not good enough?

When Cindy gets back, she does not feel like going inside. She looks at her house and listens to the whispers of the wind. The exact same bird flies over her head and disappears into the distance. When she sees how pleasant Cay is when he gets back, whistling all the way, she gets back at more upset.

They talk. Naturally, he does not want to clarify anything. He has been doing sneaky things behind her back, and has been to that lady for whatever reasons she does not want to think about. Eventually, she accepts his casual attitude and gives up. She does not sleep much that night though ... not one minute.

BANG!

The door flies open.

" What was that?" Cindy asks as she awakens.

" I don't know," Cay says. "Perhaps just the wind?"

" Go check," Cindy pleads. "Please."

" No problem," Cay answers.

He puts on some clothes and goes downstairs, to the living-room. He was right, he thought. It truly was the wind. Or was it?

He licks his finger and holds it up in the air. Weird. There is barely any wind. Did someone enter their house? He gets restless and suspicious, so he takes the stick from a broom in the corner as a weapon and sneaks through the living room, the shed, and some other spaces. Nothing. Nobody. It is empty. He goes outdoors and checks the streets.

And there it is.

Cay sees a shady figure, but it looks like if the person in front of him is green. He is wearing a blue clothing and with his red, glowing eyes, he looks straight at Cay.

" What is that?" Cay asks, but before he can utter another word, the animal runs at him. Cay steps back inside and closes the doors. Then he locks it. The animal bangs his fists on the door.

" Honey?" Cay hears Cindy shout from upstairs. "What's going on?"

" I think it's a zombie!" Cay screams back. "He's trying to burglarize our house!"

" What are we going to do?" Cindy asks.

" Oh, I am sure he will quit after a while. The door is locked."

But Cay doesn't recognize the zombie isn't alone. All of a sudden, another zombie jumps through the window.

Clash!

The pieces of glass are all over the floor, and the zombie has already sped towards Cay and is now attempting to choke him.

" H-honey," Cay says, "could you knock the zombie out?"

Cindy looks at the broomstick and puts her hands in her side. "I do not know," she says. "If I do, will you tell me what was going on between you and that charming girl?"

" Wh-what? Come on! Just save my life already!" Cay screams.

" Okay, all right." Cindy takes the broomstick and bangs the zombie on his head.

" Thank you," Cay says. "Now, could you please stop stressing over what I did at that house? I told you, I will explain it to you later."

" Sure you will," Cindy says, still suspicious of the worst.

They both peek through the front window-- the one that hasn't been broken-- and see a crowd of zombies in the village. They are substantial, almost twice as huge as people. It is as if they increased in size after rising from the dead, or as if only the biggest people became the undead.

" Oh my goodness," Cindy says. "It's an intrusion! There are hundreds of them. What will we do?"

" I know a way," Cay says. "There are a lot of them. We should not try to fight them."

" But what about the other villagers?"

" There is nothing we can do. I hope they will be okay, but for now, we have to save our own skin. |Don't you agree?"
" I guess you're right. So what is this fantastic idea of yours?" she asks sardonically.
" There is an underground passage," Cay says. "It's not too far from here. Hopefully, we can sneak by the attacking zombies and make our way there without being seen."
" Okay, let's do it. I don't feel safe here."

Chapter 4: The Secret Passage

Cay opens the back door. It's quiet in the backstreet of the area, although they hear voices and screams all around them. Cay checks two times to ensure he doesn't misinterpret the situation.

" This is our chance," he says. "The hatch is on the opposite side of the street, in a tiny barn around the corner of that home. When I say, 'Run,' we'll both run over there and I will raise the hatch. Got it?"

" Got it," Cindy says.

Cay looks one more time, both ways, and then says, "Go!"

Hand in hand, the couple runs towards the barn and turns around the corner. They see the hatch and Cay raises it up. Cindy goes midway inside the tunnel and after that asks, "How come no one else knows about this passage?"

" Rush," Cay whispers. "We have no time at all to lose. I will tell you when we are really there."

Cindy moves down the ladder and winds up in some mud. "Yuck!" she exclaims.

" Come on," Cay says. "Keep moving, please. Here I come."

He moves down and joins his marriage partner in the murky fluids that are covering their feet and shins. He takes a look at her with a smirk on his face. She is not delighted. He chooses to say nothing. Better not to make her angrier than she already is.

" So to address my questions ..." Cindy says, hoping that her spouse will fill her in.

" Ah, yes. It was actually built by my grandfather. It is well hidden, and nobody comes here anyhow. So I don't think anybody has ever discovered it yet."

" Why did your dad build it?"

" I think there were zombies back then too. I just really wonder how bad it was at that time versus now."

" Well, it sounds awful outside," Cindy says. "I am glad I am here. Have you considered how to see? It's pitch black."

" I am already ahead of you," Cay says as he lights a candle light.

Together, they walk through the tunnel. Above them, the sounds of the attacking zombies are abundant in the town, but the married couple is safely set in their tunnel. With the candle in front of them, they hope for the best.

Unexpectedly, they hear a sound.

BONK!

Cay and Cindy put their backs against the wall.

Then a male voice shouts, "Who goes there?"

" I thought you said no one knew about this place," Cindy says.

" That's right," Cay says. "But maybe I was wrong. Let's check it out."

" Who goes there?" the voice asks again.

" Uhm ... it's us. Our names are Cay and Cindy!" Cay shouts back. "We are not zombies, so please do not kill us."

" Step into the light," the voice says.

Cay goes first. Cindy is keeping his arm securely, nearly squeezing it too hard. She is a little worried, despite the fact that the man obviously isn't a zombie. When they enter the light, the man is relieved.

" Appears like you two are all right," he says. He enters the light too and introduces himself. "My name is Mason. I have learnt about this place for several years. I do not know why any person else hasn't found it, but I knew I should go here when the zombies attack."

" How did you find it?" Cay asks.

" I'm just a big snoop. Ha-ha! I just follow people and see what they depend on. One day, I just came across the hatch, and naturally I wanted to know what was below it. There is really no story to it."

" Oh, alright. So what's your strategy?"

' Zombie attacks normally last for several days. After that, lots of people will have developed into zombies themselves. It's sad, but it's the harsh truth. Honestly, I don't think I have a strategy. I am just going to wait here until they leave town."

Then Cay notices the locket Mason is wearing. Odd. It is the same locket Nana was wearing.

" Where did you get that?" Cay needs to know.

" Uhm ... I don't know. Why do you ask?" Mason asks.

" I saw another person wearing that pendant. It had red and green, and a skull and unicorn sign holding on it. So maybe you got it at the exact same place?"

And that's when Mason gets a little emotional. His self-denial phase is already over, even within those extremely seconds. In the beginning, Cay and Cindy are surprised by the abrupt change in his temperament, but when they hear his explanation, they begin to comprehend.

" Who was the one you saw wearing the necklace?" Mason asks.

" Her name is Nana," Cay says. "She has a little art store in the area."

" Nana? Who is Nana? How do you know a girl called Nana?" Cindy requires to know, still suspicious of her partner's intentions.

" Never mind that," Cay says. "I will tell you later. So how about it, Mason? Is there a connection?"

" I." Mason stutters. "Well, she is my marriage partner. We wear the exact same necklaces, just to show our love and dedication to one another. We got split up. I feel so dreadful. The zombies were coming. I was on the other side of town, doing some business. But I thought I could come here and meet her here. We discussed this before; if zombies would assault, we would go to the tunnel. But now, after being here for a while, and seeing that she hasn't even shown up yet, I am beginning to get a little worried."

" I understand," Cay says. "You feel guilty since you feel that you should have gotten her first, right?"

" Precisely. So what should I do now? Do I go out there and get her? Or do I wait here and hope that she shows up?"

Cay looks Mason in the eyes and says, "Be a man. Go get your woman. There is no time to lose."

" Seriously?" he asks. "Wow. Okay, sure. Yes, that's what I am going to do."

Cindy has a loving appearance in her eyes when she hears Cay's ideas on nerve and fidelity. She gets a little closer to him and asks, "Would you have come back for me if I was there by myself, surrounded by zombies?"

" Obviously, I would have, Cindy," Cay says. "We are married. I really love you. I would do anything to protect you."

Cindy thinks for a moment and then says, "We have to help this man. Let's opt for him."

" Are you sure? We could just stay here in the tunnel. It would be more secure."

" No," Cindy insists. "He really deserves a happy life like us."

Cay is happy to hear that Cindy still considers their life to be happy, despite the miscommunication between the 2 of them. He understands she will be even happier when she finds out what he was going to give her. But now he is not so sure it will still be there, since the zombies turned the entire town upside down.

" Take these," Mason says, handing the other two a sword and a axe. "I'm sort of a fan of the shovel myself, but I am certain you can put these weapons to good use if you see a zombie."

" Thanks," Cay says. "Ready to go?"

" Yes, I am," Mason says in a determined voice as he walks past them. "Let's kill some zombies."

Cay and Cindy are right behind him. They splash through the muddy tunnel ground and reach the hatch. They look at one another and climb the ladder. Back on the village roadways, they are surprised. In front of them, a town abides in mayhem. Zombies are running after villagers, homes are burning, screams are heard all over, in addition to howling and groaning zombie sounds. Some people are unsuccessfully making an effort to defend themselves and hack several zombies down before they get bitten. The entire view is cooling and dreadful.

" Scary," Mason says.

" Ha! You mean, Mason-fying!" Cindy says with a smirk on her face.

The two guys take a look at her with a serious facial expression.

" S-sorry. I'll stop making puns," Cindy says sheepishly.

" Let's just slip from the one yard to the other," Mason suggests. "The majority of the zombies are in the front yards, in the houses, and on the street. It's not too far from here. Let's go to my home and see if Nana is there."

The trio remains low and peeps over every fence before they go to the next yard, and the next, and the next ...

Ultimately, they get close to Mason's and Nana's house. They hop over their white picket fence and go to the burning house.

" Hey, wait a minute," Cindy says, turning to her husband. "This is the exact same house you went to, you two-faced cheater!"

" But honey, could we please discuss this later? I can clarify," Cay says.

" Pffft ... you better have a good explanation then," Cindy says angrily as she rolls her eyes. "The lady was half undressed and giggling when you were talking. Does not that say enough?"

Cay overlooks her grievances. Fortunately, their conversation doesn't raise any suspicions in Mason, because he didn't hear what they were talking about. He already entered the home and begins looking for his marriage partner. "Nana!" he yells. "Nana! Are you in here ?!"

" Thankfully, only the upstairs is on fire," Cay says. "Did I ever tell you not to run into a burning building just because of the smoke and the fire?"

" I know," Cindy says. "Hopefully, she is downstairs. Otherwise I would not know what to do, although I am unsure anymore if I want that sexy female to live."

But then she sees it. "What is that?" Cindy asks when she picks up the product in front of her.

Cindy is holding a board. It's charred, and apparently, it didn't actually survive the incineration of the upper half of the house. But in spite of the unclean appearance and horrible soot on it, she is still able to read the inscription through the faded ornamental patterns. In swirly letters, practically like calligraphy, it reads:

" Cindy and Cay Forever"

She looks at it. She is speechless. Cay scratches his head when he understands that there is barely anything left of the product he paid 4 golden coins for. Cindy's back is turned towards her husband, so Cay has not the slightest idea what she is feeling. He can't see her facial expression, so he just waits.
" Well, uhm ..." Cay says after a bit. "It was going to be something for you, for our anniversary. Did you see I put your name first? Heh-heh ... it's since I wanted to make you understand how essential you are to me. And maybe you can still see a heart or a star in there. Anyhow, sorry that it burned down. I realize it's a waste of money, since it isn't any good to us now."
But when Cindy turns around, there are tears in her eyes; tears of joy. She drops the board and throws her arms around her well-intending partner. Then she kisses him.
" Thank you," she says. "I'm sorry I was so suspicious. You're the best man I could ever request for."
Cay just smiles. It appears as if the moment lasts forever, even though it is just a few seconds long. They stare at one another and just feel like they're drifting ... till they get interrupted by Mason.
" Help!" Mason yells. "I need some help here!"
Cay and Cindy hurry into the direction where the sound is coming from. They hop over a damaged table and run into another room. There they see Mason, who is attempting to lift a heavy beam that is obstructing Nana's legs. She is mindful, and she seems all right, but she is unable to move away from the particles.
" Nana," Cay says. "Thanks for the terrific work you've done."
" You're welcome," she says. "Sorry it got burned. I can return you the 4 pieces of gold if you want me to."
" Nah, we're good. You did your job," Cay says.
" Wait a minute," Cindy says. "I'll take those pieces of gold. Why would you turn down an offer for a free refund, Cay?"
" Ahum ... okay, touché," Cay says.
They stop talking and lift up the beam. The 3 of them have enough strength to get the heavy thing from Nana, who slowly stands up and starts walking again. "Let's get out of here," she says, after giving Mason a hug. "There are still tons of zombies around."

The four survivors slip back through the backyards, heading into the direction of the hatch to the tunnel. But before they arrive, they get faced by a crowd of zombies that just happens to see them.

"Growl!" one of them says, most likely meaning, "Over there!"

"Grumble grumble roar!" another one adds.

The two couples figure that it probably means, "Let's get them!"

"Run!" Mason yells.

They start running and get closer to the secret tunnels, and the zombies are chasing them.

"They must know that we're here," Cay says. "You 3 can go. I will distract them."

"No!" Cindy says. "I won't leave your side. Don't leave me!"

It's too late to start a discussion, so Cay accepts her desire to come with him. They deviate from their course and run towards the other side of the town. All the zombies come after them, leaving Mason and Nana to hide in the tunnels.

"There!" Cay says, pointing to an empty house.

He slams through the door and hides with his partner underneath a table in the corner. The zombies quickly run by. Cindy is sitting in Cay's arms, feeling safeguarded by her strong man. He checks out the window and sighs.

"I think they're gone," he says after a long time. "Let's go to the hatch."

But when they go out of the house, 2 zombies are standing in front of them. They roar and drool and look vicious.

"You take the one on the left; then I'll take the one on the right," Cay says.

"Deal," Cindy concurs. She holds her axe beside her, all set to swing it at the zombie on the left. Cay holds his sword in front of him and stabs the zombie on the right. The zombie drops immediately. Then Cindy swings at the other zombie.

Bonk!

Unconscious, on the ground.

"Good job!" Cay says. "I do not know why you are always indicating that you need defense from me. You are great taking out the zombies."

"Thank you," Cindy says proudly.

No more zombies cross their courses on the way to the hatch. They consider themselves fortunate. When they get to the hatch, Mason and Nana are waiting for them.

"Welcome to the underground movement," Mason says. "We chose to wait here and see if any other civilians would survive. There are about 50 people there now."

"Outstanding," Cay says. "How long before the zombies will disappear?"

"Most likely a number of days. That's how it generally goes. I've seen it in other towns. Oh, and we may want to switch off all our candle lights and torches. There are little fractures in the ceiling and I don't want the risk that zombies see us."

"Two entire days without light?" Cay asks. "Whoa. Sounds extreme."

Cindy puts her head on his shoulder and her hand on his chest. She smiles and says, "I can get used to that ... 2 days in the dark with you."

Cay smiles. She is right. He rubs her hair and says, "Happy anniversary, honey."

THE END

Nasty Women

She brushes her long, brown hair and looks into the mirror.
" Why is it always so hard to keep it straight? I love straight hair. I wish I had it like Lara, with a bit of a curl at the end and straight in the middle. Her hair is perfect, but I am stuck with these frustrating brushes, attempting to align everything out. Erg ... So dumb."
Helena takes a look at the reflection of her face. "Well, at least my eyes are pretty," she says with full self-confidence, "but I do not know if that's going to convince Randall. I wish he was intelligent enough to see that I have had a crush on him for months. Maybe I will go to Lara and ask her what to do."
After she grabs her bag and runs out of the home in her striped t-shirt, Helena snatches a sandwich from the counter, yells, "Thanks, Mother!" and shuts the door. She hurries to the home of her buddy, Lara, who has consented to see her and discuss stuff.
They love to talk, these 2 girls, and they can go on and on for a long period of time. One time, it was after midnight and they absolutely forgot the time. They speak about every little thing: Looks, music, people, boys ... but a ton of times, they talk about horses.
Lara and Helena are horse girls, and they each have their own horse. Helena is 11 years of age; she got a horse from her father, who has a good job in the village where they live. Lara, on the other hand, is 13; she had to work really hard to save up, but she declares that she does not covet her female friend for getting it totally free.
Helena knocks on the front door and Lara opens the door.
" Helena! I am happy you came early. Come in."
" How have you been?" Helena asks.
" Okay. Okay. Have you been noticing some boys recently?" Lara asks while laughing.
" I just still like Randall," Helena says. "You already knew that." Unexpectedly, she looks at Lara's hair and says, "Whoa. How did you do that?"
" Do what?" Lara wants to know.
" That thing with your hair. I was just thinking about it today. I do not know how you always get it the way you do."
" Oh, you mean with the swirl and stuff?" Lara asks. "That's my little trick. Do you assure not to tell anybody?"
" Sure. Tell me."
" I will show you. Come on. It's upstairs."
Full of curiosity, Helena follows her good friend up the stairs and into her room. Lara bends over and moves some things around in her drawer. Then she gets a hairbrush from the bottom of the drawer and shows it to Helena.
" This is it," she says.
" I do not understand," Helena says. "What is so unique about it?"
" It's not just a hairbrush," Lara says, referring to the pink item in her hand. "It's a magical hairbrush."
" Ha-ha! Seriously?"
" Yes," Lara says with a serious face. "It straightens your hair immediately."
" Can I use it?" Helena asks.
" No, obviously not."

" Huh?" Helena didn't expect this response. She doesn't understand. "Why not?" she asks. "What's wrong with using your hairbrush?"

" Like I said, it's a magical hairbrush, and it belongs to me. You use enough magic as it is."

" What's that supposed to mean?" Helena asks, feeling a little upset.

" I finally have something that you don't, and now you want to have it too? No chance. You have magic spells that make pearls appear, skeletons die, or turn in circles. I am not really good at any of those things. For some reason, you have a propensity for magic. It's unfair. I have always been jealous of you; and now I have something that you can be envious of. It's as basic as that."

" I can't really believe my ears," Helena says. "You never said anything. Stop being so childish! We always share."

" You never share your spells," Lara argues.

" That's since I can't share them. You need to study the ancient arts of magic. It's your own fault that you're so bad at it. If you would have studied more, you would have been proficient at casting spells too."

" My own fault ?! That's it! Get out of my room!"

Helena gets out of the room. "So now what, Lara?"

" Uhm ... and now, get out of my home! I don't want to see you again for the remainder of the week!"

" Regrettable! We'll see one another in school!"

" Okay, absolutely nowhere else then. Get out already!"

" Great!"

Helena stomps as she descends down the stairs and slams the door. She is furious. She will avenge herself. That selfish Lara! She is going to pay. Why will not she just share her wonderful hairbrush with her? After all, her hair is always perfect; doesn't she want her to have the exact same beauty?

" And how am I going to impress Randall?" she thinks out loud. "My hair is ruined. He will see. I can't let her do this to me."

And she doesn't ...

That night, when it's dark, Helena waits until her father and mother are downstairs and sneaks out of the upstairs window. She jumps down without hurting herself.

PLOF!

" Now, let's see how I can get into Lara's room without noticing," she thinks.

She tiptoes to Lara's house and looks up. On the main floor, the lights are on, but on the 2nd floor, there are no lights.

" Good," she thinks. "She must be downstairs. Let's hope I am right."

She climbs, holding onto the drain pipeline, and checks out Lara's dark bed room. It looks like the coast is clear. Helena opens the window and sneaks inside. Then she searches in the drawer and finds the hairbrush.

" Ha!" she says, congratulating herself that she found it. "Let's see whose hair will be perfect in the early morning."

After she jumps down, she runs back to her house, but she forgot to close the window.

Chapter 2: That's What You Get

Lara gets up. She yawns. She stretches her arms. Then she rises, leaves fast her night dress, and puts on a t-shirt and a skirt. She opens the drawer and reaches inside it.

" Huh?" she says. "I thought I put it right there. Where is my hairbrush?"

She looks around in the room, just wondering if she has been careless with it or left it in a corner. She searches for several minutes ... and after that she sees the open window.

" What?!" she exclaims. "That has to be Helena's doing. She wanted the brush so badly. She took it! Oh, that ... she has every little thing! Her daddy purchased her a horse, she can use magic all she wants, and the ONE thing she will not let me have, is more lovely hair. Well, if you want to play this game, let's see who wins, girl! You're going down."

That early morning, it takes her ten times as long to get her hair done, but she doesn't care. She has a strategy to get back at her previous good friend. She puts on some additional cosmetics and leaves to school.

Sneakier than ever, she walks around on the playground and searches for Helena. She does not speak to her, but she observes her from a distance. Helena looks pretty today, and yes, her hair is perfectly straight. She walks around as if she owns the place, with her shoulders up and a huge smile on her face.

" Helena is going to get it," Lara thinks. "I have to do it at the correct moment. It has to be timed precisely." She looks over her shoulder and sees Randall. He is by himself.

" Awesome," Lara thinks. "It's time for some vengeance."

She walks over to him and strokes her hair. "Hee-hee, your name is Randall, isn't it?" she asks.

" Yes, it is. What is your name?"

" I am Lara. I don't know if you have discovered, but I was taking a look at you all the time."

" Oh, uhm ... why did you do that?" Randall asks a little awkwardly.

" Because you're handsome, silly," Lara says as she moves closer to him.

Randall steps back, but Lara won't let him go. She keeps flirting with him, getting his arm and rubbing his shoulder with her hand; and while she does, Helena looks their way.

There is no pen worldwide that can explain how Helena feels at that moment. Her presumed best friend is making a move on her crush! He was meant to be hers! How dare she ?!

By now, Randall is sitting down and Lara is sitting really near to him, nearly on his lap. He appears like he enjoys the attention, but doesn't truly know what to do with it. Then she leans over and kisses him on the cheek. She carefully touches his chest for a second and steps away.

" Tah-tah, Randall ... cutie ... see you in class," she says as she exaggerates the way her hips move back and forth while she walks away. Then she moves her look to Helena, smirks, and squints her eyes, as if to say, "That's what you get for taking my hairbrush."

Helena is boiling up inside. She dislikes her! She hates that narcissistic, insolent brat! She despises Lara! How dare she flirt with Randall like that? She knew it! She did it on purpose! Ughh ... that's it!

" Seriously?" she says aloud, not caring that other kids can hear her. "This means war." She endures the classes in school, although she wants to just damage everything around her. She will not even take a look at Lara. She wants nothing to do with her. In the meantime, she is contemplating an act of ruthlessness.

" What can I do that will really hurt her?" she thinks. "There must be something ... something she really appreciates ... something she loves more than anything, besides her hairbrush and her hair, of course. Let's see ... aha! Oh, that's dark. That's mean, but she asked for it. She started it."

After school, neither of them speak to one another. It's different than it used to be. On a normal day, they would walk home together and talk about life, about their insane instructors, or the things their peers said in the class. But this time, they calmly different from each other.

Helena heads straight for the grass fields beyond town, the fields where their horses are. The two girls have been good friends for so long that they even put their horses in the exact same area. But this time, it's only Helena who goes to the horses. Lara has no clue what she is really up to.

As Helena reaches the fields, she looks at the horses and thinks, "Do I actually want to do this?

A peek of Lara's laughter and her kiss on Randall's cheek flashes through her head. "Yes, I'm sure," she says in a low voice. "She is going to regret what she did."

Helena leaps over the fence and approaches Lara's horse. As she focuses, she mumbles the words, "Horsey, horsey that I have fed, become like one of the very dead." She waves her hands through the air to empower her magic.

Poooooof!

In front of her, Lara's horse undergoes an instant change of appearance. Its eye sockets droop down; its pupils disappear into a hollow, empty gaze; and its skin turns green as the flesh begins to reek of decomposing decay.

" Moowah-ha-ha-ha-haaaah!" Helena exclaims. "Let's see if you still like your zombie horse you saved up for, Lara! It's not alive any longer; it's not dead ... it's an UNDEAD horse! Ha-ha-ha!"

The zombie horse snorts. Its eyes are looking soulless and wicked. It's on a harmful objective. Before Helena understands it, the zombie horse begins to assault the other horses in the corral. It runs at them and tries to kick them with its feet.

" O-oh," Helena says. "I didn't expect that. I better get out of here."

She runs towards the fence and leaps back over it. Then she looks at what the zombie horse is doing.

" No!" she shouts. "What's it doing?!"

The regret conquers her as she understands that the zombie horse is assaulting her horse as well. Helena's horse installs some sort of a fight but then quits. It runs away and jumps over the opposite side of the fence, disappearing into the mountains as it gallops away.

" No! No, no, no, no, no ... this was not supposed to happen," Helena says in despair. "I wish I would have been more careful. Now I lost my own horse."
Nevertheless, the evil zombie horse isn't done yet.

The zombie horse takes a look at Helena and comes running at her.
" Stay away from me!" Helena shouts. "Help! Heeeeelp!"
But it won't stop pursuing her. She reaches the town, and some of its inhabitants come out of their homes to see what is happening.
" Heeeelp!" Helena still shouts as she keeps running away.
They look at her with big eyes, not comprehending why she is in so much panic, but when they look behind her, they instantly figure it out. The zombie horse has a scary appearance, frightening the villagers and triggering them to flee too. There is an outbreak of worry in town. People are yelling as they try to go away from the insidious-looking beast.
" Leave me alone!"
" Go away from me!"
Other comparable exclamations are being heard throughout the town. Lara steps out of her home too. When she sees the zombie horse, she squints her eyes for a moment and says, "Fall? Is that you?"
The zombie horse blinks. It snorts and breathes greatly; then it runs at her. Lara quickly steps inside and shuts the door. The zombie horse bonks its head against the door and tries to get in, ramming the door with its head constantly.
" It must be my horse," she says. "It's definitely her; I just know it, but how could she have developed into ...?"
Suddenly, it dawns on her who her only opponent is.
" Helena," she says. "It's Helena, that filthy ... oh, if I get my hands on her ..."
The zombie horse keeps making attempts to get in. Lara counts herself fortunate that this beast isn't smart enough to go through one of the windows. She locks the door and runs upstairs, hiding underneath her bed.
" If only my parents were home," she mumbles while panting heavily. "This is ridiculous. A zombie horse? That's so unsafe!"
She buries her head in her face and waits.
She waits and waits ... hoping that this problem will soon be over.
Eventually, her parents add the stairs and enter her bedroom.
" Lara, sweetie, are you fine?" her mom asks.
" I'm all right, Mother. Did you know that the zombie horse in the town is my horse?"
" What?" her dad asks. "How is that possible?"
" I know it is, Father."
" Well, anyhow, it left the town. Thank goodness for that," her mom says.
" It's my horse," Lara says, "and I want to go find it."
" No," her dad says. "It's too harmful. Even if you would, then how do you know you could communicate with it effectively? You've seen that beast. It's dead ... it's undead."
" I know, but maybe I could still talk some sense into it."
" I would not recommend it, honey," her mother says. "What if it doesn't even recognize you?"
" But I saw it," Lara insists. "It recognized me when I was standing in the entrance. Come on, please."

" No means no," her dad says. "I am done having this discussion. We are fortunate that we didn't get hurt. Leave it for what it is, Lara. I know you saved up a ton of money to purchase this horse, and it's a huge loss, but you can't just head out there and risk your life. After all, it's still just an animal."

" You don't understand," Lara says. "It's not fair."

She diminishes the stairs and heads outside. When she opens the front door, she can hardly really believe what she sees. Plants are knocked over, sheds are broken, windows are shattered, and some of the people in the town are faltering, as if they got injured somehow.

" What happened here?" Lara asks the first guy who walks by.

" That zombie horse ... it damaged a lot of stuff here. Some people got hurt, but no casualties. It's a disaster though. I am glad it's gone."

" Where did it go?"

" Into the mountains. That way. Now, if you'll excuse me, I have to go examine the children."

Lara doesn't waver. She knows into which direction to go now, and she leaves instantly, ignoring her father's counsel.

Helena is sitting in the corner of a street, behind a trashcan. She is shivering. She recognizes that she didn't know what she was doing when she turned Lara's horse into a zombie horse. The effects are even worse than she expected. What she actually wanted to do, was to make it look ugly, odor bad, and have it stay the exact same way. The aggressive side has been an unpleasant surprise.

When she searches for, she concludes that the risk is gone, and as she walks through the village, she is revolted by the damage she has triggered.

" Oh my goodness," she says. "The horse did all this? Wow."

Fences and walls are broken, trees are lying across the streets, and bushes have been ripped from the yards.

" I must put an end to this," Helena says to herself. "Hey, you! Where did that zombie horse go?"

" It's gone!" a little girl screams back. "They say it went into the mountains."

" Okay," Helena says. "Then that's where I'm going too."

She hurries home and gets some food without her father and mother seeing her. Then she runs into the open, wanting to find her own horse and the one she cursed.

She walks for hours. The sun is slowly setting, and the town is in sight, but it's a long walk from the point where she is at. Helena gets tired. She takes a look at the valley which she left. Thoughts of anger, remorse, and hope run through her mind. It occurs to her that the battle has escalated into something that is being overplayed.

It has to stop.

Lara's journey is a long one as well. She recognizes that when she sees the sun hide behind the mountains on the others side of the valley. It's getting dark, and it is beginning to rain. Within minutes, her outfits are soaking wet.

" Great," she complains. "If only I had my hairbrush now. Ughh ... I dislike the rain." Nevertheless, she keeps pushing forward. She continues to walk uphill until she sees a shade in the distance.

" Huh? Another person? Up here? That's odd."

After she says it, she hides behind a huge rock. She waits and looks, trying to find the identity of the better half. The mists and damps originating from the ground camouflage the said person.

Then it becomes clear.

She sees who it is.

Fuming with rage, Lara leaps from her hiding place. "Helena," she says in a low but determined voice. "It's you! I could have known. It was your idea all along, wasn't it? You turned my horse into a zombie horse, didn't you?"

" Err ... yes, I did," Helena replies, "but now I am searching for it."

" Ha! That's the least you should do, you, witch!"

" Take that back. I am not a witch."

" Oh, you're not a witch? Then what do you call cursing an innocent horse and turning it into a zombie? You are pure evil, Helena, and you know it."

Braaaaoooom! Brom! Brom!

The thunder in the distance is loud and lightning flashes boost the dramatic feel of the circumstances as the two girls look one another in the eyes and yell accusations at each other. The air is covered in a thick fog, and the rain magnifies.

" It's all your fault anyhow!" Helena says, safeguarding herself. "If you would have just let me use your hairbrush, I would not have stolen it."

" Oh, so now you're justifying that too? Wow. You're so innocent ... and filled with yourself."

" Do not give me that. You're not so good yourself. Why did you have to be all over the one guy I like, huh? You knew I liked him, and then you just throw yourself into his arms in front of everybody. Let me ask you this, Lara. Do you even like Randall?"

" Of course not! I just did it to get back at you. Randall is a loser!"

" How dare you? Take this, you, tramp!" With those words, Helena leaps to Lara's waste and pins her to the ground. When she has her there, she starts to beat Lara up, who holds her hands in front of her face and kicks Helena off.

" You think you're better than me?" Lara asks. "I'll show you how to put up a fight!" She pushes Helena over, who slips and falls with her face into the mud.

Lara pulls her direct by grabbing her hair and is going to pound her hard, but then Helena says something she didn't expect.

" P-please, Lara. I'm sorry. I'm sorry. Please ... let's stop this nonsense."

Lara's facial expression changes. As she checks out Helena's eyes, all she sees is the best good friend she missed so much throughout their ridiculous argument. A tear appears in her eye, and Helena stays up. "I'm sorry," she says again. "I was jealous of your perfect hair. I just wanted to be more like you. I appreciate you. And yes, I have practiced more magic, but what do you think I try to make up for? And are you envious of the fact that I got my horse totally free? Do you think I am proud of myself? You are the one who worked long and hard to pay for your own horse. I do not think I could ever do that. You're my heroine, Lara. Whenever I am with you, I try to compete as you're so proficient at so many things. That's the truth."

Lara takes a look at her, with the rain still putting down on their faces. "Do you mean all that?" the older girl asks her good friend.

" Naturally. You help me find a purpose in life. You've always been a motivation to me." It touches her, and without doubt, Lara gives her younger good friend a hug. They embrace one another for several seconds. Then she looks Helena in the eyes and says, "I forgive you. I am sorry too, Helena. Please forgive me as well."

" We're fine," Helena says. "I feel extremely guilty for what I have done. I didn't know the curse would have such an effective influence."

" Well, let's go find the horses. You do have a spell to reverse the curse, don't you?"

" Yes, I do. I just didn't use it at the time I saw the zombie horse, because I was so scared."

They stand up and brush themselves off. When they see how pointless this is, since they are both covered in unclean mud, they start to laugh. Their friendship has been brought back. Now all they need to do, is find those two animals.

Before they go any further, the two friends hide under a tree. They discuss hair, about Randall, about the weather, and the damage in the town. They are friends again, never to be separated by anything.

When the rain is gone, they advance their journey.

" Do you want a snack?" Helena asks.

" Naturally. I am starving," Lara says.

Helena reaches inside her bag and finds 2 sandwiches. She gives one to Lara and begins chewing on one herself. They walk up the mountain and take a look at the foggy view.

" Hey, what's that?" Helena all of a sudden asks.

" That looks like two horses," Lara says. "Let's go check it out."

As they approach the two shades in the distance, they begin to see something odd: The two horses are peaceably eating grass, standing next to each other.

" We found them!" Helena yells joyfully.

" Isn't my horse supposed to be aggressive?" Lara asks.

" Well, in the beginning, it attacked my horse. But now, they have become friends." She takes a look at Lara and adds, "Just like us. Ha-ha!"

But the zombie horse is still not as it used to be, so Helena raises her arms and hands and says, "Zombie, zombie, change your fur; alter back to the way you were."

The magic works. Within seconds, the zombie horse reverses into a regular horse, smelling and looking better and more alive.

" It worked!" Lara exclaims. "Thank you, Helena!"

She gives her horse a hug and says, "I am glad that you are back, Autumn. Say, Helena, isn't she looking great?"

" She looks terrific. Oh yes, and I almost forgot ..."

Helena puts her hand in her backpack and gets the pink hairbrush, the object that began all of it.

" You brought it here? Why?"

" I do not know," Helena confesses. "Maybe it reminded me of you. Anyway, here it is. I am giving it back to you. My hair is so muddy and unpleasant that even this brush will not do any good."

" You're right," Lara says laughingly. "It probably takes more than a magic brush to make us look good again. But since we have it here ... have you ever seen it being used on a horse?"

" No, I didn't think of that," Helena says. "Can we brush the horses?"

" Yes, we can. And after we're done, we'll ride home together."

" That sounds like a great idea," Helena concurs.

THE END

Zombie Killer

Chapter 1: My Occupation

My name is Sanderer, and I am a zombie killer.
I have been doing it for years.
And I do not care about anything else.
This is the life that I am familiar with. I wait, I kill, and I make money. I protect the people of this great country against the impulsive invasions of the undead. You never know where they are going to show up, and you never know how many of them there will be.
I don't know what turns human beings into zombies; I really don't. That's not my field. Scientists and laboratory men have been captivated by this their whole lives. To each his own, right? If they want to sit in a lab all the time, then that's their decision.
Not me though. I make certain those disliked derelicts remain in the status they should be in: Dead.
How do I do it, you ask?
Oh, I got my methods. I slice them, shoot them, slice them, stab them ... it's an art and an occupation of decision and anticipation. You have to be quick. Some of those zombies were probably warriors themselves before they ended up being the unclean beasts they are today, and so their alertness and fight skills are excellent ... well ... for a zombie.
I use various weapons. I don't like to stay with one specific favorite. Distinguishing makes an important difference. It keeps the job fascinating and it challenges me to improve and broaden my proficiency. Let's go through the list, shall we? I have pickaxes, swords, fight axes, shovels (to bang them on the head), knives, weapons, and maces. Okay, all right, I don't use them all the exact same amount of time, and I think I mainly wind up with a sword and several knives, if nothing else, but you get the point. My home is a weapon room, and I really love it.
I was never good with emotions. It used to bug me when kids sobbed all the time. I've learned to be tough in life. My mother and father were still together, but they were hard on me. I learned to just handle problems, not to whimper about it and pity myself. I guess that's why I chose the profession that I did. People who are too vulnerable or wimpy, don't take this job. They know that somehow, one day, they will see a zombie that has way too much of a similarity to someone they know, and then they hesitate.
I never am reluctant.
Never.
When a zombie comes running at me, I go for the kill. I don't doubt. I do not fluctuate. I know what has to be done, and I am more than willing to do it.
So now you know a little something about me. I am single, and I wish to stay that way. I am young, and I just want to get some money. Killing zombies is an exceptional way to do that. Can you think how much the city or village mayors are willing to pay me to exterminate the zombies that assault their towns? Don't even think you can guess. Let's just stop talking about it. Suffice it to say that I make a good living. It's remarkable. Incredible is exactly what I want to be. It's what I always desired become, nothing less. And being remarkable is something you can't do by talking or making claims. Talk is low-cost. Doing something about it is the only way to enhance yourself, and that's what I have been doing my whole life.

Now, are you ready for a remarkable story? A story where I faced one of my biggest challenges? Brace yourself. Here it goes ...

You might expect a brave story of impressive fights and fast, action-packed scenes when I tell you that I want to show you the most difficult kill I've ever made. You may expect a monstrous, enormous zombie who was indestructible and three times the size of the others, but it wasn't. My hardest kill wasn't such a really tough personality. It was tough for me because, for the last time, I had a difficult time with my choice to do the right thing.

Why? My emotions got in the way. It was actually type of awful. If you can't stand a little sadness or suffering, then stop reading at this moment, as this is an unfortunate story. Remember how much I dislike sobbing? So become tougher and let it go. Things happen, and happy endings are reasonable, but they can be interfered with by the occasional misfortunate incident.

It was one of my buddies ... well, he was sort of annoying, but he still didn't really deserve to die. He was the sort of guy that would burp loudly in public and hit on the women with only a disgusted response awaiting him. No, he wasn't a nice guy. He was a jerk. But for some reason, we got along quite well. And no, he didn't deserve to die, particularly not the way he did.

It was on a Friday. Both he and I had been in the pub for several hours, and we were just joking around. I came to find out that he was a skeleton hunter, and that his frequent is visiting to the Underworld matched my journeys to far towns to solve the zombie issues there. I remember it so clearly.

At a certain point, he said, "Sanderer, with your job, you can't try to connect to others too much. It will kill you mentally."

" What do you mean?" I asked.

" I mean that often, you'll need to choose between what's right and what's easy. You cannot save everyone. You realize that, don't you?"

" I didn't expect you to be so serious," I said. "You are always upsetting people with your indecent jokes. Why are you lecturing me?"

" Look," he said, "I am not happy. I am waiting for that marvelous moment when I can be launched from the tragedies of this life. The afterlife is waiting on me. Do you know why I do what I do?"

" I don't have the slightest idea, so inform me," I said.

" My partner got killed by a skeleton. Don't stress ... no kids were left, but I can't tell you how much anger I am still holding within me towards those creatures. The best way I knew how to deal with it, was to start eliminating them for a living. I have been to the Underworld, a hellish, infernal place, and I have saved several people from being overcome by the exact same fate, but in some cases, I am far too late."

" That must be hard."

" Are you listening to me ?!" he asked, as he grabbed my shoulders and shook me a little. "It will happen to you. You need to live with the frustration. You cannot let yourself go soft, friend."

" Okay, I get it. I will keep it in mind," I said.

After that, we didn't speak another word. I felt for him. I knew he had wished to die so many times, but that he survived to secure others, a worthy thing to do.

But then it occurred ...

It took place so quickly that I still remember the awe and the rush I felt. Zombies were assaulting the village. Oh, and by the way, did I mention that there were only about 30 people in that village? Yes, it was more like a fork in the road than an actual town, more like a hamlet.

Anyway, as always, I brought around a number of weapons. I had a knife in my pocket and a pickaxe on my back. I never go anywhere without something to protect myself with, and this day was no different. And that night, I made sure to use them, as when the zombies assaulted, I had no time to run home.

They stormed in.

" Wraaaaah!"

The ones in the pub were first, and I heard people yell and yell from the houses in that little hamlet. I drew my pickaxe from my back and held it in front of me. I looked at my friend, the skeleton slayer. He already had a sword prepared and had killed a couple of zombies before I could even blink my eyes. What a ruffian!

" Come and get it, zombies!" I screamed, and I took a step forward, cutting one of them in half.

" Good to see us collaborating," my good friend said. "I'll tell you what: You secure the male zombies and I'll get the female zombies. It appears like you care a bit more about who you kill anyhow."

I was a little hurt that he thought of me like some useless woos who would care about something like that, but I accepted his offer nonetheless. We hacked and slashed, and the zombies were still being available in. Within minutes, the entire club was filled with townspeople who had been developed into zombies and were now turning on us.

All of a sudden, I heard a cry from the opposite side of the room.

" Aaaargh!"

" Hey, what's going on?" I asked.

" Aaargh! One of the zombies bit me, Sanderer. You have to finish me off!"

It was my friend. I wanted to the left; I sought to the right. There weren't that many zombies left. My friend was kneeling down. His weapon had dropped. Every little thing became blurred, as if a slow-motion influence was being put on my life. I hacked at another zombie in front of me and kicked another one through the window as I ran forward.

I bent over and put my arm on my good friend's shoulder and asked him how he was doing.

" This is it, Sanderer," he said. "It was good to meet you. I am prepared to meet my marriage partner in the afterlife."

" What are you talking about, man? We can get help. You will be all right."

" You know I won't be," he said laughingly. "It doesn't matter. I knew this would happen one day. Go ahead. Finish me. Don't let me become one of them."

" But I do not want to end your life. Come on!" I said. "This isn't right. There has to be something we can do."

Then he got me by my shirt, looked me straight into my eyes, and said, "Toughen up, Sanderer. Do what needs to be done. Stop caring, and DO it!"

I killed him. I closed my eyes when I did it. Yeah, that was the toughest kill I've ever made. I still remember it so well.

His name was Jake.

Chapter 3: The Good Life

After this pleasant (ahum ... ahum ...) anecdote, I hope you comprehend that my life isn't all misery and darkness. You see, Jake wanted to meet his marriage partner again, and he strongly believed in paradise. He was ready, and he had done his part. Besides, after this, I did precisely as he said. It was an important lesson for me. I conditioned, and I distanced myself from friendships. Now, that may not be the best thing to do for everyone, but for me, it ended up being a practical way of life.

The good life; that's what I called it. Stop caring, stop thinking, and just do it. That was type of my motto.

I've lived this way for a very long time, and I don't get tired of it. Do you wish to know where I get my enjoyment from?

Action!

It's all about the action. I love it when the enemy seems bigger and unsurpassable. I love a difficulty. I really love the rush of unfaithful death over and over again, and I especially yearn for the adrenaline that flows through my body each time I chop off the head of one of those mindless, ugly zombies. It gives me a sense of satisfaction that I don't think I could find anywhere else.

And after that there is another thing: I have A LOT OF money. That's right. I am pretty packed, so when I have to choose between inns, I can afford the most glamorous one. I provide to beggars when I see them, I buy fruit at the markets when I feel like it, and I change weapons and outfits when I need a different style. It's all part of the good life: The flexibility to spend whatever I want, and not needing to care about saving up or footing the bill. My cabin, where I live, is relatively cheap anyway. I began living there as I didn't need a huge home, and it suffices.

The third thing that delights me in life is the excellence difficulty. I have yet to learn so many moves, it's not even funny. After having mastered the art of sword combating and different designs of martial arts, I went into archery, studied the ancient ways of butt-kicking without weapons, and ended up being an expert at navigating through hordes of zombies without even touching them. Every little thing is fascinating. Curiosity drives me, and I typically review my battle skills after another day of "tidying up" the streets of some victimized town by those undead creeps.

So there you have it. I really love my life, and despite the fact that you could say I am alone a lot, I do not get lonesome. I get a kick out of the action each time, I have enough wealth to keep me happy, and I enhance my abilities and knowledge about the ancient battling arts each day.

Sounds good, does not it? Well, it was, until something went extremely wrong.

It was a dawning day filled with doom and misery. It had never resembled this before. I mean, the Ferrith Lands had had their issues, but not like this, and even for me, it would be a tremendous challenge to the survival of our species: Mankind.

I woke up that day, feeling typical and ready to eat a good meal. I had some breakfast items in my cabinets, and I immediately cooked some bacon and eggs to fill my stomach. As soon as I was done with that, I went to my little training room. But as I was practicing my moves in front of the mirror, I became aware of something that was coming for me.

BANG!

The door flew open. I was shocked. No later than a few seconds afterwards, zombies were all over my house. They knocked over my properties and furniture. With my sword, I kept them at a considerable distance.

" Stay back!" I yelled as I killed a few of them.

When I glanced at my kitchen area, however, I felt truly silly. I had left the stove on. It was a miracle nothing had happened before. The gas was dripping and the zombies were running into combustible objects, making the danger something to be taken seriously.

That's when I ran out of my cabin. I took the back door, on the other end, the fire escape in my small training room, and rand as quick as I could. When I looked behind me ... Booooooooom!!!

The remains of the structure collapsed after taking off into a thousand pieces.

I fell onto the ground. I covered my head, making certain that no debris would fall on me. A few seconds later, I looked back.

" My lovely cabin," I said. "I just barely paid it off. Gggrrrrr ... I absolutely know who is going to pay for this. Those silly zombies!"

This was it. I had nothing to lose now. I think it was type of my fault, but those zombies had been obstructing my way. If they had not come, I would have done something about the stove. But it was gone now. My money had all been in that house. It was gone, all gone. I checked one more time to make certain, but I couldn't find anything valuable that hadn't been developed into ashes. I felt empty-handed, practically naked, in a metaphoric way. I was left with nothing. Where did those zombies come from? It made no sense.

" Revenge," I said. "It's not just business any longer. This time, it's individual."

And that's when I chose to get to the bottom of it. I went to the closest town, only to find that there weren't many people left. When I asked a random pedestrian on the street what had happened there, the answer was, "Zombies."

So I left. I went to another town. I walked for 2 hours and found the little village going through the same issue. Again, I asked some female, who walked outside, what was going on. Her response, "Zombies."

So I went to the city. And even there, when I came, I saw some houses lying in ruins. Others were deserted. People were terrified. The streets were reasonably empty. I wanted to know everything about it. I knew zombies would occasionally assault in different places, but not all surrounding towns at the same time, and rarely in the city. I went straight to the municipal government, wishing to find my answers there. When I arrived at the square in front of the building, the mayor was sitting on the stairs that resulted in the main entrance.

" Are you the mayor of this city?" I asked candidly.

" Yes, I am. Who are you?"

" My name is Sanderer. I am a zombie hunter, and it looks like your city has been raided by zombies. Am I correct?"

" Yes. Yes, you are. Did you just say you are a zombie hunter?"

" I did."

" Then you are who we need, my good friend. Please, come inside, and I will clarify every little thing."

I was still suspicious. I wanted more answers, and this random figure didn't have them for me yet, so I asked, "Why were you resting on the stairs here? |Don't you have better things to do?"

" Actually," he began, "I was kind of 'out of it.' I asked my therapists for a break. I needed some fresh air. There have been so many issues coming at us that I didn't know what to do, but I am grateful that you are here. Maybe you can help us. But do not worry about it now. We will answer all your questions in the meeting room."

And that's when I shut up and just followed him.

Chapter 5: The Disease Was Spreading

I went into the conference room in the great city hall. It was a modest room with seats and a table, like any meeting room should be. With my sword on my back and a knife in my pocket, I was certainly the one person that stood out among these chic bureaucrats.
" Mister mayor, who is this?" one of the counselors asked.
" This man is the solution to our issues, gentlemen," the mayor said. Then he turned to me and said, "Please, have a seat."
I sat down and gazed some of these educated people in the eyes. They weren't too sure about my rough look and my dusty outfit, and when they saw the big sword on my back, I think some of them ended up being rather worried too.
" Gentlemen," the mayor began, "this is Sanderer. He is a zombie hunter. Tell them what you do, Sanderer."
" Like he said, I hunt zombies."
" Elaborate, please."
" Well, I stab them, I cut them to pieces, I break them in half, I pound them to piec ..."
" Okay, we get it. We comprehend," the mayor said, disrupting my graphic description of the daily assault that typified my life. "Sanderer is the response to our problems. He will pursue the zombies for us and make them disappear, won't you, Sanderer?"
" Sure. But I do have a question: How come there are so many of them? It's not typical."
" That's a good question," the mayor said. "Some days ago, zombies were identified, but they weren't routine zombies. As you might know already, a human being can turn into a zombie after being bitten. But these zombies were different. All they had to do, was sneeze, and the people would become contaminated instantly. It was a disaster. The disease was spreading out like wildfire. People were panicking. Whole towns were being turned into zombie towns. Males and female left their houses and ran away to the city, but even here, we couldn't hold them all back. A lot of us hid in our homes, and the zombies vanished from the city, but I know they will be back. They are assaulting other surrounding towns as we speak. Something must be done."
" And what makes you think that I can stop that? If they sneeze on me, I will develop into a zombie too. Did you consider that?"
" We have created a vaccine. It is being given to people at this moment. A lot of my messengers and servants are taking this remedy to all people in the country. So at least that is being looked after. The disease will stop spreading. The remedy is being transported all over."
" Then why do you need me? If you're already managing it, then what's my role?"
" We want to pay you if you kill the zombies. Just because we are immune to becoming a zombie, does not mean that we aren't in danger. There still is an entire army of zombies out there."
" Makes sense," I said.
We talked about the payment and the terms of the contract. Everything else was clear to me. This was what I was trying to find. Now I could kill these zombies to get my revenge AND to get money. Wow. What else does a guy need, right?

As I talked some more with the mayor and one or two of his less suspicious therapists, I began to understand where and when all this drama with the zombies had started.
It was several years ago. Individual hygiene was pathetic, and no one knew about bacteria. It was only after this event that people comprehended the significance of cleaning hands and other safety measures against diseases. The outcome was the black Plague, a terrible illness that took the lives of many. No one knew the remedy, and in order to produce a cure, laboratory scientists started fiddling around with chemicals. Nothing could have been even worse for mankind than what they did. They injected needles, tossed potions on the floor, and integrated the elements of the Ferrith Lands to develop a remedy.
If only they knew what they would unleash by doing so ...
The first indications were increased aggressiveness and disturbed mental conduct. The researchers should have stopped with the experiments at that point, but the authorities kept pushing them to keep going, and they did.
Once the infection took over, it was too late. Zombies were a fact, and since then, zombies have become part of life. They always attack in groups or hordes, but the hordes have never been big enough to swipe out whole villages. That's why I was always able to stand my ground and kill as tons of them as was necessary without getting killed.
Fascinating, huh? Yes, I thought so myself.
But now, times have changed. The hordes have become larger. Their numbers have increased, and for some reason, they have shown different conduct than before: They stick together, forming huge hordes that crash through any town, any city, and any fortress. There are tons of them, and everybody fears them.
And then they turned to me: Their last hope. I knew not to let them down. They were going to have the best show of their lives. Bring it on, zombies!

It was early in the morning. It was the day after I met the mayor and his counselors. All of them had high expectations. The city didn't have many soldiers, and they were all too scared of the zombies. Lot of pushovers.

They depend on me, and on me only. This was my moment; my moment to shine or to die. In either case, with a sense of desperation, the gut feeling of a guy who lost everything but still wants to resist-- that sensation-- I went and stood my ground.

And if that wasn't bad enough, then listen to this: The whole city (or nevertheless many people were left in it) came to watch; lots of them. They were standing on the city walls and were cheering me on. There I was, outside the city walls, on a visible, giant grass field awaiting my doom. I closed my eyes and put my hands in some kind of meditation position. The hordes were coming. We all knew it. The city walls were air tight, and everyone hoped that I would have the ability to stop these beasts from attacking their strengthened environment. The city gates were closed, despite the fact that didn't stop the zombies last time, and the soldiers were watching with the commoners.

When I opened my eyes, I glanced at the mayor. His eyes were huge. He didn't know what to think, but when he saw the persistence in my eyes, I knew that he knew for sure that he made the right choice. It was one of those almost telepathic moments.

There they were: The hordes of zombies. In the beginning, just a couple of appeared on the horizon. Then lots, then hundreds, and this army of the undead grew larger and larger. I spat out a piece of gum I was chewing. I tightened the headband around my head and I took the sword from my back and the knife from my pocket. Its glossy surface area was reflected in the sun, and a legendary, significant moment had started. I walked forward at the crowd that was running at me. Then I increased my pace, and when I came closer, I ran towards them.

" Graaaaaaaaaaaah !!!!!" I shouted. "Die, zombies! Die!"

Tsyaack!

My sword cut through a lot of them, and within a tiny glimpse, they were all focused on me. I slashed, I cut, I punched, and I kicked. I threw some of them away and used others as a shield when they were fighting back.

Bang! Clash! Thud!

The battle continued. I had never dealt with so many zombies at the exact same time. It was a new milestone for me, and the chances of passing away were so high that I stopped caring. Occasionally, I got a fist in my face or a zombie who was attempting to eat me. Throughout my kicking and shouting and slashing, I ensured that none came close enough with their teeth.

One time, however, one of the zombies came too close. He nearly bit me, and I was glad I went back in the nick of time.

" That was close," I told myself, after which I punched him in the face.

The zombies became frustrating. They all attacked me at the same time. On a pile of dead undead bodies, I was combating them off one by one. But I knew I wouldn't last long. They jumped at me and accumulated on me, pinning me to the ground and making me lose my sword. Between the arms, the legs, and the dead bodies, I desperately grabbed my blade.

Worthless.

Too far away. I had to do something.

Then I remembered that I had another spare knife, hidden in the back of my boot. I had always kept that one there, just in case, and I absolutely ignored it up to this point. I wiggled my hand down and moved the knife.

" Got it," I said.

After almost choking beneath the dozens of zombies on my body, I was finally able to cut through several of them and battle my way back to the surface area. I dove to my sword, got it, and dealt with the monstrous enemies again.

" You thought you were finished with me? Reconsider!" I yelled loudly.

The zombies were decreasing in numbers. Stacks of zombie bodies were joined by other falling opponents. The massacre was unbelievable, the massacre immense, and the probability of this ever happening again was virtually zero. I was like a ferocious beast. I was caught up in the most adrenaline I had ever felt in my life. I hacked and slashed and stabbed as if I had a limitless flow of energy running through my veins.

And after that it practically stopped. Only a few zombies were still standing. Some of them had already run away. Others were taking a look at me with doubts in their empty, brainless heads. 2 of them came at me, in a last attempt to take me out.

Stab! Stab!

Bad idea on their part, as they died that instant. The others escaped.

" Is that all you've got?" I said, catching my breath. I wanted to yell more ridiculing one-liners, but I didn't have it in me.

I collapsed.

I fell to the ground, drained from the many strikes and the disastrous limits of the human body. I was exhausted, and I lost consciousness.

It ended up being black.

Chapter 8: Back on My Way

I awakened. I slowly opened my eyes. A ton of people were loafing me. They were the city people who had been watching. I more or less felt like a gladiator in an arena. Me against the zombies, that was what it had come down to. What were the odds that I would win this?

But when I saw all those people, I knew that I had won. I was triumphant! I acquired awareness, and I was happy to see how many of them were proud of me. They cheered. They were amazed, and they wanted to celebrate.

" Congratulations," the mayor said. "I can't believe you pulled it off. It's hard to express in words what you did here. You saved us from the zombie horde, and we are indebted to you. Tell me what you want, and I will try to organize it for you."

" Water," I said.

" What?" the mayor asked.

" Water. I am thirsty."

The mayor got someone to get some water. When he returned, I felt in heaven. Can you imagine how much I had been sweating during that severe fight? I felt like I was dying from dehydration, but when the water came, I drank my heart out. When I was done, I had renewed strength. I looked at them. I nodded, and I accepted the payment from the mayor.

Then I walked away.

" You're not going to celebrate?" The mayor asked.

" Nope," I said without looking back.

" But the people want you to socialize with them."

" Don't feel like it," I said.

" Oh, come on. Are you sure?"

" Yep."

And that was it. I got what I wanted: Money and vengeance. I didn't want to get mentally connected to all these people. Why would I care? If I did, I would only end up eliminating them or watching them die a long time in my life when they would develop into zombies themselves. Hey, do not get me wrong. I appreciated their health and wellbeing, which was part of the reason why I accepted the assignment in the first place, but part of me didn't want to have a broken heart. Makes sense, doesn't it? So yes, I left. And I kept it at that.

I know it's not over. I am pretty certain that there are still zombies in other parts of the nation, and that's fine. It keeps me going. It gives me something to do. Come and get it, suckers. I am waiting on my next objective.

My name is Sanderer, and I am a zombie hunter.

I have been doing it for many years.

And I don't care about anything else.

THE END

Digging

Chapter 1: Ralph the Digger

My name is Ralph. Pretty ironic, because this diary is all about something I dug up. I was a building worker. I lived in a decent-sized village with a lot of miners. There was a mine nearby and I went to work every day. Since I was single, I was pretty content with my living circumstances and didn't feel like I had to please anyone besides myself.

But the sequence of events that happened sometime in July, changed my perspective on life. Additionally, my little home became a symbol of everything that can fail in life.

One day, I was on my way home, when I saw my neighbor operating in his yard.

" Hi there, next-door neighbor," I said. "What are you doing?"

" My wife wants the weeds gone. It's a lot of work," he said.

" What's the point?" I asked. "They will grow back anyhow."

" I know. That's what I kept telling her, but she didn't want to hear it. Instead, she handed me a shovel, a rake, and some other stuff. I have been digging for two hours. I am permitted back in to eat supper when it's done."

" Ha-ha! That just goes to show you who is wearing the pants in the family."

" Ah, just wait till you are married, man. We'll see if you'll end up the exact same way."

" Don't try to dissuade me," I said. "I know marriage isn't everything, but I would really love to begin that happily-ever-after life at some point."

" Good luck to you. It's not for everybody. Some people die without that chance. I was just fortunate."

" I am glad you see it that way. I need to go. Have a good time in the garden."

" Yeah, right. Depend upon your meaning of fun," he mumbled, but I had already gone inside.

I put my miner's helmet on the table and sat down on the sofa. When I put my feet up, my little wiener pet dog got on my lap.

" Marco," I said. "I am happy to see you. I had a long day at work. The mines had plenty of minerals and important blocks. But now I can unwind. How was your day?"

" Woof! Woof!" Marco said.

" Of course your day was good. You're a dog. You don't need to work," I said while chuckling.

I sat back in my chair and poured some juice into a cup. I took a sip and said, "Aaaah, this is the good life."

That's when I went to sleep.

I do not know how long I slept, but it probably wasn't long, because before I knew it, I heard Marco bark.

" Woof! Woof! Woof!"

" Huh? What's going on?" I said.

Marco was running backward and forward, as if he was attempting to show me something. I followed him and wound up in the yard. When I came there, I discovered what he was barking about.

Chapter 2: Pickaxe

In the corner of my garden, there was a shiny object. It was partially covered by sand. I bent over to know what it was, but there was only a little part protruding of the ground.
" Time to get the shovel," I said.
" Woof! Woof!" Marco agreed.
I went to the shed behind my house and got the shovel. I began digging like insane, since I was curious to see what it was.
" Umpf ... I'm getting a little worn out, Marco," I said. "I have already been working all the time."
Ultimately, I made it through and pulled out the shiny thing.
" Wow!" I exclaimed. "It's a golden pickaxe! Those are pretty pricey!"
This was excellent. I had been desiring one of these for a while, but I never put the cash away to purchase one. I went back inside and put it near the front door. Pleased with life, I leaned back in my chair again and drank another sip of my juice.
" Tomorrow ..." I said.
The next day, I left my stone pickaxe in the home and took my golden pickaxe. It was great. My co-workers, the other miners gave me envious appearances.
" Where did you get that?" one of them asked.
" From my yard," I said. "It was just there and I dug it up."
" Ha! Ralph dug it up. That's the pun of the day."
" You know, one of those pickaxes recently disappeared in the village," one of the men said.
" I didn't know that," I said. "What took place?"
" Well, if we knew that, it wouldn't be gone anymore, now, would it?"
" I think not," I said. I thought for a moment. "Hey! You're not implying that I took this, are you?"
" I'm not indicating anything," my colleague said. "All I am saying, is that this could be the exact same one. If you claim that you found it in your yard, then who am I to judge you? The question you need to ask yourself is: How did it wind up there?"
" You're right. I do not know," I said. "But I am not grumbling. I like it."
" Well, you have striven, Ralph. You deserve it. Enjoy it. Maybe we'll discover where it originated from after all, huh?"
" Yes, maybe."
It made me think, but I didn't have all the answers. How was I supposed to know? I just found it. When I went home that night, I was tired. The pickaxe came in handy; it was easy to deal with, but to get more done, I worked even harder than normal. So I was just as exhausted anyhow.
I did the exact same thing as the night before. I kicked back on my chair, cuddled my pet, Marco, and drank a sip from my juice.
Then I went to sleep in my comfortable chair.

I was in the back alleys of some huge metropolis. It was dark and the streets were filled with a spooky fog, blended together with the odor of wet pet dogs and sweat. I didn't know how I wound up there. It was a secret to me.

When I sought to the side, I knew where the smells were originating from. A homeless person with his pet dog was sleeping beneath a few blankets, and his bag of stuff was filled with food leftovers from the previous day. I reached over and put several coins in his hat, which was lying next to him, upside down on top of the dog.

I looked the other way and saw a girl run at me.

" Whoa, what's going on?" I asked her as she approached me.

" Help! Help me!" she uttered. "I am being gone after by an explosive beast."

I grabbed hold of her and made sure she didn't trip. Then I gradually helped her and sat her down beside the beggar, who had gotten up by that time. He was rubbing his eyes and didn't think anything of the circumstances.

The green beast was coming. I knew it; I felt it, but I was going to protect this girl from him. The monster happened the corner. Its shape was showing against the light. It had the shape of a monster, but it wasn't just any green monster. It had a red coat.

It made me laugh and shiver at the same time. My mind was going nuts. While the cells in my brain were lining up the info in front of me and asked the question why a monster would have a red coat, half of my body ended up being numb for a 2nd or more, recognizing that this monster could run to me and blow up in our faces.

And it came.

The explosive monster ran at me.

It ran faster and faster, so I ran towards it. Out of thin air, the golden pickaxe appeared in my hand. I held it firm with my steady grip, unaware of its origin.

I ran at the beast and tried to kill it with my pickaxe.

Ready ...

" Gaaaaargh!" I screamed.

I practically hit it, but the beast ducked and ran straight previous me. I stopped. I turned around and saw the beast run at the girl. It was totally out to get her, not me. That's why it avoided me and went towards its target.

The beast began to flicker.

" Nooo!" I exclaimed.

But it was far too late. The beast blew up. The beggar and the girl died. When I went towards the scene of death, her dead hand was holding a piece of red cloth she had ripped from the beast.

I could not save her.

" Nooo!" I yelled again.

Then I got up. I panted greatly. It had all been a dream. I was relieved when reality dawned on me.

Marco was taking a look at me with a shocked face. This dog undoubtedly didn't understand what had happened in my mind while I was asleep.

" It's fine, Marco," I said. "It was just a dream."

Or was it?

The next day, when I went to work, I felt a little sleepy. I wasn't too sure of what had happened to me, but it was like the imagine the previous night was cursing my understanding of reality and was covering my eyes with a thick cloud of darkness.
I didn't like it, to say the least.
I kept digging with the golden pickaxe, despite the lack of attention from my colleagues-- it wasn't news any longer that I had one-- and went straight home after work. I opened up the door, greeted my pet dog, and ate some bread with butter and a little bowl of soup. I sat down and played with Marco for a few minutes, till he got on my lap and went to sleep.
I was next.
I dropped off to sleep as well.
Another dream started. I found myself sitting on the steps of my backdoor that led into my backyard. I looked into the distance and got up. Every little thing appeared calm till I heard a troubling, spine-chilling noise in the distance. It originated from the other side of the fence. I walked towards the fence and looked over it by pulling myself up a little.
" Baaah!"
A dark shade was screaming in my face for a 2nd and after that teleported to the other side of my yard, within the fence. I was shocked, so much that I fell over. When I looked at it, it teleported again.
Then I saw the golden pickaxe I had found previously. It was stuck in the ground. I got it and rushed at the dark shade. The dark shade teleported away and evaded my attack. Then it laughed with a laugh so wicked that it made me tremble with worry.
I looked at the pickaxe. It flew up in the air and became my direction.
" What the ...?" I said, squinting my eyes to grasp the reality of what was happening.
The pickaxe came at me! It was flying at me, trying to kill me!
" Whaaaaah!" I yelled, and I tried to open the door to the home.
Why was it locked? I didn't lock the door! Who locked the door? The dark shade? Where was the key? I need to get out of here! Let me in!
" Let me in! Open up!" I yelled.
I turned my head and saw the golden pickaxe come at me. This was it. It was going to kill me.
" Whoa!" I said, as I stayed up. The environment had changed. I was in my room again. I looked at Marco, who was still sleeping on my lap. This, too, had been a dream, a terrible nightmare in which I practically got killed by the very pickaxe I had found.
Odd.

Another day, another expectation of dull routine at work.

" Has anything happened at home lately?" someone asked me at work.

" Not much. I have just been having weird dreams," I replied.

" Ah, I've had those too. It's the season. I dislike fall. Everybody gets colds, and it's that weird temperature level when a transition between warm and rainy weather occurs."

" I know what you're talking about," I said.

When he was gone, I added, "But that's most likely not it. There is something else ... something fishy is going on here."

I looked at the golden pickaxe I had brought to work and hit it into the rocks. It was almost as if some charming power was originating from this average-looking tool. I could not put my finger on it, but I knew something was wrong. Still, I continued to use it.

That night, I went home and fell down on the sofa; on purpose obviously, as I was just tired.

Marco was in the kitchen. He was already sleeping, so I just closed my eyes and chose to space out for a while.

But I fell asleep, and another problem took place. I was in another part of our town. It was on the opposite side, where I generally didn't go. But I recognized it nonetheless. I was wandering through the streets, just wondering what I was doing there in the first place. My very first impulse was to go back home. I knew I had to get there before dark, since I didn't trust the streets in the evening, no matter how little our town was.

Something was just behind me. I didn't know what, but I was afraid to look. When I finally had the guts to turn my head, I saw a girl.

But not just any girl; it was the girl I had met in the previous dream!

" You're alive!" I said. "You didn't get killed by the monster, did you?"

She moved her head in an abnormal way, something that frightened me. Then she put her hands forward and came at me.

" Huh? What?"

She was a zombie! I recognized the odd walking pattern, the moaning, and other indications. I knew she was a zombie, and she was chasing after me.

" Stay away from me!" I yelled as I ran into the opposite direction.

She was acquiring on me, and I was getting lost in the town streets. And then it happened: I tripped and fell flat on my face.

" Ouch!"

I rubbed the dirt off my face and looked up. The zombie girl came closer and closer. She bent over and attacked me.

Then I got up.

" Pfew!" I said. "This is going too far. Where did all these nightmares originate from? I mean, just several seconds ago, I almost ended up being zombie food."

I took a look around me as if I was looking for the response to my own question. And the answer was right there: The golden pickaxe. It was leaning against the wall in the corner of my living-room.

" What does this pickaxe involve the girl I keep seeing? What are the monsters? And why is there always someone dying in these dreams?"

I was turning into a little dream investigator, and to be honest, I sort of liked finding out what was going on in my head. But, again, I could not put my finger on it. It was like a huge blur, an unsolved secret.

Would I ever find out how all these dreams were related? Maybe I had to do something myself. Maybe I needed to do something about it.

Chapter 6: Action

The next day was a Saturday. I didn't need to go to work that day, so instead, I chose to return to my backyard and dig some more.

I didn't know what I was going to find, but I was determined to find some answers. I was sick of the problems, but I didn't just want to chuck the golden pickaxe into the garbage. I had to get to the bottom of this ...

Actually ...

And the bottom of my yard was still far away, so without squandering time, I ate some breakfast and grabbed my shovel. Marco joined me outside, keeping me business while doing so. It was hot that day, and the sweat was drenching my shirt, so I took it off.

" Howdy, next-door neighbor," the next-door neighbor said as he looked over the fence and saw me dig. "What are you doing?"

I looked at him with an ironical look on my face. "What does it look like? I am digging," I said.

" I can see that, but why?"

" To get a hole in my garden," I said. "Duh."

" But what for? Are you going to build a pool, or did you lose something?"

" A pool," I lied. I wasn't going to explain my abrupt desire to dig. He would not comprehend. So he shrugged and left me.

I dug and dug. I dug throughout the day. Marco helped out a few times too, although he didn't get as far as I did. The neighbor returned in the evening.

" Still digging?" he asked. "Why don't you take a break?"

" I already have," I said. "I drank water about ten times today. Why do you think I have not lost consciousness yet?"

When I said it, I all of a sudden felt the aching muscles in my shoulders and arms. It was a lot of work, and the strange thing was that I didn't even know if I was going to find something. I just wished for the best.

" Well, do not get careless," the neighbor said. "Some of the sand got thrown into my garden. Please watch where you throw that stuff."

I looked at him and said, "You know, there are other things I can do with this shovel too, like killing, breaking down someone's fence, smashing someone's windows, striking the neighbor; and there are many other choices."

He ended up being scared and chose to leave me alone. Exactly what I was aiming for. Good.

A half hour later, I all of a sudden saw something. It was like hair or something. I kept digging around it and moved some of the sand with my hands. "Marco, come here," I said.

" Woof! Woof!"

Then I stepped back.

" Whoa," I said.

It was hair! But the worst of all, was that it was an entire head. It was a dead remains!

" Ew," I said. "Where did this originated from?"

A little nervous, I kneeled in front of the head and dug out the remainder of the body. And to my surprise, it was the girl I had seen in my dreams. One of her fists was

clenched, as if she was holding on to something. I pulled the fingers back and was surprised.
" The red piece of cloth," I said in awe. "Who would have thought?"
Instantly, I asked my other next-door neighbor (not the bothersome one) to go get a policeman.

Chapter 7: Problem Fixed

The next day, the criminal activity was solved. The policeman had shown up at my home and had called over forensics teams and investigators to find out what had occurred.

I was being interrogated, obviously, and I told them exactly what my experience was, how I found the pickaxe, the headaches, and the digging until I found the dead girl.

" Do you recognize you fixed our puzzle for us with your unusual dreams?" Officer Daniel asked.

" I don't comprehend," I said. "I told you every little thing. Why am I back here? I told you that I didn't know the girl, and that I didn't do it."

" That girl was assaulted," he began. "Obviously, a young man was attempting to rob her. He had a golden pickaxe with him, something he had taken that exact same day. But his greed didn't end, so he made an attempt to get her bag and run off with it. When she withstood, he became exceptionally violent. Still, she held onto her bag and would not let it go. So he used the pickaxe to kill her. According to his testament, he buried the girl and the said item in your yard. It was the closest thing to the crime scene that wasn't obvious and you weren't home at the time. No one saw him, so he thought he had gotten away with it. And even if you or anyone would find the pickaxe, he never thought you would be crazy enough to dig so deeply."

" I do not know what came by me," I said. "I just felt that there was more beneath the soil."

" And there was. The girl was underneath a ton of sand, and it's a miracle you found her."

" How did you catch the criminal?" I wished to know. "Since nobody saw the criminal activity, how did you find out who did it?"

" Remember the red piece of cloth the girl was holding in her hand?"

" Yes. What about it?"

" It gave it away. Our research group includes experts when it concerns tracing finger prints, objects, hairs, or any other forensic indications of who did it."

" So did you examine the cloth and trace it back to the person who did it?"

" That's what we did. Yes. We interrogated a ton of people yesterday, and eventually, it led us to him. One of the witnesses that helped us out, was a beggar."

" Really?"

" Yes. The lawbreaker's name is Albert, and he had the same red shirt the girl had ripped the piece from. Initially, he denied it, but when he found that we had enough evidence, he confessed to the whole thing."

" What was the girl's name?"

" Victoria. We pity her family. She had been really missing for quite a long time, but thanks to you, we were at least able to secure the murderer. Thanks, Ralph."

" Wow. You're really welcome, Officer Daniel. I feel for the girl's family too. Maybe I'll go visit them one of nowadays."

" Good plan. Now, please excuse me, as I have more work to do."

Officer Daniel left, and I was left alone with Marco. The benefit for the golden pickaxe I had returned to them, was lying on the table. Blood cash ... that was practically what it felt like. I had gotten some finances, but I felt upset about this discovery. An innocent girl who had been killed ... who knew where this world was going to?

" Come on, Marco," I said. "Let's give this money to Victoria's family. It's the least we can do."

I put the bills into a bag, held the door open for my wiener pet, and closed it behind me. What a world, what a life ...

THE END

Made in the USA
Las Vegas, NV
15 July 2021